PENGUIN

a cry in the jungle bar

Robert Drewe was born in Melbourne and grew up on the West Australian coast. His novels and short stories have been widely translated, won many national and international prizes, and been adapted for film, television, radio and the theatre. He has also written plays, screenplays, journalism and film criticism, and edited two international anthologies of stories. He lives with his family in Sydney.

ROBERT DREWE

a cry in the jungle bar

PENGUIN BOOKS

Penguin Books Australia Ltd
487 Maroondah Highway, PO Box 257
Ringwood, Victoria 3134, Australia
Penguin Books Ltd
Harmondsworth, Middlesex, England
Penguin Putnam Inc.
375 Hudson Street, New York, New York 10014, USA
Penguin Books Canada Limited
10 Alcorn Avenue, Toronto, Ontario, Canada M4V 3B2
Penguin Books (NZ) Ltd
Cnr Rosedale and Airborne Roads, Albany, Auckland, New Zealand
Penguin Books (South Africa) (Pty) Ltd
5 Watkins Street, Denver Ext 4, 2094, South Africa
Penguin Books India (P) Ltd
11, Community Centre, Panchsheel Park, New Delhi 110 017, India

First published by William Collins Pty Ltd 1979
This edition published by Penguin Books Australia Ltd 2001
Offset from the 1988 Picador edition

1 3 5 7 9 10 8 6 4 2

Cover design and digital imaging by Ellie Exarchos
Cover images by Stock Photos and Getty Images
Printed and bound in Australia by McPherson's Printing Group, Maryborough, Victoria

National Library of Australia
Cataloguing-in-Publication data:

Drewe, Robert, 1943– .
A cry in the jungle bar.

ISBN 0 14 100800 8.

I. Title.

A823.3

www.penguin.com.au

To James, Ben,
Amy, Jack and
Laura

I have called this principle, by which each slight variation, if useful, is preserved, by the term of Natural Selection.

Charles Darwin

This principle of soul, universally and individually, is the principle of ambiguity.

Paul Tillich

The expression often used by Mr Herbert Spencer of the Survival of the Fittest is more accurate, and is sometimes equally convenient.

Charles Darwin

CONTENTS

I ADOBO

1

AFTER THEIR QUARRELS Cullen often hid the knives. Before making up a bed in his study he would grab up the carving knife, the bread knife, and, after a particularly savage row, the assortment of sharp cleavers and fruit knives as well, and secrete them in the freezer or under a pile of laundry in the washtub next to the housemaids' room.

After drinking, despite his size and strength, he feared nocturnal stabbing and slashing. He needed the security of knowing that attempts could not easily be made on his bare, vulnerable back as he slept. His spine especially anticipated an evil little bone-handled knife which the girls used to slice calamansi fruit and papayas. In their deft brown fingers it cut, pared and quartered while they hummed sentimental pop songs and day-dreamed of marriage to blond American millionaire country and western singers.

On such an occasion, breathing heavily in the heat, Cullen lay naked, thick freckled arms behind his head, sweating out the evening's liquor on the hard bunk. Blurrily, he focused on a house lizard above the bookshelves, trying to decide whether to turn on the air-conditioner. It would clatter and whir, muffling the tiptoe of approaching feet. On the other hand he'd never get to sleep in the stifling humidity: his throat and thighs streamed, his stale pungency hung in the air. Between decisions, overstimulated by brandy and argument, he wondered again why he was frightened of his wife.

He had no evidence that Margaret was prone to violence. She had never even slapped his cheek in anger, here or at home. These days there was just something about her when she was overwrought and they had been drinking: a desolation in the eyes, a glittering potential he couldn't pin down. Perhaps alcohol heightened his perception of it, magnified this glimpse of her neuroticism. She *was* becoming more neurotic, there was no getting away from it. He saw all the signs: transcendental meditation, Rajamurti. And lately the 'mucus-free diet' fad.

Yet he was sober enough to realize that instability could seem close to craziness on a hot night after a few drinks. He rather prided himself on his magnanimity. Naturally she was unhappy in Asia, out of her element. Nothing to do and the children away at school. Depression weighed her down. She seemed to have no self-confidence lately, burst into tears at small setbacks, had difficulty making friends. Shopping, she'd snap at storekeepers, then overcompensate by neglecting to bargain with them so they took her for a sucker. Her moods were many and diverse. An example: last Good Friday she'd insisted that José drive them to see the Black Nazarene shrine. He was unwilling but she was adamant. Great crowds gathered there to venerate the carved ebony image, to watch waves of pomaded, sweating penitents carry the Black Nazarene through the mouldering streets of Quiapo. Little leathery women with peasant Malay faces trooped behind in long maroon and purple dresses, crowns of green branches in their hair. In this throng Margaret the former Catholic began snorting derisively, making disparaging mutters. Startled onlookers swung their heads, on the verge of umbrage. He hurried her away, bullocking through the crowd with his shoulders, hauling her behind him. Mortified, José followed in their wake and on the drive home hunched distressed over the steering wheel.

As it happened it was she who had articulated his fantasies of night-time mayhem, though in a different context.

'They'll have a brainstorm, those girls, one of these nights. Murder us in our bed. The *amok* is a well-known local

14

phenomenon.' She snapped her fingers, saying, 'The whole race can go berserk just like that.' At the breakfast table she read with bitter relish reports of clerks who'd gone crazy with filing spikes in insurance offices, servant girls apprehended for hacking their mistresses with *bolos*. 'Remember the Toleng brothers,' she said ominously. They were famous for having run amok on the Bicol Express in 1965 with a knife and scissors. Even though it was what their neighbour Ted Orosa might call a 'negative reality', the local newspapers liked to periodically recollect the case:

Toleng Rampage Tenth Anniv.
Twins Killed 8, Wounded 18

Cullen had an occasional quick vision of his own body, pared and quartered with the calamansi knife, floating in the storm-water channel beneath the white-petalled sampanguita in the back garden. A big negative reality, white as pork.

Such exotic thoughts were relatively new to him. He was not what he would call an imaginative person. Before this tour of duty flights of fancy had rarely troubled him. He had not suffered from excesses of emotion or creativity. Here he seemed to be thinking more; wool-gathering. This was a worry, potentially. Lately he had given free rein to a fantasy or two involving women of his acquaintance. He had strong sad urges to touch them at parties; to cup a breast, a knee, in his hand, stroke a soft cheek—mild enough depravities in themselves. But a tic fluttered in an eyelid as he perceived this degeneration; simultaneously he became aware of a hundred little recidivist itches all along his body. Sighing, he dragged himself from the bunk and snapped on the air-conditioner. He padded into the bathroom, took a can of prickly-heat powder from the cabinet and shook it over his chest and legs, patting the powder into humid, chafed corners. Its unusual texture registered in his spinning mind—gritty yet slippery, like tiny scales. The smell was high and unpleasant, somewhere between antiseptic and perfume; even its application, his own dabbing hands, had a vague adolescent wrongness.

Anointed, he fell back on the bunk. Puffs of powder rose like tiny atomic blasts. Eventually he lapsed into a twitching sleep.

Though thick-headed and with the sour aftertaste of their fight in his mouth, he woke curiously unmolested. When he returned from his trip he'd have to take her for a holiday, he decided, slipping on a T-shirt, shorts and jogging shoes, moving gingerly past their bedroom and down the stairs. Mina and Concepción were rattling softly in the kitchen. Outside José was polishing the car. Often he slept in it when his wife's relations came to stay and overcrowded their shack.

'Morning, sir.' A gold tooth showed in José's greeting. His right arm was wound about with grey bandage from wrist to elbow. It had been bandaged now for two months. He was treating an ulcerous crater with applications of a black ointment from the *sari-sari* store. Its cloying smell had permeated every corner of the car's interior. Even when Cullen drove himself, alone in the car, José's absent arm was in command. For the first few weeks he had remarked, 'How's the arm?' or, 'You want to get that looked at,' but, like José, had come to accept its constant presence as inevitable, and no longer mentioned it.

He nodded good morning to José and let himself out through the gate in the high iron fence. Various gardeners and maids looked up from trimming hedges and sweeping paths as this big forty-three-year-old Caucasian, wearing a shirt which said, in red letters, *Wanderers' Sports Club*, jogged heavily past. He was instantly dripping sweat and, though a daily sight, inspired the Orosas' smirking gardener to mutter behind his croton hedge, 'Pool!' The people often had trouble with their 'F' sounds.

Cullen's jogging route was four miles around the boundary of The Fourth Estate, the middle-class residential village where, in Stop Press Avenue, for three thousand pesos a month, they leased their two-storeyed bungalow with its high cement portico and forbidding front door carved in lauan

16

wood from a traditional motif. The village had been named by its first residents, a group of gung-ho newspaper publishers who had taken over the sub-division from a bankrupt developer a decade before. With many of the original householders now residing at better addresses or in gaol, middle-ranking foreign embassy families and businessmen had gradually moved in.

He ran this route every day, with or without a hangover. He had run with worse hangovers than this over the years: he still got headaches blamed on a Tongan kick in the ear in 1957. Combined Universities had finally despatched the Tongans 24-15 but, making their first overseas tour, the 'gay and colourful visitors from the Friendly Isles', as the sportswriters called them, had nevertheless been noted for their head-high tackling and overuse of the boot in the ruck. Today's headache was less a pain than a constriction: the sensation exactly recalled the tight maroon cap, like a pimple on a pumpkin, he had been forced to wear as a schoolboy. He actually touched his scalp to make sure.

He jogged into Headline Boulevard, along Extra Avenue, past the guard post, and headed towards home, feeling the enigmatic eyes of the guards on him. He obtained no bourgeois reassurance from their crew-cut, heavily armed presence, their quasi-American uniforms. Coming home from a party the other week, five minutes over the 1.00 a.m. curfew, they had been stopped at the barrier by two thin youths with drawn pistols who flexed their chicken biceps at him, saying, 'You are late, you are late. Big trouble, buster,' and grabbing the telephone.

'You know us. We live here,' he'd insisted obsequiously, tensely swatting mosquitoes yet deliberately calming himself, not relishing a night in the cells and the next day spent weeding the grass verges of the highway—the soft punishment allegedly meted out to tardy Westerners. He dropped Orosa's name first (his newspaper by-line carried influence), then the magic letters 'UN'. Grimacing, the guards waved him back to the car where Margaret sat tense and wan. As they drove on he glimpsed a reason for their testiness: two naked girls, as brown as Moros, one with shaved pubis, pressed against the guardhouse wall in the edge of their headlights.

Considering this brief vision made Cullen's head thump. Their bodies had been as sleek as seals.

He aimed to keep his mind clear when he jogged, away from domestic or work pressures which placed an extra strain on the body. Today this was difficult as his mind swung from last night's fracas, to his project, to his departure tomorrow on a tour of the Organization's duty stations around Asia. They were all interconnected. Cullen's field of special professional competence was buffaloes. It was a Level Two priority project, of considerable importance to the Organization and, naturally, of great value to the Third World. His first-hand observations were imperative for the publication of *The Poor Man's Tractor*, a review of all existing knowledge of the health and husbandry of the water buffalo, which he was editing for worldwide distribution.

Margaret didn't understand of course. In her present state of mind she seemed to see the trip as just a nice long junket with sexual possibilities. She would be lonely. 'How can you leave me in this humid, corrupt dump?'

It was tough but unavoidable, he'd told her. She had been eager enough for the bigger salary, the servants, the perquisites of the move to Asia. Where did agricultural and veterinary science lead if not to the Third World and its hungry millions? The argument reached lofty planes. And he blew his own trumpet for once. It shouldn't be forgotten that he was now one of the top men in his field, on a par with Agabeili of Russia, Banajee of India, El-Shazly of Egypt, even Siri Subharngkasen of Thailand; published in the *New Scientist*, *Scientific American* and the *Oxford Veterinarian*. In an introductory paragraph the *New Scientist* had even made jocular reference to his size and his record as a 'buffaloing' second-row forward in the early sixties, a parallel which had earlier tickled *Horizons*, the Organization's staff magazine, two Sydney sportswriters and *The Grammarian*, the magazine of his school's old boys' association. If the joke was

18

wearing a little thin, he was still good-natured about it. Forced to give their mutual traits any thought at all he could find none that weren't commendable.

All this he had impressed on her last night while they drank a bottle of cognac and his voice rose with indignation at the injustice of her attitudes. She seemed to absorb it all, then stared at him with that desolate intensity she sometimes showed. Her even features appeared tightly drawn across her facial bones.

'What do you think of me as a person?' she asked. 'I'm desperate to know.' Her mouth was rigidly ajar, revealing her small neat teeth.

'What?' He was thrown by conversational disjunction. He required order and logic in most things, especially arguments, otherwise he was helpless, gaping, a beached whale. His co-ordination went and he could unintentionally break glasses in his sausage fingers, drop things. Simultaneously he was swept by sympathy for her. After all, he loved her.

'Ricky, what am I?' She grabbed his hand and kneaded the lumpy knuckles, clutching with a severe pressure. He wanted to pull away, to retire to the personal territory of his own air space. He concentrated on not tensing up. He barely fathomed her questions, much less considered answering.

'Calm down,' he instructed. 'Take it easy.' One of the secrets of his sporting success had been an automatic detachment, an ability of the mind to switch into neutral while his body went through its various layered thresholds of fatigue and pain. Now he coasted with a wary smile. 'Another drink?' He reached for the bottle.

'You don't *try* to understand me!' Her exasperated cry rang out, jarred like shattering glass.

His turning off had occasionally irritated people when he did it in emotional confrontations. Funny, it was almost as if they wanted to see him lose control. She was searching his face now, watching desperately, curiously, for his reaction, and for a second his shoulders actually shook with the frustration of not being permitted to let go, to overturn the massive red lauan dining-table and fling chairs through the windows and backhand her across the room.

Then she kissed his hand. 'I'm at the end of my tether in this place. Understand me, Ricky, I don't fit in here.'

He inhaled deeply and took another draught of brandy. The boyish nickname he disliked too. Only *she* used it and only in times of anguish. It reminded him of Rudyard Kipling's mongoose. 'Nonsense,' he soothed, patting her dry hands. She had lost all lubricity lately, could make him feel a gross night-time raider. Lovingly carnal she had been ten, fifteen years ago, with the smell of fragrant lagoons hidden in her thighs. Once noisy at love, here she lay lily-white and silent, impatiently pushing damp hair from her eyes. Their bodies, though drenched with his sweat, eroded away at each other. In this country he sometimes thought—slithering wet, panting on his elbows, annoyed and embarrassed at the passage of unresponsive time—why bother?

'I don't trust anyone. Not even you. Especially you.' Her voice rose. Out in the kitchen the maids shuffled nervously. Restrained hands edged crockery around the sink. Cutlery chimed.

Trust? *He* was going crazy. Who could be more trustworthy? These fights had at least made him realize that he'd been boringly solid, dependable, all his life. Honourable. Prefect and officer material. The team captain. He had read the Bible aloud in school chapel every morning, opened car doors for all the visiting VIPs. Ex-King Peter of Yugoslavia and Douglas Bader, the legless air ace. ('Welcome to college, King Peter,' he'd greeted the exile, on instructions to diplomatically forgo the 'ex'. Booze blossoms glistened on the regal cheeks. And after he initiated three cheers for the gallant RAF officer, the airman, visibly affected, gave them a half-holiday.) Who was first at football training year after year? Who stood in for hungover malingerers on lifesaving patrol?

So now he was, frankly (here he had poured another brandy), a respected authority in the area of animal husbandry. And it wasn't as if his sporting days were over, either. He'd been a leader in the most honourable and ethical of games, he'd like to remind her. Hadn't he captained Rugby teams from the age of eight right up to the big ones? Carried on with fingers snapped like carrots, concussed, with a wired jaw, his nose alongside an ear, no knee-caps to speak of? Shot through with pain-killers he could be trusted. What did this unfamiliar woman want of him? Breath whistled fast through his restored nose.

'What do you expect me to do, Margaret?' Suddenly impossibly heavy, his arms sagged on the table. Absently he picked up her hands again and patted them. Her eyes immediately widened. They had an unusual glint. Her face was set into a stranger's lines and her chin met her thin neck in an alien fibrous arrangement of tensed muscles.

'Don't patronize me. Leave that to your mother. For God's sake don't you patronize me!' she hissed at him. Then she had snatched her hands away, piercing him with an enemy's eyes, and hurried from the room.

Oblique and dangerous ground. As his mother, the surfing pioneer, had once remarked, 'Isn't Margaret a wilful lass?' She wasn't being complimentary. They had not hit it off from the beginning. It was a genuine clash of personalities, ages, religions. At the time Margaret had just refused one of her bridge invitations outright, shown no sense of appreciation either at being nominated by Dottie for the Casuarina Club. There Dottie still held sway three times a week at a bridge table with scenic views of the same beach and surf where during the twenties she was such a familiar figure. Indeed, in the club foyer was a framed photograph of a brown, grinning Dottie, glamorous in bathing cap and daring woollen swimsuit, posed on the sand between two muscular hedonists with her twelve-foot wooden board. Sharp as a spear, more or less phallic. A caption said: 'The prowess of Mrs George Cullen, née Miss Dorothea Greenlees, on the solid surfboard was regarded as equal to that of the best male exponents of board riding.'

From the beginning Margaret had been shown plenty of other sepia representations of the sporty Dottie, just to indicate what she was up against. Dottie clearing various jumps on Sunrise, her bay gelding. Dottie volleying in tennis. Dottie knifing off the high board like the Jantzen girl. Dottie relaxing in deckchairs on ferries, jetties, promenades, showing her calves. Generally she was surrounded by sinewy tanned men with centre hair partings, some of them George Cullen, with a full head of brown curls, gangling toothily in the background.

Precipitately he had invited Margaret home for a weekend at Casuarina Bay; much sooner than he had brought her predecessors. Of course she was ill at ease. Nature required a seasoning, a hardening. Immediately there was a fear of spiders: funnel-webs in the laundry, tarantulas in the bathroom, redbacks in the wood bin. Then, even the tame birds seemed in cahoots against her. She took it personally when kookaburras snatched barbecued chops from her flapping fingers. Tense currawongs fixed on her their severe gold eyes; swooping magpies clicked beaks millimetres from her lambent head. Rising in clouds, small scarlet parrots repulsed her timid offerings of sugar water.

Naturally this amused and encouraged his father, playing the rustic bohemian on her behalf: gardening naked, a flour bag around the loins, flailing a reckless scythe through the wet-the-beds, delighting in his suntan, holiday white stubble, fly-away hair strands. How could this man be a doctor, a surgeon? His whole creased eccentric body jumped with germs.

'Here, Marg, have a go at this,' he'd offer, snapping off a banana, a passion-fruit, a pomegranate, a wormy nectarine; tossing them to her, spitting pips into the rustling shrubbery. 'We don't stand on ceremony at the Bay.' Certainly not, squatting on the front steps sucking a mango, licentious juice trickling down his brown stringy neck, knees open, flour bag agape, old exhibitionist's balls sagging in the heat almost to the step below.

She had persevered nonetheless.

At the surf club they had danced at night. Jazz was popular: swing, Dixieland. Big band and combo. In her ear he whispered phraseology gleaned from *Downbeat*. A romantic moon, romantic tepid air, saxophone, cornet, clarinet, trombone, piano, bass and novelty flugelhorn. 'What's that funny looking trumpet?' 'A flugelhorn.' (He had danced there many a Saturday night.)

They strolled romantically along the beach. Low white breakers rolled on the shore. Couples writhed in the sandhills in the corners of their vision. But not this couple. They were beginning to be in love and in the fashion of the time held hands, kissed, pressed close and took themselves very seriously.

Cullen's misunderstood heart dutifully pumped the extra emotional load as he thudded through tropical suburbs. His tricky patched knee gave his steps a syncopation: a weighty, slightly limping tempo on the road. While he ran he repeated, half-consciously, any rhythmic gibberish that was stuck in his brain. Since passing the guardhouse, even though his thoughts had moved on, his steps said, 'Mar-tial-law. Mar-tial-law.' Tossing on his bunk one night months ago his overstimulated brain had worked 'martial law' into 'marital law'.

Sterile thunderclouds had hung over the Sierra Madre for a day; now it began raining steadily. Lightning bolts slashed the highway beyond The Fourth Estate. Fungus glistened on the high compound walls. At once there was a smell of rot. Cullen splashed on. His clothes stuck to his body, his hair lay plastered down in ginger spikes. Actually, he enjoyed the rain; it was something to react against. He tackled it as though it was an opposing forward line, leaned into it, felt it strike his head and shoulders. It was cool and trickled into his open mouth.

As he squelched up Stop Press Avenue to his gate his head was finally clear of superfluous thoughts. In the front garden, on the sodden grass, he performed a vigorous exercise routine: sit-ups, toe-touching, side-bends; concentrating on his abdominals while the rain swept over him. Another exercise he'd done for twenty-five years: to toughen his shoulders for scrummaging and rucking, he approached the thick palm tree in front of the verandah, packed down against it with his shoulder, and, the veins standing from his neck and temples, grunting and heaving, body close to the ground, legs scuffling for territory, he pushed against it as if to drive it from the garden.

The fighting of the tree was the part that José waited for each morning. He had mentioned it many times to his family. Sheltering inside the car with a cigarette he slowly shook his head.

2

'ANY MAIL?' MARGARET ASKED as, showered and dressed, he joined her at breakfast. She was wrapped inside a cobalt-blue silk kimono he had bought in Hong Kong, almost lost in its folds, with the newspaper spread before her. Though her eyes were underscored with leaden circles her face had the expressionless neutrality of medium-term marriages. Her blonde hair was brushed efficiently back from her forehead. The appearance was severe, but then she had spoken first—that could be interpreted as a conciliatory gesture.

'Only bills. Power and the club. There goes five thousand pesos.'

Rustling the newspaper, folding it, bringing the loose broadsheets under crisp control, she said, 'You could cut out the club if you were serious about money.'

'The same goes for your dressmaker and the hairdresser, I suppose.' Already a thin rivulet of sweat slid between his shoulderblades. He poured himself a glass of iced water, drank it thirstily and scooped into a slice of mango. Rain still pelted on the roof. In the middle distance beyond the village wall the traffic hummed and hooted on the highway. Concepción brought him a plate of fried ham, several tiny pale-yolked eggs and two racks of rice-bread toast. It occurred to him that they must have had to hunt for the knives in order to cut the bread and mango. He felt slightly foolish.

'Finished with the paper?' he asked.

Margaret did not eat any ham and eggs. She was lately dabbling in Flehretism, the mucus-free diet healing system of the late Professor Maximilian Flehret (1856-1924), the noted European savant who had spent his last years among Southern California's growing colony of celebrities. She kept to a slice of papaya and a glass of calamansi juice. She had been introduced to Flehretism at a bridge party by Helen Carey, whose husband was at the Embassy.

Helen had been singing the praises of this new diet which eliminated the body's poisons. She made it seem like a type of exorcism. It was wonderful for the skin, figure, hair and mental attitude. Margaret had been so bored with bridge that she had paid the woman more attention than usual and gone home clutching two of the professor's books: *Sensible Fasting—For Physical, Mental and Spiritual Rejuvenation* and *Thus Speaketh the Colon—The Tragedy of Nutrition*. Both carried a cover photograph of the bearded professor, obviously taken at different ages and stages in his career. On one cover he resembled Karl Marx; on the other—his moustache waxed—Wild Bill Hickock. The word at the Polo Club, according to Helen Carey, was that the President's wife herself was a Flehretist. That explained her serenity, youthful complexion, vigour and increasingly assertive role in national and Third World affairs.

Margaret was trying to observe the tenets of Flehretism as conscientiously as possible, apart from the veto on alcohol which she had made no attempt to obey—a mid-afternoon gin being both instinctive and irresistible in Asia. She had nonetheless been struck by the professor's main introductory principle: 'Every disease, no matter what name it is given by Medical Science, is CONSTIPATION: a clogging up of the entire pipe system of the human body by accumulated mucus caused by Protein and Starch.' So she had given up meat and eggs (not so difficult here where even the butcher shops in the fashionable shopping centres stank like medieval charnel houses), eliminated fats and most carbohydrates. In four weeks she had lost twenty pounds and believed on her more optimistic days she looked better for it. (Once, younger and

26

dimpled, she had been told she looked 'vivacious'. She had not taken it as a compliment.)

As Professor Flehret said, 'Moderate eaters and frequent fasters have a very fine, spiritual facial expression. For instance, it is said that Pope Leo XIII, that great faster, had a very clear, almost transparent complexion.' Strangely, though her Catholicism was long ago lapsed and cloudy, she had derived a little encouragement from that. She had not told Richard her periods had stopped, like Professor Flehret said they would.

At the breakfast table Cullen flicked through the paper but could not concentrate. The news was not engrossing, though the nearest plane crash of the day had happened not quite a mile away. A twin-engined passenger plane belonging to Rayo Airlines had crashed into a house during a test flight, killing the pilot, two girls in a guava tree and a housemaid.

3

'AMONG THE MANY MISCONCEPTIONS regarding *Bubalus bubalis*,' Cullen dictated, 'is the belief that it is exclusively an animal of the East.' He was addressing his new secretary, Gigi Fernandez, a tiny pale-skinned fine arts graduate with sweet features and searching eyes, whom he had inherited from Personnel. He thought her gaze attentive and evidence of her efficiency; in fact, she was trying to think which movie star he resembled. She liked to fantasize that her bosses were screen heroes, and gave them movie star aliases in her lengthy telephone conversations with girlfriends. In Grain Production she had worked for a handsome fair American whose real name she forgot—he had been Robert Redford. Mr McLeod in Personnel was not aware that for three months he had become Sean Connery. The best she could come up with this time was Gene Hackman, and even that was stretching her imagination. The damaged broad nose was all wrong.

Cullen was dictating a foreword to his buffalo book. It would be, he hoped, the definitive volume on the subject. *The Poor Man's Tractor* would be a reference source for the veterinarian and animal production expert, a brief for the practical farmer and a textbook for the serious student. He believed even the general reader could find it interesting. He was anxious to stress the global *significance* of the beast, its importance in the scheme of things.

'Actually,' he dictated, 'it is found in forty countries

28

extending from Italy to Greece, to the United Arab Republic and other countries of the Near East, India, China and the whole of South-East Asia. Buffaloes are found in the West Indies, the swamps of southern Iraq, the Amazon Valley of South America and the desert scrubland of Australia's Northern Territory.'

Miss Fernandez's pencil meandered over her notebook. Her hair was velvety black, cut fashionably short. As she concentrated her lips quivered slightly. They looked soft and were sensually shaped.

His own attention was wandering. From his office desk on the fourteenth floor he looked out over the adjoining Eden Hotel on whose flat tarred roof an old woman was now hanging sheets and towels to dry on a clothes line. These days, since martial law had attracted the big international hotel chains, the Eden depended for its livelihood on the daytime trysts of businessmen and their *queridas* and on the goitres, wasted limbs and tumours of foreign invalids in town to see the faith healers. No doubt Galash was over at the Eden at this minute with one of his girls, performing dexterous sexual feats. One of his implications was unparalleled virility.

'Got myself a new beauty queen yesterday,' he'd announce over a report on Sumatran anthrax. 'Father's a Dole pineapple millionaire down in Zamboanga. Very edible little morsel.'

Certainly he had a lot of girlfriends who fell for his charm, chunky cufflinks, after-shave and such accoutrements. Cullen was slightly in awe of his American *savoir-faire*. In the company of Galash or the enigmatic Z.M. Ali, his other colleague, he could easily feel gross, hairy and ham-handed. The smell of his own thick-boned body embarrassed him. His crass meat-eater's sweat offended his nostrils. Everyone else here smelled like a rose. Fragrant Galash had taken to applying coconut-derived unguents to his hair in the local manner. He wore Brooks Brothers' seersucker and a selection of space-age digital watches duty-free from Hong Kong. The success of this snazzy image with the local girls was perhaps understandable, but Cullen couldn't fathom why the European women too saw something intriguing in his dated, slender suavity. Perhaps it had something to do with the return of his wife to New York three months ago.

'I suppose Hugh's sort of roguish,' Margaret had mentioned once.

'Roguish? Christ, roguish went out with Douglas Fairbanks.'

'He always smells clean and has nice hands,' she said.

Cullen's concentration was bad. His head throbbed as he continued dictating: 'There has been a regrettable tendency for too many years to regard the water buffalo as a symbol of primitive and backward agriculture. Despite lack of government support and years of indifference on the part of scientific organizations, buffalo numbers are steadily increasing. It is worthy of note that the present world buffalo population is thought to be at least one hundred and fifty million.'

On the Eden's roof the washerwoman strung another load of sheets on the line to dry in the tepid air. Galash had no conscience about his job either—that was another flaw in his character. Most un-American. He'd be fornicating away over there with Alice Estalilla or Gracie Mendez knowing that he, Cullen, was holding the fort, palming off inquiries about his whereabouts and keeping the sixteenth floor at bay. And if he called in for a drink after work, there Galash would be with a slyly demure Alice or Gracie sipping a San Miguel in the Eden's Jungle Bar, rosy-cheeked and brimming with *bonhomie*. The Jungle Bar had rattan furniture, bamboo screens and various mounted wild heads on the walls. It kept a cloudy glass tank of live lobsters for seafood diners; their shells rattled against the glass, a high marine odour hung in the air. 'Why, there's Dick!' Galash would call, and generously wave him over, sit him down, beckon drink waiters, proffer bowls of glazed nuts and bacon rinds. 'Have you met Alice? This beautiful young lady was Miss Davao City 1972.' In his hot frustrated hand, hers, being tiny and cool, would dissolve almost immediately.

Cullen stated in his dictation to Miss Fernandez that while

the buffalo could truly be called 'the poor man's tractor', it also had an unrealized potential as a major source of meat, milk and leather. It was of significance that it existed in greatest numbers in those areas of the world where animal protein was most scarce. He could have picked up Miss Fernandez in one hand and eaten her, she looked so frail and delectable. Already he was in love with the way her top lip subtly joined her pink gum with a tiny moist thread. Did her eyes have a shrewd light?

'In tropical countries,' he continued, 'there is widespread credence in the aphrodisiac properties of buffalo meat and milk. They are usually considered to be beneficial in their effect on libido. This belief is common in most countries where the buffalo exists.'

He thought himself bold but it went right over her head.

Miss Fernandez had never dreamed up a movie star alias for Zulfikar Muhammad Ali; she kept this habit for her Western bosses. Indeed none would have suited Z.M., as he was known. He was not easily typecast, seemed not to represent any particular culture. Neither his dress, nor his manner— not even his accent—was readily identifiable with the sub-continent. When he had been born in Dacca, Bengal was part of India. Though allegedly Muslim underdogs, his family had prospered as bankers, professors, scientists. Young Z.M. had been bright and secure, rode a British Raleigh bicycle with silver mudguards and shot at crows and wild dogs with an American Daisy air rifle. When the Muslims received Bengal and he suddenly lived in East Pakistan, things were not so good. Luxuries were short and his father's savings went on educating Z.M. and his brothers in England. Now the Ben-galis ran the country themselves, he was a Bangladeshi and matters were, if anything, less certain than ever. His nation-ality seemed not to have left its stamp on him. He had not lived in his country recently.

Now he strode into Cullen's office dressed in a khaki safari suit and oxblood English brogues saying, 'Dick, where is the bloody genetics report?' and waving his cigarette impatiently.

31

'That's Galash's area.'

'That Hughie! He's holding up procedures again.'

As he spoke Z.M. grinned, tapped ash into Cullen's waste-basket and gestured out the window towards the Eden. 'Over there, huh?'

Cullen shrugged. Miss Fernandez gazed dreamily at her notebook. With a quick thrusting forefinger Z.M. made a sly in-and-out motion into the O of his other forefinger and thumb. 'That Hughie!' he said again. Miss Fernandez blushed and perused her shoes, then, Cullen noticed, glanced up with a small twitch of the lips. Had he been right about the shrewd eyes? 'What about pelota tonight?' Z.M. asked him.

Though still torpid he said, 'Fine, why not?' and cheered up considerably. Ever since he was a boy, a big child with a deceptive rangy ease, he'd used sports to erase his problems. At least momentarily. The day after Lindy died he'd turned up for football as usual, scoring three tries and delighting the coach of the under-twelves. But when he trotted from the field flushed and proud despite the other numbness two of his team mates' mothers were tutting, 'It's not right,' and he moped off sobbing guiltily for not having hung around the house behind drawn curtains; perhaps for not having died himself.

Still his deepest contentment came from athletic competition. Even here, a heavy man in the tropics, swallowing salt tablets and nursing his old talent and wily injured body through sweltering contests against younger men, it was pleasurable. Playing the cruel game of experience and guile and laughing about it later. The boisterous nude democracy of the change-room. Munching hard-boiled eggs, downing a bottle or two of San Miguel at the bar after a game. Heavy-legged from the spongy ground but serene in his exhaustion—this was when he harmonized with Asia.

Their cars and drivers were waiting in the parking bay at five o'clock, José leaning against the driver's door reading a Tagalog comic book. 'The Sports Club, José,' he instructed.

Z.M.'s car followed them out on to the boulevard and along the bay, past the airline offices and tourist nightclubs.

At the Mañana Club a flashing neon sign proclaimed the current attraction, a local pop group called—incredibly, he had thought on first being struck by it—*Boy Camera and the Afterbirth*. Soon after his arrival, following several hours' drinking at the Eden, he'd gone there one night with Galash. Hugh had been a most attentive guide those first weeks. The nightclub retained a prominent sign in the foyer from the wild days before martial law: *All Weapons Including Handguns Must Be Deposited Here By Government Order.* Galash was known there by the manager, hostesses, waiters. Attention was paid them and a table arranged near the band. Along the corridor to the men's lavatory they passed a long glass-walled room like the viewing nursery in a maternity hospital. Inside rows of bored girls were perched like stenographers on upright chairs, reading magazines, smoking, knitting. On their way back from the toilet, zipping up their flies, businessmen would stop and casually select girls, tapping on the glass to attract notice, and lead them back to their tables.

Cullen, drunk enough to be fleetingly stirred by such exotica, politely convivial, commented, 'Some good looking little girls in there.'

'You sex maniac!' It appeared that Galash remained playfully dapper even after hours of drinking. Cullen recalled snatches of his advice that night. 'They're on an M.I.T. kick at the moment. Parade your degrees at all times. Of course this country is crazy. Who wouldn't be after three hundred years in a convent and forty in Hollywood? Arrive on time and the rest of the day's yours. Sure you can play sports. Get a mistress. But lay off the office girls—don't shit in your own nest.' All this while a thirty-man band of idiosyncratic guitarists and brass players performed jarring pop music, strobe lighting sent electric impulses through his brain and a glossy boy in sequined cowboy gear sang pensively, '*I shot the shereef. But I did not shoot the deputee*'. A whiff of urine fanned down the corridor to their table. The brass section, after a long struggle, eventually defeated the guitars with a strident flourish.

'Actually, it's a waste of time and money,' Galash went on. 'Their boyfriends pick them up at closing time. Purely for dancing and drinking with. A quick squeeze of the buns is all you'll get.'

'It's not my scene, anyway.'

'You wouldn't want a nice little knife in the gut, hey, Dick?'

'Hardly.' Galash was an over-explainer with, he was quickly learning, a slick habit of making him feel ill at ease sexually.

'But if you need that sort of thing I suppose they're handy for the ego.'

'Not me.'

'Boy, a fellow like you should have been here before martial law. Anything you wanted. Some very questionable entertainment. All sorts of exhibitions—dog shows, the occasional Shetland—you wouldn't credit it. All tightened up now, naturally.' Galash poured the dregs of a San Miguel into Cullen's glass, pulled his chair confidentially closer. 'Things can still be arranged though. Cleanest little girls in Asia. And like a mouse's earhole, if you know what I mean.'

Big, uncomfortable Cullen, teetering on his matchwood chair between cultures, said, 'Is that so?' and beckoned for unwanted drinks.

4

Z.M. HAD A GOOD EYE. In shorts, T-shirt and snowy towelling headband he dashed about the pelota court with thin-limbed *élan* and little expenditure of body heat. His rubber soles made pinched squeaks of restrained proficiency. He had a neat, precise service and an ability to sidle close to the walls and scoop up Cullen's hardest ricocheting shots.

'Good shot,' Cullen muttered. Sweat ran into his brows and dripped on the floor. His head pounded. Z.M. carried only a light dew on his top lip and was covering more territory. With his reach Cullen could get to most shots from centre court, and he could thrash the ball with greater force than Z.M., but gradually his opponent's springy strokes wore him down. Z.M. won the first game. A salt tablet under the tongue, Cullen bore down on the ball with intense strength and concentration and won the next game. The effort cost him the third game: his eyes began to go, little paramecia wavered at the edges of his vision.

'You've got it, you've won it,' he said at the end. He hated to lose, always had, but was always gracious. 'Played like a champion,' he said. 'Don't know what's the matter with me.'

'What do you expect, with the abstemious life I lead?' Z.M. laughed. A spicy odour rose from his body as he towelled himself, removed his sweatband, ran a comb through sleek hair.

'Ha! We know all about you,' said Cullen, who actually

knew very little. Knowledge of the Ali lifestyle was slight within the Organization. He was a bachelor, with a Chinese girlfriend. He lived in one of the new condominiums within walking distance of the office, overlooking the bay. He broke the tenets of Islam by drinking Scotch enthusiastically. Another buffalo specialist, with London and Karachi degrees, but one with a more personal interest in raising the standard and numbers of the animal. His submissions to *The Poor Man's Tractor* had surprised Cullen somewhat with their emotive tone, but only because of Z.M.'s customary remoteness.

'Like its masters, the Bangladeshi buffalo has suffered the ravages of war, earthquake, typhoon and flood,' Z.M. had written. 'Where human diets are the poorest in the world, livestock also suffers from malnutrition.' His article complained that even though his country suffered severely from protein hunger buffalo meat was not esteemed. 'Even during the Muslim festivals, the time of animal sacrifice when hundreds are slaughtered in the streets of Dacca and given to the poor, they shun the buffaloes. Few, if any, are paraded for slaughter.'

They drank glasses of calamansi juice in the garden at the edge of the pelota courts, lounging with their racquets at their feet at a cane table under a ubiquitous Cinzano umbrella. Accents of assertive American mothers came to them from the swimming pool, and the answering chatter of children. Nearby other noisy children fed nuts to a cramped cage of monkeys, then ordered a waiter to bring more.

'You have a chit? You must have a chit for more nuts,' the waiter told them.

'Just bring the nuts, you understand?' directed a small American boy. 'Those little monkeys need more nuts.'

'You must have a chit.' The waiter wriggled with embarrassment. 'Your father here? He sign a chit.'

'I'll sign for them.' Z.M. motioned to the waiter. 'Give them the nuts.'

The children looked across at him, shrugged, and ran back to the cage giggling.

'Spoiled little bastards,' Cullen said, draining his glass of juice. 'What did you do that for?'

Z.M. leaned back in his seat with his arms behind his head, pushing out his feet in front of him. 'It wasn't for them,' he said. 'It is a luxury to feed worthless animals. It gives me pleasure.'

'You should have been a maharajah.'

'Aha, yes. With leopards on leashes and peacocks everywhere. One appreciates trivia when one is vulnerable to repeated catastrophe. You wouldn't know, Dick, the sensuality in the possession of a fresh *Time* magazine or a block of Fry's chocolate.' He stretched again.

Cullen frowned. 'I can understand that.' Languor made him uneasy.

'And there is the added titillation of waste.'

Vaguely Cullen disapproved of Asian hedonism. He certainly was strongly against prodigality. It went against the mood of self-improvement he liked to see. It countered the spirit of their work. He equated Asian comfort with black markets, corruption, fingers in the till and life-sustaining protein traded over various Oriental borders for the products of Helena Rubinstein. 'I'm surprised to hear you say that, Z.M. I always thought you were a sort of socialist, if you know what I mean.'

Z.M. raised his eyebrows but did not offer to elucidate. 'Actually,' he said eventually, 'I am quite sorry for the monkeys in this country. The wild ones are no better off. There is a local species of eagle which eats nothing else. Occasionally it has mistakenly carried babies off.'

'Really?'

The women and children had drifted from the swimming pool. Only two middle-aged Europeans were slowly and erratically stroking up and down. Cullen stood and removed his sweat-soaked shirt, socks and tennis shoes. Self-conscious, he felt. Smelly, hairy; a ginger and white mountain. 'Race you to the other end,' he suggested.

Z.M. brushed away the challenge. 'I don't swim well. I am helpless in the water.' In the gathering dusk his outline was becoming blurred but his teeth showed when he spoke. 'You people are all-round sportsmen,' he said. His tone was enigmatic. 'You have an aquatic predilection.'

'Not all of us.'

In his voluminous shorts Cullen dived into the pool with a wide splash and swam several lengths, forcing his arms and legs to carry on for a final lap when he wished to stop. At the shallow end he stood up, snorted water from his nose, hitched up his shorts and hoisted himself from the pool. Z.M. had left for the dressing-room.

5

AFTER BREAKFAST MARGARET HAD SHOWERED, dressed in a caftan and sandals and, when José returned from taking Richard to work, had him drive her into the tourist district, ostensibly to shop. She got out of the car, resisting the entreaties of boys selling lottery tickets and cigarettes along the pavement, and browsed through the stores selling cheap tennis shoes, embroidered *jusi* and *piña* clothing, abaca rugs and bags, Muslim brassware, Igorot fabrics, Wrangler and Levi jeans. She stepped around puddles left in potholes by the morning's downpour. There was a concentrated smell of vehicle fumes, humid mud and overripe fruit in the street, the occasional stench of fish, a pomaded sweetness from passing youths who now and then gawked at her fair hair, nudged each other and giggled.

The street was crowded. People sauntered around her, hurried across her path, pressed past her: bustling, indolent, self-absorbed, mildly curious. She was in the crowd but not of it. There was a blur of black hair, pale brown skin, a uniformity of physique and sleekness. She stood out, to the casual observer and to herself. She was in no way threatened by the crowd; rather she seemed a trivial novelty, an object of fleeting interest immediately forgotten. She moved as in a dream still retaining the clear, consecutive details of last night's lifelike dream in her mind. . . .

They drove with the children from the city through *barrios* of palm-thatched stilt houses, coconut plantations and *padi* rice and sugar cane fields. In each village they passed one or two children riding a *carabao* and realistic roadside stands of pineapples, mangoes and papayas. Bright laundry was spread on bushes to dry. Weaves and patterns were sharply defined. At Pagsanjan they stopped with a group of noisy Japanese for the traditional tourist lunch of *lechón* and to change into bathing suits. Richard joked with the children, flicking them lightly with a rolled towel. He kept chanting: 'One potato, two potato, three potato, four.' Curiously, he was dressed in his white laboratory coat.

On the Pagsanjan River they climbed into two *bancas*, Richard and Mark in one and Louise with her in the other. Each canoe had a forward and aft boatman. Hers were old and wiry and their shrivelled faces were photographed in her mind. Gold was prominent in both mouths. One man wore incongruous wrap-around sunglasses, the other had a line of grey stubble on his chin.

Kneeling in the *bancas*, the boatmen began paddling vigorously up-river. Even these details were precise. The water was grey, their paddles sliced its surface. Soon they came to rapids and the men jostled the canoes over them. Richard's boatmen had to heave harder because of their heavier load; their efforts made him laugh embarrassedly. More rapids were ahead, ten or twelve, and at each one the straining boatmen worked the *bancas* over the rocks against the current. When it was too shallow or when they came to a tight squeeze between boulders the boatmen jumped from the canoes and, grunting hard, actually lifted them over the rapids.

'Wow!' Louise exclaimed.

Between rocky gorges hung with curtains of begonias and orchids they passed. Excited, Louise pointed out cascades tumbling down the cliffs. Like a jungle sound-track cries of monkeys and birds split the stillness; thick snaking vines and bamboos grew to the river's edge. Gradually the thundering of the falls grew closer and the *bancas* came to a deep lake beneath the main waterfall. On the bank they stretched their legs, and from a small makeshift stall bought bottles of Coca-Cola which had been kept cool under water. Disappointingly, her drink turned to air in her hand.

Mist from the falls settled in drops on their skin as they started back down-river. Surprisingly, it was warm, like sweat. To distribute their weight more evenly Mark had joined Louise and her in their canoe, leaving Richard a lone passenger in the other. The children yelled, 'Yahoo!' as their speed increased.

The boatmen steered them into turbulent white water. 'Hang on,' she called in a shrill voice she recognized as her mother's. They clung to the *banca's* sides as jungle foliage flashed past, its sounds smothered by the river. Ahead of them bobbed Richard's canoe; his laugh rang back on the flying spray, his laboratory coat whipped around him.

In their *banca* the paddling of the forward boatman became unreasonably and suddenly weaker; his paddle jabbed ineffectually in the water. Despite the stern boatman's flurried correcting manoeuvres the canoe started to veer obliquely downstream, sheering faster as the river narrowed and fell over series on series of rapids. Now both boatmen were panicking, gibbering at each other in some dialect, and the children began to sob.

'Ricky!' she was shouting soundlessly for him, laboratory-coated and secure in the canoe ahead, as they overturned in slow motion and she and the children were thrown silently, passively into the torrent. The inevitability of it! Sucking and whirling currents inundated them. A sensation of going down the plug-hole in a giant bath. Worse. When she woke, babbling his name, she threw out a desperate arm and he wasn't there.

Aimlessly she perused shopfronts to clear her mind, eventually buying gifts for the children: carved Moro sailboats, a wooden *carabao*, savage miniature tribesmen with threatening war axes; unsuitably frail toys whose purchase nevertheless helped to counteract the dream and were proof of their continued existence.

Then in a store window she came across a range of men's

clothing: snappy knit golf shirts, Californian leisurewear and a display of indigenous fashions. Most of the other European men in their party circle had adopted the local custom and wore the loose-fitting *barong Tagalog* at night or on formal occasions. She had never found one big enough for Richard and he wouldn't be bothered having one tailored. But here this store window advertised 'European Sizes—Big and Stout Shirts for all Occasions'. She entered and asked the clerk for the biggest size in *barongs*. From an armful of shirts she selected two, holding each in turn before her—the light from the street milky through the diaphanous cloth—trying to imagine his bulky shoulders and ginger-haired chest within its embroidered outline.

'Yes,' she decided. 'I'll take these.' Suddenly she was sufficiently elated with the idea to enter into the spirit of commerce and bargain cursorily with the clerk. He dropped the price the customary ten per cent.

'Your husband is a very big man,' he commented, wrapping the shirts. 'Our very biggest size. Only for the big wrestler and boxing man.' He giggled curiously as he handed her the parcel.

Buying the shirts gave Margaret an unexpected degree of pleasure. She was delighted. When they were younger, before the children were born, she had bought him a gift every week; sometimes just a pair of socks or a paperback, but occasionally, particularly after a squabble, she had made up with a new briefcase, a couple of Italian silk ties or a record album out of the blue. The anticipation of giving had excited her then. Now, with the habit lost, she recalled those days with poignancy. He was at his most loving then, still young, but his energy was tempered by heavy exercise and a thoughtful gentleness. She dwelt on sentimental visions of Saturday night love-making: when the afternoon's game had taken the abrupt edge off his aggression, given him a tired and lingering grace and occasionally a rare passivity when she could slide over him administering healing kisses to bruised and curiously shy skin.

Travelling home in the car, the parcels beside her, Margaret felt nostalgic for romance. This was a culture of sweet-hearts: love was always in the heavy silted air. For once she felt in tune with the whole honeyed passionate state. She had José pull up at a European supermarket and bought two bottles of white wine and a fresh chicken. They had pork in the freezer, she remembered. Professor Flehret could take a back seat tonight. She would have Mina make a special farewell dinner and she would give Richard the shirts as a farewell present. He would like them, she was certain. They would be useful, for one thing. But he would also be touched by her thoughtfulness and would see the gifts as a generously apologetic gesture for last night's scene. She envisaged him, surprised and grateful, receiving the parcel, kissing her thank you, unwrapping it, perceiving that it was two attractive shirts, getting up from the table to try them on, returning wearing one of them. The fit would be accurate. He would parade in a pleased, awkward way before her. The delicacy of the fabric would contrast nicely with his physique. The girls would grin shyly from the kitchen doorway. He would sit down again to dinner cool and classy in a new pineapple fibre *barong Tagalog* and they would eat Mina's special *adobo* and drink German wine together.

Considering this image with pleasure, Margaret lay back in the rear seat tapping her fingers lightly on the parcels beside her. Out the closed car window beyond the air-conditioning the muted hubbub of the highway grew louder. Ahead of them a jeepney breakdown was causing the traffic to bank up. The horns of trucks and jeepneys blared restlessly. All around them ornate polished klaxons were hooting the tunes of 'Mame' and 'Chicago' and there was one which approximated a cow mooing. Beneath a huge sign at the side of the highway proclaiming the First Lady's 'Green Revolution' a man sat in the crusted mud fashioning religious trinkets from discarded tin-foil. Two small boys darted urgently into the traffic to sell them. Unfortunately José accelerated into a clear space before she was able to wind down her window to buy one.

6

BAREFOOT ON THE COOL LINOLEUM FLOOR of the kitchen, Mina Evangelista took the cleaver and, with quick, even blows, cut the chicken into pieces. With a knife she trimmed the pork shoulder of excess fat and cut the meat into cubes. Then, using a small serrated vegetable knife, she sliced two tomatoes into wedges.

Mina combined vinegar, water, garlic, salt and pepper in a heavy casserole and stirred until the salt dissolved. She added the chicken and pork and turned the meat with a spoon to coat the pieces evenly with the vinegar mixture. Bringing the casserole to the boil over high heat, she reduced the heat to low, covered the pot and let it simmer. Then, inhaling the savoury steam, she stirred in some soy sauce, covered the pot again, and let it simmer for a little longer, until the pork was tender. To test that the meat showed no resistance she pierced it with a skewer.

Briskly, she transferred the chicken and pork to a warm plate. She increased the heat to high and, stirring occasionally, boiled the cooking liquid remaining in the casserole until the sauce thickened. She removed the casserole from the heat, let the sauce settle for a few minutes, then skimmed off the fat and poured it into a skillet. She tasted the sauce for seasoning, was content, and covered it to keep warm.

Mina was nearly finished. She added a little lard to the skillet, and placed the pan over high heat. When the fat was very hot she browned the chicken and pork, turning the pieces frequently with tongs and regulating the heat as they coloured richly and evenly. As they browned she deftly transferred the pieces of meat to a heated platter and covered them.

Satisfied, she wiped her hands on her apron, then passed them through her hair. The woman came into the kitchen and was pleased. She was happy for once and not making an ugly face. Her yellow hair resembled the hair of Faye Dunaway, the Hollywood *artista*, and today fell softly around her face. When the man came home and was ready to eat, before he was *gago* from drink, she would pour the sauce over the meat and garnish the platter with tomato wedges and parsley. Then she would serve her special *adobo* with boiled rice. She and Concepción could use the rice-water to boil their milk-fish and vegetables.

7

A RAW SKELETAL DOG was slinking at the front gate as Cullen arrived home. José sounded the horn at it but it remained trembling in their path. José made as if to drive over it but Cullen said, 'No,' and got out of the car. 'Psst!' he hissed, and waved his briefcase at it. 'Shoo!' With a grisly glance the dog cringed away.

As he was already out of the car Cullen wearily swung open the gates and waved José through. He closed them and started up to the house.

Through the darkening hibiscus shrubbery a voice called, 'Hey, Dick! You got a moment?' Ted Orosa peered over the dividing wall. 'I'd like a word with you, if it's OK. Bring Margaret over for a cocktail.' He was smoking a long cigar and tapping ash into the garden. Backlit by the garish light from his own garden, his small head was lustrous in a golden aureole. 'We'll chew the fat,' he went on.

Cullen sometimes wondered whether Orosa had picked up his brand of Western familiarity from his Australian wife or from the American correspondents with whom he came into contact. He was a columnist on the *Post*. The Teodoro G. Orosa by-line carried a curious weight, chiefly because he was rumoured to be the President's pipeline. Perspicacious politicians and businessmen read between the lines of 'As I See It' and heeded the warnings they saw in critical references to 'fat cat exporters' and 'unwelcome *filibusteros* from over the sea'. Certainly Orosa's taut, old-child face exuded the contentment of a man who had backed the right side. It may have been the fact that many of his contemporaries' careers had failed so dramatically that had also given him a self-conscious affability. Cullen always felt that the little man was aching to clap him on the back, put a comradely arm around his shoulders, but, frustrated by their height difference, was forced to engage in the alternate body contact of the hand-shake and elbow clasp.

'Hello, Ted. I'll check with Margaret. Perhaps for just a moment. I'm pretty bushed.'

'Sure, sure. Me too. Just a couple of quiet drinks. See you both in a moment.'

Still overheated from the exercise, he was struck by the marble coolness inside the house. A faint odour of garlic wafted from the kitchen. Rustling about, Mina and Concepción were setting the table. Margaret was not downstairs but as he changed into a clean shirt he heard the shower running in the bathroom. Bone-weary, he went downstairs again for a drink. He opened a bottle of San Miguel and took it out on the verandah to wait for her. The idea of packing was exhausting; he put the trip out of his mind for the moment. Slumped in a cane chair he drank from the small bottle, poured the beer into his throat, peered out into the tepid shadows.

Insects clamoured, fragrant ilang-ilang scented the air. But the night struck him as not so different from countless summer nights of his childhood and adolescence. The humidity was higher but the temperature and sounds brought memories—after-dinner games of Donkey in the street; he and other kids pelting tennis balls at each other, shrieking with the abnormal excitement of night play; going unwillingly, hot and red-faced, to bed. Later, the exquisite anticipation of similar warm evenings: scat-singing under the shower before a party: the sprucely shaved and sanguine expectation of the seventeen-year-old for the company of girls, and jazz tunes hanging in the genial air.

If you
Take the A train
You'll find
You get where you're goin'
If you hurry. . .

Coloured light bulbs would be strung from trees and the
sweet gassy wine would allow several boys to fake
drunkenness.

He felt middle-aged and melancholic whereas only recently
he had been the youngest person around—the fittest, strongest, quickest. How had this sudden disappointing change
occurred? There was still no sign of Margaret. He rose
wearily from the verandah, sensing unhappily that all his
movements these days were ponderous and deliberate. A kind
of resolve solidified in him, however. During the trip he
would sort things out in his mind. Perhaps the separation
would be beneficial.

He went inside to tell the girls the Orosas had invited them
for a drink. 'Tell Mrs Cullen I'll see her there when she's
ready.'

A combination of floridness and airy symmetry, the Orosa
residence could be approached only along a sinuous path of
marble chips. This wound around a sculptured arrangement
of gardens and fish ponds. Obscene carp moved torpidly in
the glare cast by electric lamps in the style of old London
gaslights. Bathed in false light Orosa stood proprietorially on
his verandah holding a martini in each hand. Smiling, he
handed one to Cullen as he came up the steps.

He said, 'Think me presumptuous, but I make a mighty
fine martini.'

Cullen was still two steps below him so they were the same
height. Orosa raised his glass. 'To friendship,' he toasted, and
his tight mouth nipped at the glass.

'To friendship.' The strength of the martini surprised him.
'Whew!' he said, looking quizzically at his host.

'Between our peoples,' Orosa continued. Habitually he
broke the ice with a hands-across-the-sea gesture. He steered

Cullen inside by the elbow to a den decorated in wood panelling and leather. 'Sit down, Dick. Put your feet up. Relax.' He motioned him to a padded stool at a bar simulating the interior of an English inn, complete with a brass footrail and a mirrored backdrop against which stood a multi-coloured assortment of bottles. Etched into the mirror was the statement *Guinness Is Good For You.* 'Is your good wife joining us?'

'Directly.'

'Good, good. Hazel is also. But beforehand I want to ask you a little something. A thing I am curious about, you know.' His teeth were like porcelain separating the dark lips. How beseeching was his smile as he refilled their glasses from the martini pitcher! It spoke of deep familiarity and also of the formality of ritual. 'When you are out in the boondocks, at your duty stations in the provinces and so on, presumably dissidents occasionally come to your attention? Perhaps at grassroots level? Middle echelon maybe? Examples of agitprop?'

'What? Muslims, you mean? Down south?'

'Oh, those crazy *Juramentados* sure, the Moros in Mindanao, obviously. Highly visible, that crowd. A tradition almost. Savages, naturally, and a great problem to the President.' He pursed his lips. 'They are of interest, sure. But others interest me also. In Cebu and Iloilo perhaps. Less prominent groups in small *barrios* who might have been more forthcoming to you people because of your neutrality. Subversive rather than blatant, people of that nature.'

'I wouldn't know one if I met one. We're not political, you realize.'

'Of course not. Forget I asked. It's no big deal. Another drink?'

He was all a-jig with hospitality and the silken third-degree. Cullen was mildly surprised at the questions. They represented a new direction in their neighbourly relationship. A peculiarly unsubtle one. He sipped his martini. If anything it was stronger than the first. 'We deliberately keep out of all that stuff. Your *negative realities.*'

Orosa giggled. 'Of course. I have many friends in the Organization, in the top echelons in New York. They entertain me on my visits, show me a good time, arrange tickets for Broadway shows. I meet old friends, top newsmen, publishers. The Algonquin. Tea in the Rose Room. Ha, ha . . .'

'I'm just in the buffalo business.' He was beginning to sound defensive to himself.

'The backbone of our nation, the trusty *carabao*. Don't think we don't appreciate the meaningful work you people do, Dick.' His hand made conciliatory pats at Cullen's sleeve. 'My information is probably wrong. We will say no more on the subject. Enough.'

His 'information'? Leaving the matter hanging in the air made Cullen feel headachy and testy. Orosa implied that he was graciously letting him off somehow. He finished the martini and asked, 'Who wants to know anyway? The CIA?'

'Dick, how melodramatic. No, nothing like that.' He refilled Cullen's glass.

'What information, anyway?' His graceless tone grated on his own ears but he was irritated by the questions. Political talk made him uneasy, especially any suggestion of his involvement in politics. When he smelled politics in something he pulled out, always had. It was distasteful. He'd gone through university easily able to resist the membership drives of the campus political clubs; he'd be forever grateful that in his representative days the issue of South Africa's racial/sporting morality had not yet arisen. Fancy putting your sport on the line! But bumper-sticker philosophy rubbed him the wrong way, too: *Don't Make Sport a Political Football*, that sort of slogan. And at home the guys from the club had stuck the stickers all over their Volvos and gone out looking for anti-Springbok demonstrators to beat up.

'Aha, that must remain confidential.' Orosa wagged a devilish finger. His eyes were alert with interest. He was enjoying himself, it seemed; his antennae receptive to all signals. 'Why do you mention the CIA?'

Cullen made a sour face. 'No reason.' He was suddenly aware that his crack about the CIA might imply a political consciousness he neither possessed nor wanted. He took an unhappy swig at his drink. Worse, if it contained a grain of truth Orosa would note it and remember.

Mark, on his last school vacation, had christened the black American Embassy limousines 'Batmobiles'.

'Put it down to a reporter's curiosity,' Orosa was saying. He winked. 'That's the thing about us old newshounds. Ed Bonner of *Newsweek* said to me once in the Foreign Correspondents' Club, "Ted," he said, "you are a relentless ferret for sniffing out the news that embarrasses the powers-that-be."' He grimaced modestly. 'True. I am the nemesis of the high-ups.'

Hazel Orosa's entrance spared Cullen comment. 'You boys have everything you want?' she asked, plopping down beside him on a bar stool. She and the leather cushion sighed in unison. The motion stirred up a wave of perfume. 'I'll have a gin and tonic, Ted,' she directed, and placed a cigarette in her bright mouth. She waited expectantly. Orosa hurriedly leaned over the bar and lit it with a gold lighter. Slanting toward the flame she presented Cullen with a slow view of puffy cleavage.

He averted his eyes, but surreptitiously took in the remainder of her. She was an object of some fascination to the Cullens. Her marriage to Orosa, her background (she was a former Brisbane nurse who in the early fifties had parlayed Caucasian dumpiness and peroxided hair into surprisingly negotiable assets), her assertive role in local society, all held their interest. Tonight she was wearing a peasant blouse, tight slacks and gold sandals. Her hair was swept up into a high and durable helmet in the bouffant style favoured by the local socialites. On her wide-pored face she wore cosmetics with great zest. Margaret had mentioned how during Hazel's afternoon bridge and canasta parties she often held court in her pink, plumped-up bedroom where a huge dressing-table displayed every conceivable brand, variety and shade of cosmetic. 'Help yourselves, girls,' she'd invite off-handedly, as if the arrayed jars, tubes and bottles were sweetmeats for their casual pecking. Reclining among fat pillows she would initiate gossip of lovers and failing careers.

To Orosa she was a treasure beyond his fellows' ken. Because of her, the Cullens believed, his self-appreciation was boundless. They felt that he basked in the good-natured envy of his political and business friends: that she was living proof of his machismo, his relentless *cojones*. Ted Orosa had regularly known the soft white flesh of a blonde!

He felt less tense, but after the martinis, and the beer earlier, Cullen was light-headed. Probably dehydration, he thought. Margaret had still not appeared. He declined another martini.

'Give Dick a beer,' Hazel directed her husband.

'Sure, sure. On the way.' Orosa, briskly efficient in the barman role, snapped the top off a San Miguel and poured it into a pewter tankard.

'*Muchas gracias.*' Cullen felt a sudden gratitude to Hazel for some reason. Icily metallic, the beer scoured his throat, made his teeth ache, produced a chill in his stomach which settled there for a moment. 'Not too much of this for me,' he said, swallowing a belch. 'I've got a busy few weeks ahead.'

'Oh?' said Hazel. She blew smoke into the air with authority.

'Six or seven countries in five weeks. I shall be making home calls on the buffaloes of Asia.'

'That sounds like heavy going. I don't know where you get the energy.' With a wily touch Hazel suddenly squeezed one of his biceps. The sharp tips of her nails astonished him. 'You must be in good condition.' Her cigarette smoke hung over them. 'I've never got used to the heat myself. I don't know how you boys do it. Rugby and cricket every weekend in the mud.'

'We're fortified by this stuff,' Cullen said, almost embarrassed. He raised his tankard.

'Mad dogs and Englishmen,' Orosa muttered from behind the bar. 'No offence, Dick,' he added quickly.

'I went with a footballer once. He always smelled of liniment on Saturday nights,' Hazel announced. 'It did nothing for me.'

Cullen laughed. Alongside her he had a view of her white fat back, exposed by the low neckline of her blouse. It looked malleable, as if the slightest finger pressure would leave indentations. Glancing away he saw Orosa grim with jealousy, tortured by his momentary isolation from the conversation. Casually Cullen peered out the window into the night, sipping his beer. Drenched in glaring light, Orosa's swimming pool shone like an aquamarine amongst the tailored vegetation. Jagged glass slivers glinted along the top of the garden wall.

Loudly Orosa said, 'Dick, we must have a game of golf one of these days. I am slashing my handicap lately.'

'Sure, Ted. Golf's not my game though. I wouldn't be in your league.'

Orosa perked up. 'Sure you would.' He grinned. 'Did I tell you I played in a foursome with the President the other week? That man has the smoothest swing! He is still the best athlete in the country. Steel in his wrists and shoulders like a boxer. A welterweight, you know?' He shook his head in wonderment and flexed his own narrow shoulders.

'My glass's empty.' Hazel made this statement with a coquettish flounce which produced a small quiver above her breasts but did not stir the rigid hairstyle. At the same time, adjusting her buttocks on the stool, jiggling, she leaned briefly to steady herself on Cullen's knee. There was a vague pressure from her fingers. He saw her hand was clustered with rings—some of them bit into the soft flesh—and the nails were voraciously bright. Her husband refilled her glass, splashing a large amount of tonic on to a minute measure of gin and dropping in a handful of ice cubes.

'Thank you, Ted,' she said sharply, 'for looking after my welfare.'

Orosa refilled Cullen's tankard, hastily, the beer falling from several inches above the rim. He had to hurriedly sip before the foam surged over the side.

'Ted certainly looks after me,' Hazel went on, as Orosa sipped his martini, doleful again. Cullen gulped at a collar of steely froth. 'Would you believe that he sheltered me from the cockfights for years?'

'Pah! They are too sordid for ladies. Women of any breeding don't go there.' Orosa, smiling ferociously, looked to Cullen for confirmation but he took refuge in his drink.

'I didn't know that Jaime our driver was a *sentenciador* at the cockfights. Ten years he's been with us and no one told me. I insisted he take me to his *barrio* last Sunday. I enjoyed it. I won two hundred pesos, too.'

'Why wouldn't you?' Orosa shrugged. 'Jaime is the *sentenciador*!'

'He played it straight down the line!' she protested.

Her husband raised his eyes to the ceiling.

Cullen had been once himself during the festival of Santa Cruzán but had not enjoyed the fights. For some reason he had expected a sporting atmosphere. The money tension, the dynamics of contest seemed wasted on the grubby barnyard surroundings. The procession of quick battles, the evil-eyed birds, the flash of steel fighting blades, the incessant ringing of the starting bell, the squalid bookie in basketball sneakers, held no sleazy charm for him. Oddly he had been reminded of his father beheading pullets for Christmas thirty years before—fowls he'd raised from yellow chicks, semi-pets; the bodies squirming headless in the dust, then hanging from a branch of the banksia in the backyard. Dripping on to the grass. The axe ominous on the chopping block.

'What about the blood?' he asked. 'It didn't bother you?'

'Blood?' Hazel wondered. 'There wasn't much blood. They're only birds. Actually,' she confided, exhaling smoke, 'what I'd really like to see is those stallion fights the old landowners used to have. That would beat chickens for a spectacle.'

Orosa sat, still silent, at his side of the bar. When Cullen caught his eye, however, he tittered like a schoolgirl. 'Fighting horses! Put a tasty mare in a nearby corral and they will fight all right.' And he winked elaborately, man-to-man. 'We are all stallions, eh?' He seemed to draw good cheer from that idea, sighing blithely. 'The problems of being a man! The eternal contests . . .'

54

'You bring them on yourselves,' Cullen exclaimed. He tempered his interruption with a grin. 'You fellows spend too much energy being gallant and dashing.' He swallowed a mouthful of beer and tasted emptiness. 'You should be more phlegmatic, like us Anglo-Saxons.' Gas rose in his gullet. His tongue and lips seemed coated with a tinny substance he could not dispel.

'Take your typical businessman,' he went on, tapping the bar for emphasis. 'He's part of the *querida* system, maintaining a mistress. As well he's conducting affairs in three countries at once. Dirty weekends in Taipei, so-called business conferences in Hong Kong . . .'

'Sly devils,' Hazel muttered breezily.

Orosa twinkled behind the bar, shook his lubric head. 'Ha, ha. That is not the view of the poet Lord Byron. "What men call gallantry, and gods adultery, is much more common where the climate's sultry".'

'The slogan of the expatriate.'

'Lord Byron was not your typical Englishman. Not at all.' Orosa abruptly stood upright, steadying himself with a hand on the bar. He was taller than he should have been, exuberant.

Cullen supposed he was standing on the bar rail for added height.

'I am something of a Lord Byronist,' Orosa announced loudly, pausing as if for applause. 'He was like the great Rizal and del Pilar. Full of life, passion and fight.' He wagged a finger. 'I am also a Brooklyn Dodger. Now the Los Angeles Dodgers as you well know. Oh, am I a fan!' He shook his head, in wonderment it seemed to Cullen.

'Well, you and Byron are both worried about the sword outwearing the sheath, I'll give you that.'

A high giggle started in Orosa's throat. He slumped back on his stool. ' "So we'll go no more a-roving by the light of the moon",' he spluttered, collapsing into coughing fit. Black-faced, he buried his head in his hands.

'For God's sake drink some water,' Hazel ordered, and slid a jug across the bar.

Cullen himself felt weak, as if from some emotional attack. A fresh bottle of San Miguel stood before him. He surveyed its icy dew, touched cool fingers to his temples, then poured beer into his tankard, paying studious attention to its collar of froth. He drank deeply. The liquid pierced his throat and plunged down through his chest. His head and the area behind his right eye were aching. The realization suddenly came to him that relations were again deranged: she had not joined him here, she had ignored him on his last night. A pulse began thumping. He felt appalling. Alone. Suddenly in sight of death. A familiar feeling occurred to him.

Once he had been at an air terminal—Hong Kong, no Tokyo, in transit. He remembered his mood perfectly, his exact physical state. He had run almost ten kilometres that morning through foreign streets, had a good relaxing breakfast, felt like a million dollars. He was serene, content, on the ball. His body hummed. With a half-hour to fill between planes he encountered a machine which tested blood pressure. Japanese electronic wizardry had struck again; he was amused and mildly curious. He placed the armband around his bicep and fed the machine coins. Suddenly the band gripped like a vice. Still he was calm, in good shape. The armband tightened while he sought the machine's decision on a glowing panel. It was slow in coming. *It's getting a second opinion*, he smiled to himself, his arm throbbing in the relentless grip. In red lights his diastolic and systolic figures suddenly appeared. An adjoining chart warned that his blood pressure was high, in the danger zone. Diminutive passers-by peered smugly at the flashing public announcement of the giant European's imminent demise. He tore off the armband, his heart leaping, and hurried from this formidable airport toy. On his way to the departure gate twenty minutes later he passed the machine again and his circulatory future was still on display. He was in a state of anxiety for days after.

Absently, Hazel said, 'You boys, I don't know,' and lit herself a cigarette.

Shortly, with exaggerated ceremony, Orosa brought out a bottle of coconut sap spirit. '*Tuba!*' he cried. 'The savage

56

tribesmen were drinking *tuba* centuries before the arrival of
the Spaniard. Try some for a novelty. Puts strength in your
bolo arm.'

Later, returning shakily to his dark silent house, Cullen
imagined he saw the starving dog lingering at the gate but,
fumbling with the catch, he was merely confused by tropical
hallucinations of light and shadow.

II   BUBALUS BUBALIS

1

MUCH TO GALASH'S DISGUST they arrived in Bangkok, their overnight stopover, late on a Sunday night. By the time they drove into the city and checked into their hotel it was too late to hit the nightspots.

'Anyway, I'm too exhausted for the fleshpots,' Z.M. said languidly. 'A nightcap and bed for me.'

Galash complained, 'I know this extraordinary bath-house in Patpong Road.'

'Oh my God,' Z.M. muttered. During the flight he had slipped into the jovial role of the seasoned traveller. He had the inside dope on all the recent coups, a fund of scurrilous anecdotes about leading regional personages. He wore a new pale green safari suit that combined elegance, comfort and launderability. The air of the modest voluptuary also clung to him. 'Better your bloodstream than mine, Hugh.'

Cullen didn't commit himself to disappointment. He was determined to stay relaxed on this tour. He had a dim idea that travel, a rigid schedule, the break itself, by some osmotic process would bring them back to a previous happier stage. It weighed on him that he and Margaret had parted miserably, but what could he do but make the best of things?

Anyway, stifled opportunities were also hangovers nipped in the bud. And there were consolations next morning in the simultaneous unfuddled appreciation of the Royal Nepal Airline's champagne and his first view of the Himalayas. The glimpse brought out a strong sentimentality. Margaret should have been there. She was a good traveller, always got something out of it. Scenic wonders softened her and produced a youthful ingenuousness that he liked. To sunsets, gorges and waterfalls she paid homage with her Canon, capturing gesturing tree branches in the corners of all her snaps. The scenes in her photographs seemed to snatch at you.

In the row ahead a young American couple exclaimed 'Wow!' repeatedly and clicked photographs out the window. Rosy with health, they wore expensive trekking clothing. During the descent into Kathmandu, with mountain peaks hanging eerily over their wingtips, they turned back to Cullen saying, 'Man, isn't this something?'

'Sure is.' The Himalayas. There was a phrase used about him once in his school magazine: 'The Everest of a Himalayan career'. This article had laid it on with a trowel. 'For Dick Cullen it was the Everest of a Himalayan career to be named captain of the Schoolboys' Team to play Britain. . . .' He remembered that sentence and several literary allusions in the piece. The author had been the English master, one F. E. Turkington, known as 'Gobble'. He had been astonished to see that Gobble was such a fan. Gobble had even referred to him as Yeats' 'wise and simple man'. More. He'd called him a warrior, admired him 'for the dangers he has passed'. His article finished with the line: 'He is a young man whom, as Emerson said of Thoreau, "It took generations to make".' Rugby affected some of them like that, especially bachelor school masters, but this grandiloquence had stuck in his mind for twenty-five years while he had forgotten every newspaper sporting story ever written about him. There was a hint of something there that had niggled at him ever since. Not that the previous generation, Dottie especially, hadn't lapped it up.

At the airport a man from the government met them. He wore a black topi and dusty city shoes. Smiling a welcome he hawked up a considerable gob of phlegm at the same time.

'*Namaste,*' Z.M. greeted him.

In second gear their official Toyota lurched through narrow ancient streets to a briefing session at the Agriculture Ministry, a square brick block set in a gravel courtyard spotted with dawdling and spitting men. Most were agog. Up four flights of cement stairs, bare except for a spittoon at each landing, they were led into a boardroom where a dozen officials in topis sat around a long table under a tinted portrait of King Birendra. Introductions were made. Old men brought in trays of tea and hard pale cake. Above the tinkling of crockery polite chatter was conducted, on common ground. A stubbled waiter hovered at each elbow.

Declining a Yak brand cigarette Cullen announced sociably, 'I understand you have four million buffaloes in Nepal?'

'Approximately,' said the leading official, nodding his head gratefully. 'That is the figure we get from your *Production Yearbook.*'

Galash accepted a Yeti brand cigarette, lit up. 'You gentlemen are fortunate,' he commented, removing a twig from his tongue, 'that your buffaloes have this outstanding adaptability to high altitudes.'

'Ah, one advantage of natural selection,' Z.M. contributed, smoothly neglecting to mention that the nondescript animals were thus ideal for neither milk nor meat. He sank into a smiling silence, almost a trance.

Around the table the officials also smiled politely. Some cleared their throats in a muted way. Others lit cigarettes with businesslike masculinity, and rustled papers. Fingernails were perused, cake crumbs brushed from shirt fronts. The air was electric with expectancy. All faces gradually turned to the head of the table. At last the leading official produced a sheaf of maps and building plans and spread them across the table.

'These are the projects for which we seek your help,' he murmured shyly. 'Some new livestock stations.'

They pored over the documents.

'Very interesting,' Cullen remarked, adding that they could be used as focal points for nucleus breeding units aimed at achieving more constructive breeding programmes.

'Your advice is most welcome,' the top man whispered.

'It is extremely valuable,' said another official. His sing-song voice rose. 'The buffalo is our meat supply, our milk supply, our machinery of agriculture. . . .'

'Gentlemen, we are here to help,' Galash soothed.

A general enthusiastic handshaking took place as they left. Corkscrews of dust twirled in the courtyard. Several officials anxiously covered their faces with scarves. In his farewells the leading official mentioned that they were fortunate to be in Nepal during October when the country's biggest festival, Bade Dasain, would occur. Much ritual slaughter of animals would take place in honour of the goddess Durga.

He smiled. 'A stream of blood flows,' he said.

'*Namaste*,' said Z.M., crinkling his handsome eyes.

They were then permitted to check into the Hôtel de l'Annapurna, where Cullen was to discover that mountain swallows nested in the ceiling of his room and that the birds were early and noisy risers. The lobby also twittered with elderly American widows tyrannized by a thyrotoxic tour guide in a red hairpiece. All this activity encouraged Galash to make a mild inquiry of a barman. Where was the 'action', as he termed it, in Kathmandu?

'Our girls do not mix with foreigners,' the barman said tersely. His frown of disapproval covered the embarrassed Cullen and Z.M. as well as Galash.

'Of course not,' Z.M. agreed instantly.

'There are the folk dances in the Rana Palace and Dilli-bazar. But perhaps you could go with the hippies,' the barman suggested disdainfully. He mimed the smoking of *ganja*, rolling his eyes theatrically.

'Oh my God,' Z.M. snorted. Imperceptibly he was now aligned with the barman against the two crass Westerners.

'Oh great,' muttered Galash, crouching over his Scotch. 'Folk culture or drug fiends!'

Instead, rugged up in sweaters, they strolled through the city that night. By 9 p.m. the snappy air had cleared the streets, but as they left the hotel a tiny girl fastened upon them. She was wrapped in skins and a helmet made of animal fibres was pulled over her ears. Relentlessly she stuck to their heels, defying all attempts to shoo her away. She had a precocious wisdom and brown medieval eyes. In a reedy lilting voice she sang:

'You are rich man.
I am poor man.
You give me money
I happy man.'

Naturally sentimental Cullen was reminded of his daughter Louise, a pale fair girl like her mother but with, more was the pity, a growing tendency to his freckled gingerness and, worse, a physique modelled after his own: broad shoulders, thick waist, sturdy thighs—even at ten. Often he sighed for her sad years to come, for the inevitable rebuffs, for her loving nature, for all her useless co-ordination and redundant athleticism. He could easily torture himself exaggerating her forced future as a rollicking leathery Phys. Ed. teacher in perennial blazers and tennis shoes or, nightmare, overalled bull-dyke garage attendant.

Mark, on the other hand, though a genuine W. H. Sheldon mesomorph, seemed to inhabit a soft and dreamy pre-adolescent world of skidmarks, green teeth, odd socks and crusty ears. His son could not pull himself together. He still cried. He had no tenacity, for God's sake. He did not wish above all else to tackle the man, to capture the ball, to possess it, to *eat* it! True enough he would rather win than lose, given the choice, but only just. Twelve years old and not enough imagination to change his underpants or brush his teeth! He wanted him to hurry up and be a man. He was also terrified of this prospect.

'Piss off, darling,' instructed Galash, giving the girl a handful of paisa. She retreated only a short distance before catching them up again. Cullen handed her a couple of rupees for being an amusing little urchin, but she would have still clung to them if Z.M. hadn't suddenly turned on her growling something dramatic in Hindi. She stopped singing as if struck and raced away up the street.

'Boy, that must have been charming,' Galash said.

Wakened by the swallows at 4.30 a.m. Cullen had long since breakfasted and dressed when, passive and shivering in the chill dusty dawn, they were in the hands of their hosts again, piling into a Cessna for a ninety-minute flight south-east to Biratnagar, near the Indian border. Here, it was suggested, were major points of interest for them: a large buffalo farm, a dairy, and also a jute mill of which the Ministry was obviously proud.

Their pilot was a devil-may-care Swiss who deviated from the government's schedule and flew them north-east towards the top of the Himalayas.

'You got to see these mountains up close,' he shouted back at them. 'So what if you miss appointments? Who gets to see Everest every day, huh?'

Who could disagree? Even their tame government companion shrugged and smiled proudly. The sky was a travelogue blue. A dazzling sun rose above the very Himalayan mountains of childhood geography book fame. Abruptly out the port windows there they were: Gauri Shankar, Cho Oyu, Nuptse, Everest, Lhotse, Makalu, crisply etched against the sharp early sky. The Ministry man chanted their names like a mantra.

Sitting across two seats at the rear of the plane Cullen experienced a range of feelings at this vista. There was the requisite soaring of spirits, the elation at viewing one of the world's classic pieces of topography. The uniqueness, he liked that. Then, he urgently wished Margaret was with him to see it—again for the sake of the shared experience. And yet he was just a shade disappointed that Everest wasn't, well, taller. Viewed in its surroundings its outline wasn't singular enough. Every peak around it was high, too.

That was always the story. Not the anti-climax exactly, rather the vague let-down. In Peking, lucky Cullen, arriving from Osaka with one of the first Food and Agriculture Organization ice-breaking teams and finding Chinese animal husbandry a miracle of medieval efficiency, its thirty million buffaloes the picture of health, had focused his emotional energies on unique traditional fixtures, like the Great Wall, long celebrated in his Arthur Mee's *Children's Encyclopaedia*. Pounding in his Adidases up the steep slate incline toward the top turret, he was astounded to see that over the centuries its visitors, not content with chiselling their graffiti (in every language but English), had also left behind little petrified pyramids of faeces, wall stains of urine, in every quiet nook. Jogging up into the clouds he puffed away, spirits alternately soaring and sinking, until after almost two kilometres, at a high turret, the wall suddenly crumbled and was no longer traversable.

Rejoining his tiny girl interpreter and puffing Red Guard attendant, the view of a lifetime in his vision and the reek of a country dunny in his nostrils, he said, 'You should put in a few toilets here.' It didn't register.

But you had to admit the Himalayas were a noble sight. As a draught of Himalayan air shot up his trouser legs from some undercarriage cranny he thought he could understand, as a sportsman, the because-it-was-there syndrome of the mountaineer. Similarly he admired their pilot's aggression and co-ordination, but could have done without his current abrupt plunges and general risk-taking. He was now treating his passengers to some barn-storming tricks in the valleys, stomach-turning dips and climbs, showy half-corkscrews and other death-defying skills. He was a solid man with a buccaneer's confidence.

'Eh!' he called back from the cockpit. 'How's the trip, eh? You lose your guts on the top of the world yet?'

Nearly. Cullen's breakfast steak and eggs sat heavily. Galash had provided the information that it was buffalo, not beef, steak. Even as an advocate of this alternate protein source he had not necessarily welcomed the news. When yet another outcrop of jagged Himalayan mountainside rose rapidly to meet them he gulped and called, 'Hey, Captain. Cut out the funny business and let's get going.'

'OK, Tiny. Non-stop to lovely Biratnagar.'

Biratnagar turned out to comprise an airport with a bare phlegm-specked cement terminal, the brick and tin headquarters of the Biratnagar Jute Corporation (where scores of hawking Hindu jute workers shuffled through dusty buffalo pats to peer curiously at the foreign trio) with its suitably dark and satanic nineteenth-century mill, and the buffalo farm. This, they discovered, was less a farm than a way station on the overland trek from India. Its scraggy beasts were mostly curly-horned Murrahs destined for the Kathmandu slaughterhouses. A fortunate few bulls would be permitted to breed here with Nepalese buffaloes to boost local milk, ghee and curd production. The others, joined by unwanted local calves and exhausted work animals, would be trekked to the capital.

The backwardness of this system was noted immediately by the visiting buffalo specialists. They exchanged glances and jotted on clipboards. Cullen noted: 'A radical change in husbandry methods is essential, with close attention to nutrition and breeding.' Then, within sight, sound and smell of the stockpens they were served tea laced with buffalo milk and pale fibrous biscuits.

'Made from the local jute, I presume,' Galash muttered, through a benign smile.

In lieu of impolite criticism Cullen sucked on a *khoa* sweetmeat, a favourite with the populace, prepared from condensed buffalo milk. Z.M. conducted small talk and offered around his Camels. Blessedly they were shortly back in the hands of their Swiss air ace who flew the direct return route to Kathmandu.

Next on the schedule were lectures, passively received, to a group of intense snuffling husbandmen. After his talk on 'The Management, Conservation and Use of the Domestic Buffalo' (Z.M. spoke briefly on 'The Buffalo as Milk Producer', Galash on his old standby, 'The Problems of Foot-and-Mouth Disease and Rinderpest'), Cullen rang Margaret, wrongly gauging the time difference and bringing her sleepily to the telephone.

'Greetings from Shangri-la, darling.'

'Hi, you know it's almost midnight here.'

'Sorry, the altitude's got me.'

'You certainly sound very chirpy. On top of the world literally, eh?'

'Oh so-so. I was quite good tonight on the varied uses of buffalo faeces, but they knew most of them. Listen, I saw Everest today and I wished you were with me.'

'Thanks. I was making paper hats for the division's children's Christmas party.'

'This early? It's only October.'

'You underestimate the efficiency of the Ladies' Committee. I'd rather have been sightseeing around Everest, I can tell you.'

'It was good but not tall enough. I guess I was expecting something like the old Paramount Pictures' trademark.'

There was a moment's silence and in a lower voice she was saying, 'I haven't been too well. I can't keep anything down.' Her voice trailed away.

'What? Are you sick?'

'Don't worry about me. I'll be all right.'

'Have you seen the doctor? Don't go to that Martinez quack. Ring old Hopkins in Personnel Medical.' Better a doddery BMA man than Martinez, who ran advertisements in the papers saying: 'TB, VD, and Circumcision Specialist—Painless, Bloodless German Cut'. He had a reputation as an overenthusiastic advocate of the cervical examination for his European patients.

An extended crackling like radio static was on the line and behind it Margaret's voice, faint and airy, murmuring ' . . . appointment on Thursday. I'm OK really. This line's terrible. Goodnight, darling.'

'Take care of yourself. Sweet dreams.'

Ringing off, Cullen had the clearest image of her replacing the receiver of the extension phone by their bed, wide awake now, sitting tousle-headed, propped up by both their pillows, frowning and going furiously at her nails with an emery board. She would be thinking, 'I'll never sleep now,' and would flip through *Time* for ten minutes before turning out

69

the light. Her sleep would be instantaneous though jumpy. She would murmur and utter half-words and perhaps sit bolt upright with an awry breast outside her nightdress. He knew the thick sleepy smell of her breath, the small opening of her parted lips and the angles of her limbs. He could see the position of her black-framed reading glasses on the bed table. He could not, however, imagine her dreams—sweet or otherwise. Perhaps they were beyond his sort of imagination.

More stomach trouble? From time to time she complained of pains, nausea and general discomfort. He advocated barium meals, X-rays and so on, but no physical causes had been discovered. Since childhood she had regularly exhibited the symptoms of major diseases. Her parents, the Catholic hypochondriacs Pat and Ruth Lynch, had brought up their only child in a sterile atmosphere: on milk warmed to blood temperature, Oslo lunches and soft-boiled eggs. She had been born in their middle age, after a series of miscarriages and a still-birth, a small baby of pale beauty. Little Margaret received a daily delicate thermometer in the armpit. Her drinking water was boiled and refrigerated. Meals and bowel movements were scheduled like Mussolini's trains. As a toddler she picked at raisin sandwiches within an insect-proof playpen positioned to catch the sun. Mosquito-netted, she was safety-pinned into bed in case of night-time tumbles. At those few friends' houses trusted to safeguard her she would ask surreptitiously for chocolate biscuits and Coca-Cola.

By the time they were engaged she was just able to joke about her parents.

'I suppose they'll want to sterilize me,' he'd laughed one evening after football training, planting germy kisses on her.

Downstairs, Z.M. and Galash were in the bar drinking brandy. Z.M. ordered him one as he entered. 'A cognac for Dick,' he said. 'Hang the expense.' The barman raised a superior brow but served him speedily.

'A dashing pair,' Cullen remarked, sipping his drink. 'What's the occasion?'

Z.M.'s eyes twinkled. He wore one of the local woollen jackets with the fleece innermost, beloved of tourists; also sturdy corduroys and fashionable boots. He looked like a Nepalese matinée idol. Galash was rugged up in an Irish polo-neck sweater. Both heads gleamed.

'Mr Ram will show us the real Kathmandu,' Galash said. Beside him stood one of the earnest young throat clearers from the husbandry lecture, drinking Coke.

'*Namaste*,' Cullen said.

'Hi,' said Mr Ram 'You've come to the right man.' He winked. His topi edged slightly down his scalp and back again.

As they moved out into the street Z.M. nudged Cullen. 'That's it, Dick. Just keep saying "Namaste"—"I salute all divine qualities in you." One cannot go wrong with that.'

Galash clapped him on the back. 'You'll get by, won't you Dick?'

He raised a jocular fist. They seemed excited and well-organized. Already he felt uncomfortable.

In the gutter the little girl beggar was bailing up a group of Japanese, singing at them while they flapped their arms at her and clicked their tongues. She left the Japanese and ran to them, her layers of clothing swaying about her. Avoiding Z.M. she sidled up to Cullen and Galash trilling, 'You are rich man. I am poor man. . . .'

Coerced again, Cullen fished for rupees. 'She really does have a sweet voice.' She gave him her historic angel's face. He could have kissed her, delicately, on her cinnamon eyelids.

Mr Ram glared at her. '*Pugyo!*' he muttered.

'*Theek, theek*,' she mewled, sinking into her garments. 'You give me money, I happy man.'

'Aren't we all, baby?' Galash said.

Relentless, she stuck to them for several blocks, Mr Ram finally raising his hand at her. Z.M. did not repeat his earlier Hindi threat, possibly out of deference to Mr Ram.

A block further, just past Durbar Square, Mr Ram gave a funny smile and ushered them into a doorway. He removed his topi, his badge of bureaucracy, and then secreted it somewhere on his person. 'Welcome to the Pleasure Room,' he announced.

Inside there appeared to be a sort of restaurant. Young Westerners and Nepalese with long hair slouched serenely on low chairs. There was sitar and mridanga music coming from hidden sources, and an extensive smoking of hashish. Slow and happy conversations took place as they entered, but gradually faded.

'It's a drug den,' Galash whispered. He nudged Cullen, who nodded unhappily. Mr Ram muttered to a smiling Nepali who led them to a space in a corner and motioned them to sit. On the walls were Tibetan carpets and Chinese deities, some of lividly ferocious aspect.

Cullen was always disorientated by mystic surroundings. Religious art threw him out just as much as political posters. Religion was a secret he did not particularly wish revealed. He browsed through the broken English of the menu. In his fingers the menu felt tiny and flimsy, like a bus ticket.

Mr Ram recommended the cakes. They were, he suggested with many winks, just like Mother used to make, as the saying went. 'Joke!' he said. 'They are perhaps a little different in their effects.' He ordered for them: three plates of cakes, some *chang*—the local beer—and four buffburgers.

'Buffburgers? You're kidding,' Galash said.

'Murrah or Surti?' asked Z.M. 'Oh my God.' His eyes darted around the room.

'I'll have a Kundi with cheese and hold the onion,' Cullen joked. He laughed loudly. His nasal guffaw hung in the room. Even to him it sounded callow.

Spots of dark pigment showed on Mr Ram's cheekbones. He was embarrassed. 'I'm afraid I cannot specify the breeds of the burgers,' he said seriously. 'They are popular here. I thought they would be of interest. We are not beef eaters, as you know.'

'No offence, old chap,' Cullen said distractedly. 'Obviously we're all great supporters of the buffalo.'

Mr Ram drew silently on a thin yellow cigarette. The sweetness of *ganja* hung over the customers, mingling with

72

the smell of frying meat and the steam from curried vegetables, rice and lentil soup.

Incommoded in body and spirit, Cullen crouched on a flat cushion, his thighs pressing uncomfortably up against the sharp table edge. He was twice the size of anyone in the room. Soon an old knee injury began to throb from the cramped posture. His awareness was acute of his short hair, his age, his Western-ness, his Rugby club tie, his lace-up shoes, the 65/35 nylon-wool mix socks which, creeping down his white shins, exposed orange curly hairs. He removed his tie, sipping tentatively at the atmosphere, taking tiny shallow breaths. It couldn't possibly do you any good, he thought. At the least it made you indolent and puny if these kids were any indication, lying around passively blinking their soft eyes. Eyes like Bambi, they had, or religious personalities; and chests like sparrows. He foresaw Mark among them, as sure as God made little apples.

Things were getting away from him.

'God knows how they get the energy to hike around the Himalayas,' he said, exerting a trace of his substantiality.

'Hmm?' Galash murmured. The food had arrived and he was leaning back on a pile of cushions sipping *chang* and munching a little brown cake.

Helpful Mr Ram passed plates around. Cullen took a mug of *chang* and, more hesitantly, a cake. Dubiously he nibbled at it. At the next table a blonde American girl in Tibetan jacket and hiking boots announced loudly: 'You can say what you like about Dhulikhel, man, the views and temples and all, but I say seven rupees is too much for a dose of the shits, sunrise or no sunrise.'

A bearded boy said serenely that a trek was a trek, man. 'You don't like hills, you should stay outa the Himalayas.'

Cullen peered about for Z.M. He was lounging against a wall-hanging in conversation with a freckle-faced girl. She passed him an ornately carved pipe. Crinkling his eyes at her he drew on it and passed it back. Next they were smiling and exchanging cakes, in a cute and romantic tableau.

His ease with this drug paraphernalia was disconcerting.

Cullen feigned ennui. 'Hey,' he said jealously to Galash, 'Ali's bridging the culture gap.'

Galash cast a calm and opportunistic eye around the room. 'This *chang* is quite powerful booze,' he said. 'It's not a bad drop, man.' He nibbled at another cake.

Cullen did not know what to do with his hands. He took another cake, too. It dissolved in his mouth almost immediately so he took another, washing it down with *chang*. He was thirsty, the *chang* went down like water, fell on his empty stomach. He sighed resignedly. Even in Casuarina Bay these days, according to his mother's letters, advantage was being taken by 'hippies and undesirables' of the subtropical climate and rich morainal clays to grow marijuana. Though a fervent gardener Dottie naturally disapproved ferociously. She grew orchids without a glasshouse, had nothing against horticultural imports such as bananas and bougainvillaea, but believed this other plant would attract a 'bad element'.

She went through life sniffing out bad elements. These included people with red cars or foreign accents and women who smoked cigarettes in the street. Already, she hinted, a notorious drug dealer had moved into the neighbourhood. There were suspicious numbers of young people at large. They wore loose-fitting clothing and carried babies.

Her position seemed quaint and eccentric to him, an old woman's bourgeois view. But he couldn't countenance the alternative: it was mysteriously blocked off from him. He swallowed more cakes. They were tasty but insubstantial—interestingly, he could detect each individual ingredient. There was a spicy after-taste of intriguing diffused herbs, each delicate flavour occupying the attention of his taste buds.

Abruptly he smiled at the thought of his mother's letters. She disapproved of him being 'overseas'. 'Overseas' to her was England, Europe at a pinch. She wouldn't visit them and lately he noticed a seductive nationalistic note creeping into her letters. She waxed lyrical about 'noble' grey gums and the 'sturdy' she-oak. She presented up-to-the-minute arboreal reports on the state of the red angophoras, spotted maculatas and jacarandas. His mind raced around his old garden, made up a dreamy botanical list. Hibiscus, oleander, camellia, gardenia, poinsettia, lassiandra. Geraniums in pots. Lavender. These nostalgic smells were not impossible to recollect. And spring-blooming freesias popping up through the lawn, their wild scent so sweetly intense it seemed to invade the skull.

The buffburgers remained untouched. Mr Ram hovered over the plate like an anxious housewife. He cleared his throat. 'A point of interest,' he said. 'Nutritionally they are tops. Two per cent more protein than burgers made of beef. And yet prepared according to the American tradition!'

Galash chuckled. 'We'll mention them in our report,' he said.

Propped up by cushions, Cullen repeated, 'We're all great fans of the old buffalo.'

Mr Ram selected a buffburger and began to eat it, slowly, looking over their heads.

Watching Mr Ram's jaws move, Cullen began to consider the immense folklore of the buffalo: the vast range of rituals, the incredible jumble of sympathetic magic governing the entire life span and occupations of the agricultural peoples. His vision encompassed the room and its young customers, the street outside, Nepal, the Himalayas and a large proportion of the earth. He spread his hands in a fatherly gesture to include it all. He was smoking a *ganja* cigarette—with great aplomb considering he could not remember being given it—and drinking *chang* from a fresh bottle. His thoughts were as mellifluous as spoken words, the vowels rounded, the consonants crisp. In Sumatra for example, every aspect of life, every occupation, every waking conscious action was affected by *adat*, the folklore of the buffalo. He mentioned this to Mr Ram.

'Probably you are correct,' he murmured, munching still.

'Mr Ram, you are a gentleman and a scholar. Did you know the buffalo has three magical functions: to carry the weight of the world, to make rain and to originate earthquakes?'

Mr Ram grunted.

Cullen had more privileged information to impart. Facts burned in his head. There was the buffalo team which had pulled heavy cannon from Edirne to Constantinople in 1453. There was the legend behind the Sumatran buffalo headdress. He was dimly aware of prodding Mr Ram in his thin chest once or twice, of repeating portentously, 'To carry the weight of the world.'

'The endless slow plodding in a circle seems more suited to the character of the animal,' said Mr Ram.

2

RAJAMURTI MADE A LOT OF SENSE, thought Margaret, placing his *Commentaries on Existence* on her bedside table, removing her reading glasses and settling back on her pillow. For a moment she did not turn out the light. Richard's pillow beside her still exuded his slightly sour male smell, an odour she would know anywhere; a trait as personal as his fingerprints. She thought of him, unhappily, among a sea of strangers, head and shoulders above them as usual; strangers whose lives he now shared. Whenever in his absences she imagined him he was always smiling, buoyant, gregarious, attractive to women, surrounded by new witty friends. She was excluded.

This attitude was not helpful; with a fixedness of purpose she turned off the bed light and put him to the back of her mind. Not only did Rajamurti speak wisely, she considered, it was strange but she derived some peace of mind from reading him. He went some way towards filling a gap. She was surprised that he could strike such a responsive *personal* chord. And he wrote so serenely, so lyrically. The man was a poet as well as a philosopher and spiritual leader. His commentaries, anecdotes really, usually began with a vivid physical description of the particular garden, lake or mountainside he was visiting. He would introduce his stories in a long, slow, sweeping curve and then suddenly produce an insight so intuitive that she would read it over several times just to absorb the wisdom of it. She appreciated his honesty. Please understand, Rajamurti said, here is no panacea for your difficulties. All I can do is provide certain guidelines—the rest is up to you. All the outsider can do is guide you a little, inspire you a little, console you a little. Empathize completely.

Well, that was a start, Margaret thought. She often worried that she was not intelligent enough, that she had no insight. In company she believed she was uninteresting and fell into silences. Everyone was so creative these days. Pottery and jazz ballet had a lot to answer for. Sometimes she felt as thick and sluggardly as mud. Rajamurti, however, said that to be intelligent *was* to be simple. You hindered intelligence in yourself by your convictions, opinions, assertions and denials. You were the result of what you had been taught. You were like a gramophone (there was a word you didn't hear much these days), playing different records perhaps, but still a gramophone. Conditioning.

Give us the child for the first seven years, said the Jesuits. When she thought of her own conditioning she could squirm. Sometimes she felt her past life—her childhood, adulthood, marriage—was a tightly wound, skeined ball inside her head, like the inside of a golf ball, and she had to concentrate deeply on keeping everything in control, on not letting go a high banshee scream, or the ball would unravel and burst her head open in an explosion of writhing nerves.

She had felt like that for years. Looking back, there was really only one time when she didn't have that omnipresent tautness. She was a fresher at university, smart and pretty, studying hard yet revelling in the freedom from the nuns. On the one day, a Friday in May, she'd received an A-plus for a European history paper and then, in the refectory at lunch-time, had been asked out, in front of her friends—before witnesses!—by the dazzling, duffel-coated Sam Considine, a very big man on campus. Ridiculous, trivial now, but things had never come together like that before or since. She could still remember the crisp temperature of the day, her Black Watch tartan skirt and white polo-neck sweater, the savoury smell of pies and pasties, the waxy paper cups of tomato soup, the hiss of the new espresso coffee machine, the pale lipstick and rings of dark eye make-up they all wore, the self-important, pseudo-intellectual chatter of her friends. 'Kafka-esque' was a big adjective that year. 'Very Kafka-esque,' Sue Leighton and Jenny Rothwell would say, about a film, a play, a book, a dance—a boy, for God's sake. As it turned out Sam was a long way from surreal, grabbing her breasts as soon as he parked the car, sulking at the knock-back, angrily quaffing bourbon from the bottle and complaining peevishly of his martyred aching groin.

A vivid image of herself, viewed with the utmost detachment, would remain with her forever: returning home that night, going to bed naked for the first time in her life and, her bottom in the air like a baby, a hand between her legs in flushed need, guilt and disappointment, rocking, rocking, rocking.

On her pillow the memory still made her cheeks hot.

3

AGAIN THE SWALLOWS SCREECHING in the ceiling woke Cullen early. He got up stiff and smelling *ganja* smoke in his hair. He remembered dimly that it was Dasain, the major day of festival, the ninth after the new moon or somesuch. Unfestive, scratchy-eyed, he nevertheless felt a dull hangover lust, peering outside into the thin light. Travel was an aphrodisiac, Galash often said. He sometimes theorized on the symbolism of the traveller's arrival in the new city or country, the entry into the fresh hotel room, even the hygienically sealed toilet lid; also on the professional subservience of stewardesses, maids and waitresses, usually foreign. The traveller had a masculine power. 'As soon as I'm on a plane I'm horny,' Galash said.

Cullen's susceptibility differed slightly. Travelling, he developed urges that were romantic as well as erotic: he had a tendency to fall secretly and briefly in love. Occasionally he was clumsy enough to attempt to requite these impulses, once or twice, in drink, telling the women in question, usually Embassy or Organization wives, they had wonderful eyes or sensual mouths. Mostly they enjoyed these banalities but were of a type and class to suffer embarrassment, hastening to join their husbands, linking arms and jabbering loudly. Expatriate wives as a rule were nervous of the over-the-canapés compliment.

That it was a day of great celebration was not immediately

80

apparent. In the street greatcoated men rode bicycles. Hunched pedestrians in scarves and topis exhaled steam and spat in the gutter. Light crept up the slopes of Ganesh Himal and Dorje Lakpa, bringing, Cullen presumed, faint warmth to the sleeping bags of loose-bowelled children from Cincinatti, Melbourne and Frankfurt. He performed his ablutions, the dawn rising recalling his old National Service corporal's daily barked command: 'Rise-and-shine! Shit! Shower! Shave! Shampoo! Shag!' The shag part had been an ironic inclusion of the corporal's. The irony held good now, over twenty years later, he thought, showering, shaving and dabbing on some optimistic festive after-shave.

After breakfast Mr Ram, wearing a new topi and clean white jodhpurs, again led them cheerfully toward Durbar Square. 'Returning to the scene of the crime,' he said and laughed. Z.M. grinned and looked abashed. Cullen had left the others in the Pleasure Room at midnight in a condition of relaxation and confidence. 'We are well this morning, I hope?' Mr Ram continued.

'Fine,' Cullen muttered. 'This is the big one, eh? The stream of blood and all that.'

'Indeed. Tonight every household in Nepal eats meat. By the courtesy of the King.'

'That is generous of him,' Z.M. commented affably, brushing hairs from the collar of his safari jacket. His eyerims were red and his facial skin had not yet tautened with the morning.

'He is a god, after all,' Mr Ram said.

In the dirt courtyard behind the square a crowd had already gathered. It had a governmental air: there were numerous black topis present, and many hawking soldiers standing about trying to keep their toecaps clean. Some held hands unselfconsciously. Beyond the courtyard wooden swings had been erected for the children. There was a medieval atmosphere hanging over the square and the old Royal Palace abutting it. Musty draughts wafted around its lichened pillars. Dust hung in pale sun streams. Among the pitted stones and eroded bricks swallows flitted.

In the courtyard there was an anticipatory clearing of throats and noses, a shuffling in the dust. An old flute seller in a checked headdress warbled through his range of toys. A stone tethering post stood in a central position and, beside it, wearing singlets and flapping khaki shorts, five Gurkhas waited. Squat, solid, with close-cropped hair and grim cheekbones, they shifted from one bare foot to the other, nonchalantly spitting to pass the time. Each silent and expressionless man wore a kukri in a scabbard at his waist.

'I don't know how entertaining this is going to be,' Cullen whispered to Galash. Galash shrugged. Cullen noticed he had a pale tension about the upper lip, however, as from the far side of the palace an old army truck drove up. It braked at the edge of the courtyard and discharged ten or twelve buffalo calves into a small pen.

Mr Ram began to mumble amiably to himself. The flute seller tootled an aimless tune.

'Only a dozen. I thought your gods were more bloodthirsty than that,' Cullen commented, with a show of casual quiescence. He wriggled his toes inside his shoes. He had an absurd fear of suddenly fainting, of falling head first in the dust like a felled tree. Parade ground fainters he'd always regarded with amused contempt, now he stretched his arms and legs and shook the juddering spots from the edges of his vision with some urgency.

'Goddesses,' corrected Mr Ram. 'It is perhaps interesting that sacrifices are made always to goddesses, and with young male animals. And they are *very* bloodthirsty.'

'Very symbolic,' Galash said. 'My wife should be here.'

Mr Ram smiled. 'Kali the Terrifying for example requires the slaughter of hundreds. These are just the beginning.'

Cullen's senses were raw and vivid. The sweet reek of straw and animal faeces hovered over him, and the pungency of his own body odour and after-shave. The heat was rising. Dust hung higher in the air. Z.M. popped a breath freshener into his mouth and the peppermint scent also cut sharply into Cullen's impressions. It was as if he were in the dressing-room before a big game, nose smarting with the smell of nervous bodies and liniment; rubbed down, limber, keyed-up but strangely fatalistic. The same dim crowd noises. The acute feeling of loneliness amid camaraderie. Why am I here? His mouth was as dry as cardboard.

Crunching peppermint, Z.M. was saying philosophically, that life was a series of rituals. 'As you know, Parvati, the wife of Shiva, can often be seen in her various manifestations killing a demon in the form of a buffalo.'

'Jesus,' Galash murmured.

A curious but not unfriendly glance from Mr Ram seemed to say: *You curious Muslim!* 'She has a peaceful side also,' he said aloud. 'A peaceful and a fearful side.'

'Don't they all!' Galash cracked, shifting from one foot to the other.

Meantime the Gurkhas had selected one calf from the pen. They bustled it over to the tethering post. It propped along on stiff legs, obstinately bleating and rolling back its eyes. Cullen was surprised by the daintiness of its hooves, like those of a little Pan. Two of the Gurkhas placed cords around its neck and muzzle and pulled its forehead hard against the post. Two others pushed at its hindquarters, struggling to hold it immobile. The fifth man removed his kukri from its scabbard and positioned himself, legs wide apart, at the calf's side. He bent low over his savage knife.

Heart drumming, Cullen waited for the sense of ceremony to hit him. From the impassive crowd, shuffling and snuffling in the square, he sensed nothing. At least let there be awe. He had the fleetest impression, dreamlike and anticlimactic, of executions: scaffolds, guillotines, firing squads. A bell rang. From nowhere in particular came a guttural direction. The straining men holding the calf grimaced, pulled and pushed; there was a simultaneous intake and exhalation of breath, a quick upward and downward swing and the scheme of things was miraculously changed. A headless beast stood upright before him, and a disembodied head supported itself in mid-air. The head completed a bleat and fell. The Gurkhas wiped blood specks from their faces and allowed the body to crumple at their feet.

'Just one blow,' commented Mr Ram, full of nationalistic pride.

Another young bull was despatched, and another, the Gurkhas taking turns to be executioner. A pool of thick blood was forming around the tethering post. At Cullen's suggestion they left to have a drink somewhere. Considering that no one was buying his handiwork the flute seller piped an extremely optimistic note.

4

THE LOBBY AND ELEVATORS of the Dacca Inter-Continental swarmed with East Germans and Russians. The East German Prime Minister was in town on a goodwill visit to their leader, their government guide informed them.

'The guns boomed salute nineteen times! They are discussing the whole gamut of bilateral relations and international issues of common interest,' he said proudly.

The guide, sent by the Development Council, was named Mr Uzzerman. He was an unfortunately pigmented man. His eye-catching face was basically a shrill and vulnerable pink, with several dark blotches on the forehead and neck; his hands and thin forearms were the normal brown skin tone. He greeted Z.M. with wary familiarity. 'It is a big week for us,' he said, smiling. 'Visits from the GDR and our own Mr Ali.'

Z.M. crinkled his eyes at him. 'Acha, Yusuf.' Going up in the elevator while Mr Uzzerman waited in the lobby, he commented: 'His career is going OK now but you have to watch that one.'

Cullen checked into his room out of sorts. He'd rung home again from the Hotel Oberoi Grand in Calcutta, their overnight stopover en route to Bangladesh. He had been struck by the need to call Margaret while he and Galash fended off importuning toothy youths offering 'neckked' Kashmir girls in Jawaharlal Nehru Road.

'I wouldn't even touch them with yours, man,' scoffed Galash, waving away the most persistent tout.

Returning to the hotel after this abortive walk around the block, Cullen feeling harassed and guiltily underexercised, they were still brushing street hawkers from them when, amid the smoke of street fires and car exhausts, they stopped to let a procession pass. It was made up of young boys, emaciated and with shaven heads, pulling floats illuminated with lucky symbols: stars, hearts and diamonds. A bell clanged harshly somewhere in their midst; its rhythmic ringing seemed to foreshadow some further major stage in proceedings. So strong was this sense of impending event that Cullen let Galash go on ahead while he waited for the tail of the parade to reach them. Behind each float trailed fifteen or twenty expressionless boys aged from about eight to twelve, each carrying a live fluorescent tube mounted on a wooden T-shape, and behind them, linked by frayed electric cord, more boys struggled to pull handcarts holding throbbing generators. Eventually the end of the procession came into sight. It was a gaunt boy carrying a sign announcing that the floats were electrified by Das Brothers of Dum Dum Road. No further explanation was available as to the procession's meaning.

The stream of grim children unnerved Cullen. They had the look of the institution about them, of acute hunger and pessimism. Meanwhile he was flatulent from his dinnertime asparagus vinaigrette, mutton shish kebab and coupe Jacques. He had a paternal urge to see his own kids, undergoing their particular form of institutional suffering in expensive Anglican boarding schools.

'You sound depressed,' Margaret said to him.

'Just listen to that.' He held the receiver up to the open window and the life-struggle cacophony of the street. He imagined the smells and sights could reach her too. The conversation was not a success. It was interrupted by an ingratiating old bellboy, presumably left over from halcyon Mountbatten days, returning Cullen's glossy shoes and hanging around for his tip. And he could not properly

86

express his malaise to her. She gave off emanations lacking empathy while suggesting that all the tough times were at her end.

'Have a good time,' she said, preparing to ring off. She couldn't resist it.

'This isn't exactly Las Vegas.'

'I'm sure you'll make do.'

'Why the sarcasm? Some long-distance serenity would be nice, Margaret. I'm missing you and you treat me like this. What's up?'

There was silence. Her famous silences. Unstated disapproval was her specialty; it sped as quickly and effortlessly over oceans as across a room. The deadness in her eyes, the icy incuriosity of her repressed features were as clear to him as if she were present. He could have touched a finger to the pale poker face. He took several deep breaths, aware of his racing pulse, of the steamy, used street air invading his room. Was the merest hint of weeping coming over the line? Had she shifted her position yet again? Leaving him dangling, on marshy ground, treading water. Had he misunderstood? He wished for insights, for her deeply female subjectivity.

'I'm sorry,' she whispered. 'Take care,' and hung up.

He slumped where he was for some time watching life from behind the safety wire of his window, remembering he hadn't asked after her health. Then he had a compulsion for a long cool bath, to wash Asia down the plug hole. He took one, soaking there for an hour, his big unhappy body displacing water all over the bathroom.

Twelve hours later, sipping improbable coffee, they were overlooking the pool from the Dacca Inter-Continental's coffee shop being 'familiarized' by Mr Uzzerman on their brief role in the enhancement of Bangladeshi life. On the itinerary were visits to the Development Council, a buffalo dairy, the university and various animal husbandmen and a dinner to be given for them by the Agriculture Minister.

Poring over the schedule, Z.M. instilled remarks on the various personalities mentioned. 'Rahman's doing very well.

Habibur's taken a tumble.'

Mr Uzzerman gave pink nervous smiles, made no comment on these career vagaries and worked his way through Z.M.'s Camel filters. 'It would be wise,' he suggested as he left, 'not to leave the hotel grounds. You might be getting lost.' He laughed, displaying thin teeth. 'We will send a car for your appointments. Mr Ali, of course, is knowing his way around.'

Shortly they were taken in a Volkswagen to meet the Development Council. The meeting took place in a wood-panelled boardroom overseen by a serious double-chinned portrait of the Prime Minister. The chairman, a Mr Chowdhury, was plump as a stockbroker, with silky hair and prominent teeth. He beamed at Z.M. and pumped his hand.

'Your brother the engineer was just in to see me about employment the other week,' he enthused. 'Nice chap. Unfortunately we could not use him.' He swung around as if to embrace Cullen and Galash in the magnanimity evidenced by his granting audiences to job-seeking Ali relatives. 'And may I welcome you gentlemen to our troubled but fascinating country?'

Mr Chowdhury smoothly introduced the other ten members of the council. Each had a soft quick handshake. Cullen caught only the name of a Mr Hussein who suffered from a variation of Mr Uzzerman's pigmentation problem. In his case his face was the normal brown except for the skin around his lips, which was the lightest pink, giving him a duck-billed effect.

A nod from Mr Chowdhury brought in six waiters with refreshments: bottles of 7-Up and Fanta, dishes of firm fruit cake and handsome bananas. There was a condition of utter silence as the officials fell upon the fruit. Avoiding Galash's eye Cullen peeled his banana as neatly as any clown or monkey. Around the boardroom table each executive sat upright with banana in hand. In half a minute the bananas were demolished.

'7-Up or Fanta?' Mr Chowdhury asked Cullen solicitously. Waiters hurried banana skins out the door. Technocrats snatched at plates of cake.

88

'7-Up, thanks.'

'Good,' said Mr Chowdhury approvingly. 'Fanta is a child's drink.' Then, clearing his throat, he began to read a speech about Dante being escorted by Virgil through the Seven Circles of Hell and being astonished to see so many who had been undone by Life. Mr Chowdhury said that of course T. S. Eliot had alluded to this in 'The Waste Land' in depicting the sad, strained faces of workers crowding over London Bridge after the devastations of World War I.

'In the same way this can be said of our country,' he intoned in a sing-song voice. 'The weariness of war, not only in its primitive form but against its aftermath of poverty and want, is writ large on the faces of the people.'

Solemn faces ceased chewing cake as he looked up.

'Smiles have grown less plentiful and light-hearted banter has vanished altogether from our midst,' he said.

Waiters produced saucers of loose cigarettes. Hands reached for them, lit them.

Mr Chowdhury was saying that life had become a grim business. It was almost as if the people in the streets had read Dante's well-known inscription over the Gates of Hell: 'Abandon hope, all ye who enter here', for there was a look of hopelessness in their expressions and a lethargy of movement that appalled him. His voice rose in a shrill inflexion. 'Not on honeydew have they fed nor have they drunk the milk of paradise!'

Pink-lipped Mr Hussein grunted something and picked edgily at Cullen's neglected cake.

'They have gnawed at the crust of poverty,' cried Mr Chowdhury, 'and drunk the dregs of despair.'

Galash was staring intently at his clipboard. Z.M., imperturbable, leaned back in his chair and blew smoke at the ceiling. Surveying his cuticles, Cullen desperately fought off sleep.

Mr Chowdhury said that while they were all presently going through the Valley of Despond they should remember that all trials were a test of endurance. The struggle was worthwhile if they had faith in the future, faith in humanity

89

and faith in providence. 'As for circumstances,' he said, winding up, 'let us all be little Napoleons and say: "Circumstances? I am circumstances!" and by that means ensure our victory over our present foes.'

A round of applause seemed almost warranted. Z.M. struck the right note by calling, 'Hear, hear.' Other hear, hears sounded politely around the table. Beaming, Mr Chowdhury sat down, calling on Mr Hussein to speak.

The Hussein speech was unemotional and technical, with details of agricultural projects planned, international assistance sought, jute export figures and rice import quotas. He described it as an 'overview'. In flat tones he discussed the setting up of 'infrastructures' and the carrying out of 'drastic measures'. He paid tribute to the aid given in the past by the Organization, anticipated considerably more in the future, and mentioned the gratitude the whole country felt for the presence of the 'visiting specialists in the field of the water buffalo' and their 'obsession for raising our protein intake'. This brought polite chuckles from the Bangladeshis present, led by Mr Chowdhury.

Then came a strange change in Mr Hussein's behaviour. For a moment he seemed to be weighing up some decision, then he reached under the table and produced three copies of a thick report which he presented to the visitors. A frisson of discomfort occurred around the table. There was coughing and a scraping of chair legs. Mr Hussein pursed his lips defiantly. 'The onus for synthesizing this report fell on my lone shoulders,' he cried. 'I alone shall stand or fall by the wayside on it.'

'Hussein!' called Mr Chowdhury, grimly.

He ignored the chairman. 'For too long it has been gathering dust on bureaucratic shelves. I have the honour now to present it to the world! Free, gratis and for your sincere perusal.'

The report in front of them was titled 'Integrated Agricultural Development Programme: An Evaluation.' Embarrassed, they flipped cursorily through its pages while Mr Hussein struck a heroic pose at the head of the table. In full voice he said it had been his urgent hope to optimize the use of resources by bringing the peasant farmer into the decision-making processes as set out under the nation's charter. But the status quo had continued through many dark nights! Their socialism was a mere paper commitment! The government fought shy of the simplest possible measures for land reform! Private ownership of land was a sacred cow! The demand for national self-reliance was mere polemics. . . .

'Ffft!' Mr Chowdhury was abruptly on his feet, hissing through his large teeth, muttering soft oaths to colleagues, shaking his head agitatedly. Others stood up too, shuffled their feet and sat down again. Waiters were under foot and roundly abused. Clerks from nearby offices poked curious faces into the room.

Cullen and Galash sat bemused through this fracas while Z.M., regarding events with a small smirk, mumbled 'Oh my God!' The hubbub came to an end only when Mr Hussein, bristling with self-consciousness, his rare mouth set in a firm pink line, forced his way through the crowd and left the room.

With a giant effort of will Mr Chowdhury stretched his face into a smile. 'Well, gentlemen,' he said. 'Would that our Mr Hussein were like the frustrated Wittgenstein! "Of that which one cannot speak one must remain silent".' He sighed, deeply and philosophically. 'In life, gentlemen, one must let Edgar Allen Poe's raven fold its wings and perch soundlessly on the sculptured head of Pallas.'

Still smiling tightly Mr Chowdhury reached out and took their copies of Hussein's report from them, shook hands and showed them out.

'Well, how about that?' Galash said as they squeezed into their official Volkswagen again. 'Revolution in the air. Technocrats with their balls in a knot. Z.M., would you say Hussein's career chances are not the brightest in the nation?'

'Perhaps.' Z.M. appeared distracted suddenly. He held back so he got the front passenger's seat.

Mr Uzzerman was bright with embarrassment. 'A little disagreement. Nothing of importance,' he said optimistically.

A moment later, halfway to their next appointment, while the VW braked to avoid a stream of bullock carts and bicycles crossing Bangsal Road, Z.M. abruptly jumped out saying, 'Oh my God, I've forgotten something. I'll catch up with you,' and disappeared into the turmoil of the pavements.

For a minute Mr Uzzerman seemed smitten, squashed up against Cullen's thighs, a victim of events. The driver looked at him wonderingly. Mr Uzzerman eventually grunted and waved him on to their destination. There he left Cullen and Galash to tour a buffalo dairy and conduct a stilted interview with its overawed administrator while he slumped unhappily in the car.

Cullen, frayed and squeamish, nonetheless took notes on daily milk yields, butterfat content, calving intervals and lactation periods. Galash inquired about rinderpest vaccination programmes, enzootic foot-and-mouth and calf mortality. Frowning over his clipboard, Cullen recorded local castration methods (by the knife, performed by neighbourhood 'specialists', with a survival rate of seventy per cent), noted the habit of piercing the nasal septum—and was suddenly grabbed around the intestines in a powerful and painful grip. Squatting over an open and feculent earth closet a few minutes later, exposed to the passing curiosity of gumbooted Bangladeshi dairy personnel, he knew his lowest ebb for some time.

Crouched there in humiliation, a sultry sun on his face, green shiny blowflies crawling on his knees, he could only thank God for the great horse-needle of anti-hepatitis serum old Hopkins had forced into his buttock, the cocktail of other miscellaneous vaccinations. Light-headed, hollow, he puddled wearily to the administrator's office where he joined Galash, accepted a dusty warm bottle of 7-Up, declined buffalo-milk sweetmeat snacks of *cham cham* and *rashagulla* and gingerly passed the half-hour before they could rejoin Mr Uzzerman.

Back at the Inter-Continental they spied Z.M. in a huddle with five young Bangladeshis in the coffee shop. He was speaking in a low and serious fashion; they seemed to be hanging on his words while draining their American ice-cream sodas and licking the last crumbs of their nut sundaes. Cullen perceived that Z.M. had treated them to these luxuries and that they regarded him as an authoritative figure.

They approached Z.M.'s table. 'What are you up to?' Cullen asked jocularly. 'You were greatly missed, you piker.'

'What? Oh, how was the tour? I am sorry, something came up. My relatives and I are just talking about old times here. I'll be with you shortly.'

Z.M. made no attempt to introduce them so they ordered drinks by the pool. There, late afternoon shadows fell across the pale shoulders of two girls, possibly Germans, tossing a plastic ball to three French businessmen. A couple of giggling Japanese in sneakers played table tennis on the terrace; a group of Russians in shirt sleeves sipped ideologically impartial beverages and passed quiet remarks about the girls. Cullen willed his stomach to behave, dousing its fires with a gin and tonic. Galash stretched out on a chaise-longue with a bottle of Tuborg lager.

'God knows how much this costs here,' he said. Belching softly he seemed to gain grim satisfaction from the thought.

Fat crows flopped between the lush lawns and the branches of a large tree-of-heaven which shaded a corner of the terrace. Other crows, cogitating on the high brick wall surrounding the hotel, shambled away at the approach of two workmen with stepladders who were fixing coils of barbed wire along the top of the wall.

5

FROM THE OLD BROADWAY TUNES coming over the Orosas'
wall, Margaret guessed that the party was already well under
way. *Carousel, Oklahoma!, South Pacific*: Ted Orosa's fav-
ourites were getting another airing tonight, she thought
resignedly, smoking a cigarette on the verandah, bracing
herself for the party. A steel guitar and saxophone rendered
'I'm Gonna Wash That Man Right Out of My Hair'.

They were always so boring, the Orosa parties. Crypto-
American cocktail parties with tiny slick men quaffing Scotch
and bourbon and displaying their hormones; their decep-
tively steely wives, all mothers-of-ten, unctuously sipping
Coca-Colas and pretending to be madonnas. All the
European women she would know already: their whines and
gripes and the names of their children. And most of the men:
the Americans in drip-dries and seersucker, the Australians in
sports shirts or *barongs*, the British in their strangely timeless,
shapeless tropical garb. Even the *real* Europeans, the Italians
and Germans, would look uncomfortably wrong in their
modish casual clothes: their loafers and understated tailoring
rendered them anonymous in this flashy place.

A bat surprised her, breaking out of the big palm in the
front garden. Its screech was like a bird's, it flapped and
scrabbled for another position but was driven off by a rival.
Amazingly, she thought, the local fauna no longer worried
her. She concluded that in this jungle atmosphere everything

had a natural enemy and that there were no creatures left over to sting and bite, to hide in shoes or to appear out of the plumbing waving hairy legs and fatal nippers. The trusty geckos kept down the spiders and mosquitoes, thank God.

No need here at least for those claustrophobic nets beloved of her mother-in-law. Dottie had nets bunched up above the beds in all her bedrooms and over the divan in the sunroom. Casuarina Bay attracted mosquitoes in clouds, for all its casual sub-tropical charm. On one of her early tense weekend visits, allotted the chaste spare bedroom, Margaret had unrolled the high beige net over her bed and down had fallen a small jewel box and a bank savings book containing two hundred pounds in ten-pound notes rolled inside a rubber band. Inside the jewel box were two strings of pearls and various rings, gold brooches, necklaces and bracelets of old-fashioned design. The savings account showed deposits in Dottie's name totalling eighteen hundred pounds. For some reason she'd hurriedly wound up the mosquito net again and replaced Dottie's valuables in her hiding place. There was a feeling of absolute secrecy about it, as if it were being kept hidden not from strange intruders but from intimates: a nest egg jealously hidden, a source of independence. Mosquitoes had savaged her that night but she couldn't bring herself to release the net again and she hadn't mentioned the cache to Richard.

But Dottie had known somehow. Perhaps by the different arrangement of the mosquito net. Next morning knowing glances were passed, a certain florid, embarrassed geniality appeared in her cheeks as she tinkled her little breakfast bell for the kookaburras. She threw them mince and chop tails, assuming a most proprietary air, scolding and crooning. There was a smugness in the way she fed them, in the observance of a habit, as if she were on top of Nature.

'Morning, Marg,' she'd said. 'Aren't you looking summery this morning in those tiny shorts.'

She flicked her cigarette into the garden. It glowed for a moment like an animal's eye. The cloying fragrance of the ilang-ilang rose from the shrubbery. A jagged clattering of drums, frenzied yet amateurish, suddenly overwhelmed the steel guitar and saxophone next door.

'Bong Bong' she said aloud. The Orosas' teenage son Teodoro Junior, nicknamed Bong Bong for reasons she neither knew nor cared, but which pre-dated his interest in percussion by ten or twelve years, owned an expensive set of drums which Orosa would prevail on him to play for guests. Orosa set great store in Bong Bong, a large, apparently boneless boy whose maternal genes seemed to have provided only increased size. His features were a rounder, plumper version of his father's, his colouring the same, his shrewdness still discernible despite the innocent fat cheeks and page-boy hair. Concepción and Mina had once complained, twisting their hands, blushing, that Bong Bong was frequently hiding under the servants' lavatory and peering up through the ventilator at them. Their embarrassment at telling her this had been immense. His spying had been occurring for many weeks. He would call obscene remarks through the ventilator and was wholly without shame, they told her.

To each other they hissed in the laundry: '*Hijo de puta madre!*' Son of a mother whore.

Orosa had beaten his son when she told him, loudly and flamboyantly. Theatrical sounds of punishment had come over the wall, shouts from both father and son. But he had managed to imply in his dark eye glints and clever pursed mouth a great amusement at this chip off the old block. And now Bong Bong looked at her in a new light, ever since then venomously polite in his exaggerated American accent ('Good morning, Ma'am') but with an arrogant chubby panache that she found infuriating, swaggering around in his tight denims and always, it seemed to her, on the verge of slyly expressing some lewd hand gesture or other.

Margaret walked next door. A black Batmobile waited outside. Her heels rang sharply on the pink marble path. Laughter came to her from the patio by the swimming pool. An American voice told a joke and there was another burst of laughter, shrill and obeisant. Hazel Orosa was smiling and patting the arm of Henry Beaumont from the American

Embassy. Three women in formal *piña ternos* gossipped together and darted savouries into their mouths; their eyes missed nothing.

'Margaret!' Ted Orosa, looking like a haggard child in his immaculate *barong* and black trousers, hurried across the patio to her with his arms outstretched. For a moment she thought he was going to embrace her, but he grabbed the nearest of her hands in his small dry ones and squeezed it.

'Aha, we're especially gathered tonight to entertain the grass widow,' he said, clapping his hands for servants, hissing 'Tsst!' until a maid came running. 'What will you have to drink? Bring Mrs Cullen a delicious drink. Tell the band more music. I want Rodgers and Hammerstein, Lerner and Lowe, all the top men. Bong Bong can sit in. We'll all have a jam session. Oh, we're having a ball!' *Sotto voce*, he said, 'The First Lady's cousin is here!' His face was distracted and feverish with excitement. Already his eyes roamed beyond her, seeking more fascinating company.

'What do you hear from Dick?'

6

BEFORE LEAVING for the Agriculture Minister's dinner, Cullen, by now trying to quell his stomach spasms with some charcoal tablets recommended by Z.M. as well as his own Organization-issue Enterovioform, placed a call to Margaret. Concepción answered the phone, giving the information that she was at a party at the Orosas'. This stymieing of his good intentions for some reason made him irrationally agitated. He was also annoyed at her being *there* specifically.

He had no enthusiasm for the evening ahead. Exhausted, fragile, he took an immediate dislike to their host, a plump fellow with a high-collared pinstripe suit and wily eyes. The Minister's voice was like a comedian's parody of the southern Asian accent and the Minister liked the sound of it, chirruping away rapidly whenever one of the other guests—government officials, technocrats, no women of course—made oblique reference to corruption, famine, armed gangs or other unsuitable dinner topics.

Peering around the eating hall—a long, bare cement room over a dry goods warehouse—clearing his throat discreetly, surreptitiously ridding his nostrils into his napkin, the Minister then began to pick unenthusiastically at his brown fish and rice. He had the look of a man who had already eaten. Going through the spartan formalities, he gave his glass of tepid Fanta an ugly glance.

Beside Cullen was a Professor Ahmad, a garrulous old

dean of agricultural science. 'I come here direct from a meeting of "Intellectuals to Resist Famine",' he announced. 'Held at the Bangla Academy. A throng attended.' He puffed on a cigarette. 'At last perhaps a ray of hope, the way out.'

Cullen looked for a trace of irony.

'It was a nice environment, nicely suited to the occasion,' the professor continued, dropping ash on the table. 'All immaculately dressed, some of the softer sex in Jamdari sari and printed Japanese chiffon. An ideal atmosphere for variety performance. Some expressed deep resentment, some hurled blames. The demand for honesty was high, also for combination and cohesion for combating famine.'

'What was the outcome?' asked Cullen politely. How serious was he?

'The mighty river of life flows on,' said Professor Ahmad loudly, 'eroding one side and raising the other. Maybe poetical, even philosophical, but this is the way.'

Across the plywood table the Minister glanced at them, smiled viciously and muttered a barrage of words at Cullen's companion. The professor took no notice. Ash fell lightly on his fish.

'The numbers of uprooted and malnutrited grow daily, similarly a set of miscreants, dacoits and blood-sucking parasites on the ruins,' he said. His food was untouched. 'True but staggering.' He gave Cullen a bitter grin.

Again the Minister gave them a sharp glance. Cullen had a twinge of embarrassment for Professor Ahmad but he merely saluted the Minister with a nonchalant nicotine-stained hand.

'They know I say what I like. I'll tell you something. I am a widower, sixty-six. My son Ekramul, the Assistant Professor of Physics at the university, died of barium poisoning three months ago. He was thirty-two only but he was having stomach aches so he arranged for a barium meal X-ray. Ulcer, he thought, Western disease. Ha! The substance was adulterated, naturally. This brilliant boy was being engaged only the day before and the date of his marriage was to be November seventeen.'

'I'm sorry.'

'Yes, there are many oddities on which to dwell. It's not only the poor who suffer.' His snort may have been laughter. 'Two compositors of our university press were stoned to death last week for printing a booklet called *Literacy in Thirty Hours*. It was seen as an insult against the Prophet.' Professor Ahmad shrugged. 'Maybe Kissinger was right. Maybe we are an international basket case.'

'Oh, not at all,' muttered Cullen, the polite and unconvincing dinner guest, picking at a mound of sticky rice. Already the air in the eating hall was thick with cigarette smoke. The single phlegmatic ceiling fan had revolved for several minutes and then stopped. Through the haze he saw Mr Chowdhury of the Development Council removing a fish bone from his lips. He looked for Mr Hussein among the guests but was not surprised at his absence.

Shortly, strangely, he heard his own voice discussing cricket. 'Look, you just can't go past the West Indies,' he was saying firmly. 'Even we haven't their fire-power and I'm the first to admit it.' He was slipping into a sensation that he realized he was experiencing more and more often: a surreal and blurry negativism. It ranged through frustration, anger and despair and ended in a feeling of comic futility. Again he marvelled at these perverse humorists. At their suicidal religions and inherent madnesses. The avoidance of existing animal protein! The resistance to birth control! It was as if they existed only to be difficult. What about his role? The Organization's? How ludicrous did all this make them! And their bloody gods, he thought. Harbingers of the worst luck in the world.

Meantime another Asian feeling, lamentably also familiar, welled up inside him. He lurched from the table, urgently sought directions, and crouched in some misery over an indoor closet whose walls, while providing a welcome privacy, also served to guard a dozen trays of familiar small brown fish and three buckets of boiled rice.

Around the table on his return a great fuss was being made of Z.M. Chuckling attractively, he was displaying both the frank and shrewd versions of his smile. He was generous with his Camels, for which there was some demand.

'We are not seeing so much of Mr Ali these days,' the Minister commented, benignly accepting a cigarette. 'We are missing his intelligent political conversation, the benefits of his enlightenment.'

'Oh my God,' Z.M. laughed, smiling plausibly.

Mr Chowdhury said, 'Hear, hear.'

'It seems only the day before yesterday when he was the Romeo of the bus-stop sheds and the gates of the girls' schools,' the Minister reminisced. His eyes darted into neutral areas, skipped on. 'I can still see young Ali loitering in his multi-coloured flying shirts, whistling and singing cheap film songs. He rode a Honda at breakneck speed.'

'You have a long memory, Minister.'

'Of course.'

They exchanged supple smiles.

'Later of course the poor became his hobby,' the Minister said softly. 'Very commendable.'

Nudging Cullen, Professor Ahmad sprayed ash on the table and mumbled, 'For a time your friend was being sidetracked from science to journalism, then to student politics. But he found it more dangerous even than journalism.' The professor's smoky breath carried an old male sourness, with traces of whisky. 'Only science is safe, they say, but look at my boy's example!' He inhaled smoke, meandered thoughtfully. 'Animal science seems the only secure area. Animals, food—a wise choice, yes.'

'An important area,' Cullen agreed. He was giddy and jelly-legged. For his dehydration he sipped gingerly at aerated orange syrup. It was warm and seemed to have divided up into its various chemical components. Sugary sediment coated his tongue and the roof of his mouth. Around him flew bewildering snippets from the conversations of technocrats and officials. One was animated about kerosene and powdered milk. Another mentioned bidi leaves, cycle parts and malta fruits; a third, groats, chili, tendu leaves and local shampoo with foreign labels. It sounded like a code.

'They released them after shaving their heads,' Mr

Chowdhury said, and sniggered. 'And closed down the den of course.'

'The Soviet medical team's medicine is being worth fifty lakh taka,' said another official.

'Four thousand six hundred and eleven maunds of wheat were missing when it reached Kushtia.'

'The salt movement situation in Sadar sub-division is remaining unchanged.'

Cullen became aware that the Minister was on his feet, looking at his watch. 'It has been most pleasant,' he announced in his high comedian's voice. People immediately stood and formed a farewelling phalanx at the door. Limp, small-boned handshakes were again offered. Even Professor Ahmad's square nicotined hand turned to cool pulp in his as if to repudiate his earlier intractability.

The Minister showed them to their car. The arcade abutting the dry goods store was full of waiting beggars. The Minister's eyes rolled but he kept smiling. From the corner of his mouth he hissed, 'Tsst! Tsst!' This had some effect, except on two children and a legless man balanced on hessian hip pads. The man scrabbled toward their trouser cuffs. He had dervish's eyes and a wild shirt tail hanging to the ground. The children cried, 'Taka, taka!' and plucked at their sleeves. With a smile like steel the Minister gave a long 'Tsssst!' and waved his arms, breaking the momentum of the beggars' onrush. He ushered Cullen, Galash and Z.M. into the Volkswagen. 'Goodnight, goodnight,' he called gaily. He dropped his smile at Z.M., closing the car door firmly on him. The beggars' hands pattered on the sides and roof.

'Back to the Inter-Continental,' Z.M. directed the driver. 'I need a drink,' he said as they moved off.

7

AS WELL AS HIS INTESTINAL PROBLEMS Cullen suffered from an acute whisky hangover which had left him with a sharp ache behind his right eye. His brain fizzed. His body was drained by the humidity. He sat with his companions in a cement government office which smelled of creosote and stale papers, under an andante ceiling fan. Hawking civil servants padded along the corridor outside; Cullen anticipated the sound of spitting whenever he heard footfalls.

Galash and Z.M. seemed in better shape, following the demolition of their duty-free Scotch supplies. Their resilience amazed him. Certainly they were younger but Galash especially was a wonder. He surrendered to all his appetites and never seemed to suffer for it. The sly, amusing tales of contretemps with angry husbands, the narrow escapes from fisticuffs, the snatched moments of passion with perfect strangers on trains, in theatres, on one particular Air India flight over the Timor Sea after lights out. He was a wooer of young girls, ageing grannies, women of every nationality: a walking, talking phallus. Cullen had a vague schoolboy curiosity to see *it*, he'd heard so much about its multifarious adventures, but after tennis or at the club Galash always slid privately into his boxer shorts, eschewed the shower.

'You hearty rugger buggers,' he muttered once to Cullen. 'Can't wait to all get in the shower. No bending over for the soap with you guys around.'

Now, apart from some slight rheum about the eyes, he was as chipper as ever. Taut skin, sleek head, suave Yankee mannerisms—an occasional glint of gold from a side tooth—even steady hands. A drinker, a debaucher, he kept late nights, smoked cigarettes and came up trumps every time. Bilious Cullen envied him many things.

With gusto Galash drew on a fresh cigarette and chattered amiably to three civil servants from the Agriculture Ministry on off-season buffalo breeding efficiency. They were all agreed, he said blithely, on the value of providing the cows with half-wall sheds of gunny sacks so they could develop oestrus during the height of summer. 'But—ha, ha,—it should be recognized that males are more difficult to keep in full sexual capacity. Well, we all have our own view on that, don't we gentlemen?'

The Bangladeshis chuckled uncomfortably. They drew nervously on cigarettes and fiddled with paper clips as Galash went on.

'Seriously, they lose libido unless jute curtains are hung in their sheds to diminish hot and cold draughts and to minimize radiation effects. In summer they should be liberally sluiced daily and allowed to wallow morning and evening. At night they should be tethered in an open yard and exercised in the early morning. In winter they should be kept in the open during the day and bedded down on straw at dusk. Throughout the year they must be stall-fed before being brought to service.'

Cullen's contribution to this discussion was meagre. Sweat slid down his face and trickled down his chest and back, pasting his shirt to his body. Shakily he doodled on his clipboard, took shallow breaths, loosened his tie. He prayed for the cool of his hotel room and the security of adjacent American-style bathroom fixtures. The proximity of icy European beverages was important, even the dubious creamy greenness of the swimming pool. He willed his bowels to bind, his headache to vanish, his nausea to settle, the morning to end.

It did eventually. Pleading dysentery Cullen foreswore the

afternoon's engagements, gingerly placing himself on the terrace by the pool with his reports. Mr Uzzerman was offended by his non-attendance; it seemed hard for his mind to encompass a departure from the itinerary.

'Arrangements have been made at the university,' he insisted. 'You are coming of course.'

'Sorry, not this time.'

Anxiety passed across Mr Uzzerman's unique features. Finally he gave a grim smile, saying, 'All right then, you are having your way. You don't come.'

Cullen sighed. 'Exactly.'

A little pinker today, one of the pale German girls breast-stroked languidly up the pool holding her head high to keep her hair dry. Through his sunglasses Cullen observed her cautiously. She had no male companions this time. The international business community was represented this afternoon by a table of trim-bearded Germans and debonair Indians talking over coffee. From time to time they dipped into briefcases at their feet. A gold fountain pen caught the sun. There was no air movement to rustle their sheaves of papers. Around the tree-of-heaven, across the spongy lawns, their blond and dark children played chasings, shrieking in variegated English and scattering slow crows from their path. At the hotel's boundaries workmen placed further strands of barbed wire along the top of the wall. Metal grilles lay in stacks beneath the windows.

Ordering a Coca-Cola, Cullen asked the drink waiter about these reinforcements.

'For *hartal*,' the waiter said. 'Tomorrow is a day of protest. Damages can be made so precautions are necessary.'

'Violence?' A flash of danger and disarray touched him.

'Oh no, sir. People are staying home.' The waiter giggled. 'Stay home safe from the brickbat and no harm can come to you.'

His stomach clenching around the cold liquid, he thought he would have to ask Z.M. about this *hartal* business. Actually, he found the anticipation of vague physical threats not unsatisfactory. This whiff of excitement cleared his head for a moment, stirred up the adrenalin. It had all the earmarks of an incident worth relating later to Margaret; initially in a casual throw-away fashion, then in awe-inspiring detail with a body-count and all. Momentarily he considered other events to tell her. Perhaps he should ascertain roughly the numbers of starvation and disease fatalities per day, week, et cetera, and hadn't someone mentioned the growing habit of desperate family members of administering fatal doses of endrin to hungry children and ageing grandparents? Immediately he wondered why all this should occur to him, this juvenile wish for her sympathy and concern; to perversely broadcast his proximity to danger. Like a show-off child on its bicycle: 'Look Mum, no hands!'

At least his headache was easing. Optimistically he determined to go for a calm walk. The breakdown of his exercise routines worried him; maybe later he'd be up to a light jog or a few push-ups. For a moment, however, a stroll was all he could manage—a bit of quiet sight-seeing from behind dark glasses. As he passed through the lobby piped music played:

> Take back your samba, ai.
> Your conga, ai.
> Your rumba, ai, ai, ai.

Past mosque after mosque, all with a seedy and extravagant beauty, he sauntered. Through gritty parks with the appearance of having been picked over by legions of scavengers, from sparrows to men. Ancient black bicycles crossed his path, pedalled by sombre students in white shirts. Rickshaws passed his vision, and bullock carts ground along at a pace slower than his own. He carried his hangover like one of their high swollen loads. No one noticed him, or at least appeared not to do so. Beggars were not evident; the streets lacked even their hopeless energy. Men with black eye sockets passed by, and quick anxious women staring straight ahead.

Around the bigger, more modern buildings cursory barricades had been nailed up. On one tin fortification was a freshly pasted poster which announced mysteriously in

English, in large black type:

Begum Akhter is dead.
The queen of ghazal and dadra
is no more. And she was no mean
performer of thumri!

That sort of obituary was more than enough for his present apperception. Perversely, the plodding rhythm of his steps now insisted on repeating, 'No mean performer of *thumri!*, no-mean-per-for-mer-of-*thum-ri*.' *No mean performer!* For block after block a thick and sluggardly lust dogged his steps. One of life's mysteries—the randiness of the ravaged. If he was romantically, sexually susceptible when drunk, how much more so when barely ambulatory from alcohol's aftermath? Dyspeptic, broken-winded, spavined from many old leg injuries, a breath could blow him over. Yet though wobbly in the head and pins, his trousers roared. Flush, staunch and robust, idiotically optimistic.

The familiarity of feelings! Erotic urges. The throbbing blood rush of hangover and frustration. And suddenly another instantly recognized sensation: the high mustiness of confined animals. Adjacent to him, its fetor now surrounding him, was the city zoo. He paid two taka to enter its dry lawns and dusty asphalt. A scattering of quiet children and their teacher peered into its narrow cages—otherwise the zoo was empty. A sign indicating the direction of the carnivores lay splintered on its side; it was unnecessary anyway as their low captive coughs sounded from the centre of the gardens.

Cullen approached a cage. Inside four scraggy deer rested, their tongues showing, in the shade of their walls. One nibbled at a scrap of newspaper. A young one lay dead, strangely extenuated, on the asphalt in the sun. He passed through the ruminant section. The giraffe pen was empty. Two Bactrian camels slumped on their shins. They exuded a bad odour and their ribs were sharp against their hides. The coughing of the carnivores drew him on past other woebegone beasts into the middle of the zoo. A hagged lioness was the animal making all the noise. She stood shakily in her pit, sores on her flanks, and hacked up at the world.

Nearby a sign said BENGAL TIGER—in several languages including Latin—*The Rare Pride of Our Country*. As he peered down into the tiger pit, at an animal in better condition than all the others, two keepers approached and tossed the body of a deer, perhaps the one he had seen, down to it. The deer was so light it landed soundlessly, only faintly stirring dust. The tiger padded over to the body, picked it up and carried it off to the rear of the pit.

The keepers stared vacantly down at the tiger, muttering softly and wiping their hands on their trousers.

'Excuse me,' Cullen addressed them. 'Apart from this fellow your animals are in very bad shape.'

The men glanced at him, grimaced. His size and manner seemed to daunt them.

'I'm an animal specialist. I have an interest.'

They shrugged. One man said, 'Thirty-four have died this week, not including birds.'

'Is there no food?'

'The food contractor has stopped supplies due to the non-payment of his bill.' The keeper grinned proudly. 'Only our special tiger is not unusually reduced for want of food.'

'That lioness will die soon.'

'It is likely.'

The tiger ripped a haunch from the deer. Cullen, troubled, tense across the scalp, left the zoo. He arrived back at the hotel in a rickshaw, the jolting of the journey having reactivated his intestinal worries. The metal grilles were in position on the windows.

8

WHEN THEY WERE YOUNGER they often went on picnics on Sundays, he recalled, torpid on his hotel bed, rubbing his stomach and trying to conjure up serene thoughts. (He could feel a pulse there like a pregnant woman's. God, when would it settle down? It babbled like a brook now; yesterday it had gurgled like a storm-water drain.) More often than not he'd be bruised or limping from Saturday's game. With other couples they drove to picnic spots near waterfalls. There they barbecued meat over rock fireplaces, kicked footballs, drank beer from mugs, picked wildflowers and dozed in the sun on tartan travelling rugs until the mosquitoes came out. They used to own, he remembered in a state of near delirium, a little double-lidded plastic container which provided either salt or pepper depending on which lid was lifted. He recollected that it was red and white. How handy it had been for picnics! How efficient a receptacle! In those days they had also possessed a large and ubiquitous plastic tomato. Not so efficient, it allowed air in through its nozzle and the tomato sauce inside congealed like blood. Whatever had become of those things?

One picnic, on a dry late spring day drifting to summer, they had walked after lunch along a stream toward a small waterfall. The children were playing elsewhere. Margaret picked flowers. Crickets rasped. He felt suddenly changed and could hardly endure it. He saw her bending happily over clumps of freesias, smelled their high sweet scent, and did not recognize her. Her face and arms were still pale from winter. Faint crows' feet were beginning under her eyes, hints of creases above the lips. He fought against his mind. Holding hands they walked upstream along an uncomfortably narrow path. Branches scraped him. Warm air flowed around the eucalypts. Swinging her arms she made contented remarks about encroaching summer. Lizards climbed stones. He had to stop himself standing fatalistically still, looking her in the eye and saying intimate damaging things. There was a risk of him turning suddenly and walking away into the depths of the bush. Instead he spoke neutrally, affectionately, and when they came to a warm slab of rock they stretched out and dozed. Her plump hand rested on his side.

He recalled his lack of decision whenever he smelled freesias.

Now he fell asleep, without attempting dinner, and had homesick bloated dreams.

9

WHEN THE MiG-21 FIGHTERS buzzed the city at dawn Cullen abruptly remembered *hartal*. Military helicopters also sharply scrutinized the streets. The Russians in the elevators and lobby were grimly jocular about this flag showing. The hotel relentlessly pursued a cheery atmosphere. Happy show tunes were piped over the broadcasting system and the drink waiters erected the badminton nets earlier than usual.

'OK, Z.M. What's going on?' He and Galash joined Z.M. in the coffee shop where he was breakfasting on toast and marmalade. His red eyes were evidence of another late night. His cheeks gave off waves of English Leather.

'The bloody Russians wake you too?' Z.M. asked. 'I haven't had much sleep myself.' He chuckled coyly.

'Who did you prey on last night?' Galash queried, pouring coffee. 'Not the German girls?' He sniffed his cup suspiciously. 'There's something very wrong with this stuff.' Then he muttered, 'You sly bastard.'

Z.M. grinned. 'As for today, this *hartal* is called by the JSD. A general strike you could say, sponsored by the Jatiya Samajtantrik Dal, the National Socialist Party. Shops will close down, vehicular traffic will be lean. That sort of thing. It won't affect us.'

'No danger, eh?' Cullen considered tentatively the state of his health, again decided that he wouldn't shy away from recountable Asian adventures. Mentally he flexed several

111

muscles. 'By the way, Z.M. What does *thumri* mean?'

'A traditional form of singing.'

'And *ghazal* and *dadra*?'

'Much the same. Absorbing our culture, eh Dick?'

'There's some of it now,' said Galash. Over a myriad of outlets a recorded crooner, from his accent Indian or Bangladeshi, was singing:

> *'Gotta get my old tuxedo pressed,*
> *Gotta sew a button on my vest,*
> *'Cos tonight gotta look my best.*
> *Lulu's back in town.'*

'We have a good sense of humour, if nothing else,' Z.M. said, and they laughed.

Galash was twitching with vague tensions, however. His feet tapped, he sipped dubiously at his coffee, looked keenly around the room. 'Those girls haven't surfaced yet, have they?'

'Oh my God,' Z.M. snorted, with a small smile.

Mr Uzzerman's pink face peered through the doorway. He plopped down beside them. He appeared harried and flapped a negative hand at the offer of coffee. 'I am doubtful about subjecting you to *hartal*. I am cancelling this morning's appointments as a precautionary measure.' He grinned insincerely. 'Some of you will be pleased, I am sure.' He glanced at Cullen.

'Don't take it like that, Mr Uzzerman.'

Picking at a thread in his sleeve, then tucking it from view, Mr Uzzerman said, 'Fishplates on the line to Rangpur were removed and a train derailed. Only the fireman was killed. Otherwise life seems normal.' He looked shamefaced about events.

In a trance Cullen gazed through an expanse of glass to the pool. No more than fifteen feet from them, on the other side of the window, two Japanese businessmen were doing calisthenics on the terrace, running on the spot in thick-soled rubber sandals which slap-slapped in clockwork rhythm. He watched them, becoming guilty at his own inactivity. Their legs were solid, thick-calved but hairless. On their serious faces was no trace of self-consciousness.

'Amazing people,' he said. 'They play a workmanlike game of Rugby, did you know that? Small but tenacious. Their club championship final last year drew a crowd of sixty thousand. Sixty thousand! Won by a team called Kinki Railway.'

'Seriously?' said Galash. 'Man!'

'Tomorrow you leave, eh?' Mr Uzzerman said abruptly. The pink parts of his face flushed with apparent pleasure. 'Onwards with your journey.'

Low over the garden three MiGs swooped suddenly, leaving crows flapping in their reverberations. The Japanese paused in their exercising, exclaiming softly. Stepping out on to the terrace just then, with colourful silk coats wrapped loosely over their bikinis, the German girls, very animated, stood on their toes and followed the jets' vapour trails with pointing fingers.

'Here they are,' Galash said, nudging Z.M.

Whether it was the return of the MiGs, the girls' arrival, the coffee or a combination of all, Cullen's current emotional-visceral responses suddenly forced him with quick excuses from the coffee shop. Foolish chirpy music followed him outside.

When he returned Mr Uzzerman was gone. Galash and Z.M., on the other hand, had moved out on to the terrace and were chatting with the girls from an adjoining table. In his suavity Z.M.'s eyes almost disappeared into his cheeks. Galash, the gallant, was leaning over lighting the girls' cigarettes. As Cullen joined them they moved their chairs around the girls' table.

They were discussing the MiG barrage. 'I almost fell out of bed when they buzzed us this morning,' said the pale girl Cullen had observed swimming alone. 'For a moment I was frantic.' This was hard to imagine: her crisp English indicated a cosmopolitan confidence.

First names were exchanged.

Eager Galash asked, 'Can we buy you a drink?'

113

The pale girl, whose name was Ilse, raised an eyebrow above gold-framed sunglasses. 'Just a Coke this early.' The green-tinted glasses smudged her irises. Short brown hair was stylish and bright around her face. A thin scar on her jawline did not detract from her symmetry. 'Are you as well one of these UN fellows?' she asked Cullen politely.

'Yes indeed.' No doubt Galash had exaggerated their status. Fair enough. He eased himself gingerly into a deck-chair. 'We're birds of a feather.'

'So you flock together?'

'Right. And yourselves?'

'Oh, we are secretaries only.'

Ursula was the name of the other girl. Her accent was thicker and her manner lazier, more relaxed. She was blonde, carefully slim, with a similar international appearance and demeanour. She ordered a Campari and soda. 'No ice,' she stressed to the waiter. To the trio she said, 'We watch our stomachs, you know? Cleaning our teeth with Vichy water all the time, naturally.'

'Naturally,' Z.M. agreed.

'Old Dick has been a victim himself,' Galash volunteered, to Cullen's embarrassment. 'Montezuma's Revenge or whatever the local equivalent is.'

'Yahya Khan's Revenge perhaps,' said Z.M. smiling.

Ilse tutted sympathetically then looked archly at Cullen. 'We are not keeping you, I hope?'

Ursula giggled. 'Needing to run fast in Dacca!'

'No.' He smiled tightly and changed the subject. 'How did you girls turn up here, if you don't mind me asking? I would have thought it the last place for a holiday.'

'A holiday, no,' said Ursula. 'No fun here for a holiday, but to travel is interesting.' She sipped her Campari delicately, stretched elegant legs out from beneath her robe. Above one knee was an almost circular birthmark. 'Meeting different people.'

Appearing out of the sun a military helicopter clattered over the garden wall. It slanted low over the hotel, turned and heeled again over them. Ursula gave it a gay wave. When it had gone Ilse said, 'Actually, we are here with our employers. They are making feasibility studies for the gas pipelines. To see whether they will invest big sums.'

Cullen recalled the French businessmen gambolling in the pool, their physical familiarity with the girls. 'I saw you all swimming the other day,' he said.

Ilse gave a light laugh. 'Very possibly. They are travelling now to Bakhrabad, Chittagong, Chandpur—in the remote places.' She shuddered prettily. The expression gave her a spoilt, sensual look. 'We said we would stay here in Dacca. It is only for two days we are alone.'

Cullen caught Galash's vibrations even before he spoke. 'Well then,' said Galash, ebullient. 'Now the sun's over the yardarm we'd better have proper drinks.'

It was Cullen who, some time later, suggested venturing out into the street. Z.M. demurred, becoming serious, but the others, blithe with drink, agreed at once. The girls went up to their rooms to change: they returned wearing cool dresses, espadrilles, sun hats and bright lipstick and strode sportively through the foyer.

'Let us see the action,' Ilse demanded. She tossed a khaki shoulder-bag over her arm. 'I am ready for battle.'

'Beware Mr Molotov's cocktail,' warned Z.M., mock-stern. 'Don't take rickshaws or taxis. Stay on the main roads.'

They moved in giddy convoy along the street. Ursula brightly took Galash's arm, Ilse Cullen's. Cullen was heady at the touch of her hand, as foolishly optimistic as an adolescent. Her nails lightly pierced the skin on his bicep. From the delta pungent muddy air encompassed them. On her upper lip a faint dew rested. Her mouth looked edible. How cleverly her chic body combined both languor and humidity!

Several blocks from the hotel they paused on a corner. The intersection was peaceful. An auto-rickshaw buzzed past. A furtive boy scrambled by pushing a handcart laden with flattened cardboard boxes; his sandals slapped on the asphalt.

'Very quiet so far,' Galash commented. He spun around in

his tropical shoes, scanning the crossroads. 'No one any-where.' His cheeks were pink with heat and excitement. His hair shone with hope. Suddenly a bent man slanted from a carpenter's doorway, picking his nose. 'There's some action,' Galash whispered, and snorted.

Tittering, the girls clung to the men's arms with the detached eroticism of *Vogue* models. The heat drew wisps of perfume and body scent from them. Hips occasionally brushed lightly, bare arms slid together briefly. Meanwhile lively chatter continued over this subtle activity.

'A big fellow you are,' Ilse said playfully, nudging Cullen in the side with her elbow. She whirled her hat around her finger. ' "Gotta get my old tuxedo pressed," ' she sang. Her accent was husky; her breath sweet with toothpaste, gin and health. Cullen was infatuated, ravaged by awe and lust.

By the headquarters of the Anjuman-e-Mafidul Islam they rested in a sandy park, perched tentatively on the edge of a cement bench. It was stained in several murky shades.

'That friend of yours is amusing,' Ilse said, adjusting her sunglasses on her hair.

'Z.M.? You met him last night I understand?'

They shook their heads. 'No, but he has a wicked smile,' Ursula said, and giggled.

Cullen was surprised. 'This is his home town. He likes to keep to himself.'

'Something smells bad,' Ilse announced then. 'Perhaps it is this dirty seat.'

'Don't touch anything,' Cullen warned solicitously.

The girls wrinkled their noses, nonchalantly rebuffing cholera, and dabbed at their shiny foreheads with tissues. They produced cigarettes. Galash was again attentive with his enamel and gold lighter. The Gitanes pack, raising spectres of debonair French employer-lovers, jarred Cullen abruptly with jealousy. Elegant streams of smoke rose in the stuffy air.

Its reek preceding it, a bullock-cart rumbled up the alley beside the park and stopped by one of the buildings adjoining the mosque. The driver climbed down from the cart, walked

116

across to a nearby shed and banged several times on the door. He called, 'Hah! Hah!' The door opened and a man came out grumbling and adjusting a scarf over his face. The driver similarly pulled up a rag mask over his chin and nose.

Still muttering, the second man assisted the driver to pull back a tarpaulin from the cart. The fetid rush of air that swept across the lane struck them with a blow almost physical. As they gagged under this onslaught the cart driver gave a muffled shout and a little fox wriggled from beneath the canvas and lurched drunkenly from the cart. It fell heavily on its distended stomach. The driver kicked it into the gutter where it lay writhing and biting the air. Awkwardly, on a length of hessian that nevertheless easily supported its burden, the men then began to carry one livid human body after another from the cart into the shed.

'It's all right. It's starvation,' Galash said suddenly. The thick words broke the silence. When the others looked at him he appeared to be thinking his announcement was somehow significant.

Throwing away their cigarettes, the girls rose together, pale and grim. Cullen and Galash followed. They headed hurriedly for the Inter-Continental. Ilse and Ursula linked arms and strode urgently ahead. Their long legs marched in step. The men did not attempt to take their arms; their bodies seemed to be resisting any outside contact. A barrier of frozen air surrounded them. All the way back they muttered in German. A hundred yards from the hotel a rock thrown from behind some scaffolding hit Cullen on the thigh. It surprised him but hurt hardly at all. No one was to be seen. The girls did not look around at his exclamation. He realized his head was aching.

That night Z.M. was seen treating the young Bangladeshis to a farewell dinner in the dining room. They ate what appeared to be big sirloins, shish kebabs, apple pie and ice-cream. The group was as self-centred as it had been previously, but light-hearted, jovial. Toasts were made in Coca-Cola and occasionally the youths clapped Z.M. or one another on the back.

117

10

OVER THE THAR DESERT, Karachi-bound, Cullen browsed distractedly through *The Buffaloes of Pakistan*. The sour relations remaining between Bangladesh and Pakistan had caused transit difficulties and the waste of a day each in Calcutta and Delhi. The Organization's travel department had allowed for this but not for the nineteenth-century pedantry of some Indian airport clerks. And their schedule as arranged had netted them no more than four hours' sleep each night in India. Now Z.M. and Galash, in the seats ahead, slept. Z.M. wore an airline sleeping mask like a dark highway robber. Galash's right foot, in comfy Pan Am socklet, stuck out in the aisle.

Unstrung, he envied them. Despite deep fatigue and boredom he couldn't sleep. Air travel threw him into circadian discord; his biological clock was haywire. In *The Buffaloes of Pakistan*, one of his own division's publications, he read that bells and amulets were commonly worn by working beasts and sometimes by milch animals as well. A hollow ornamented brass ring containing pebbles was often fitted around each fetlock; it would emit a musical jingle when the buffalo moved.

His attention wandered. He put down the pamphlet and thought of Margaret, closing his eyes and leaning back in his seat. The night of the *hartal* he'd telephoned from Dacca. Keyed up, emotional, he mentioned the wagon-load of bodies, then quickly stressed that they had not been victims of violence. He sounded a little odd to himself, just like Galash had earlier that afternoon..

'I was also assaulted on the leg by a miscreant. Or maybe it was a dacoit.'

'A what?'

'Someone threw a stone at me, that's all. No damage.'

'Thank God you're leaving there.'

'Mm. What's been happening your end?'

'Nothing much.' Usually Margaret said that. Her voice lingered in the region between reserve and warmth. The endearments 'darling' and 'dear' were perhaps lacking tonight. Deliberate intent? These days he often believed she was restraining some commitment to affection, as if such a show would leave her exposed and helpless. 'The Orosas said to say hello,' she said.

'Oh, really? They seem to be inundating us lately. How was their party?'

'Concepción said you rang. The party was up to their usual form, I suppose. The First Lady's cousin propositioned me. Bong Bong played the drums. Hank Beaumont slipped on the patio and put a disc out.'

'Sounds familiar.'

'Ted wanted a run-down on your movements. He sat me down and played the perfect host.'

'That's odd.'

'He was just being affable, flirting a little. He was all wound up with the cousin there, and some top Americans.' She cleared her throat. 'How are the buffaloes?'

'Plodding along.' This was a familiar line of banter, perhaps ten years old. It didn't necessarily infer good humour or even interest. But it was one of the few questions she asked about his work and showed an amiable trend.

He inquired after her health and asked some general physiological questions. 'Did old Hopkins give you the once-over?'

She hedged. 'Oh, he's about twenty years out of date.'

'Well, did you see him?' Honestly, she could be a trial.

119

'I'm well enough now. I'm eating better.'

'Not that mucus-free crap, I hope?'

'Good nourishing food,' she said crisply. Her voice was in neutral again.

'Lucky you.' He mentioned his own digestive problems. 'You can drop ten pounds after a cup of coffee here.'

The conversation had been conducted on this level. It hadn't had the depth of intensity he required, yet he felt powerless to change either his side of it or his responses. She surprised him by not asking about the dead. *He* would have, if their positions had been reversed. He had in fact beleaguered Z.M. with questions that same night.

Z.M. was cagey. 'I can't answer questions about the *hartal*, Dick. I haven't lived here for years. It's the people's affair.'

'Not that. I'm not talking politics, I'm talking about a bullock-cart full of bodies being unloaded not a mile from here, outside a mosque.'

Z.M. raised his brow at him, leaving him feeling greatly naïve. So where was the dispassion of science?

'It is charitable work,' Z.M. said. 'Rounding up the bodies of the dead for burial. A daily affair around the streets and parks, outside the gruel kitchens, surely a common practice.'

He was struck by his own gormlessness, yet he rambled on. 'There was a fox in the cart!'

He hadn't mentioned the fox to Margaret; that it had crept under the tarpaulin to eat the bodies. Perhaps he would later, but it was an image he was still considering: whether the animal was itself starving, what fears it had overcome to jump up on the wagon, and suchlike. Later he might also recount his visit to the zoo and the favoured treatment of the Bengal tiger. The relating of these anecdotes required a degree of intimacy. He felt surprisingly involved in them and wanted to do them justice. Actually, he wanted to tell them to Margaret right now, in person, but he was momentarily frightened that she didn't love him enough. He couldn't bear to feel stupid.

'Hmm, strange,' Z.M. had remarked about the fox. His voice sounded bored.

Another Inter-Continental hotel embraced them in Karachi. This time the foyers rang with mid-Western American accents. Plaid jackets and lurid trousers filled the elevators; service haircuts were apparent. On the premises also was a party of Chinese officials, in town to donate a sporting stadium or hydro-electric scheme, led by two tiny female interpreters whose faces remained impassive to GI badinage. Dacca's Mr Uzzerman had a counterpart in Mr Haq, an equally serious guide and mentor. Mr Haq, though, displayed a public relations bent: his schedule for Karachi, Rawalpindi and Lahore had time set aside for museums, shopping and the general absorption of local colour. This programme gave nothing away in steely efficiency, however. Within thirty minutes of their arrival they were whizzing along a tarmac road in a government Chevrolet towards a military dairy farm outside the city.

Scratched desert moonscapes sped past, clumps of scrubby foliage and khaki plant life of hardy characteristics. Cullen and Galash lay back in exhaustion, scarcely speaking. Z.M., on the other hand, was surprisingly genial and garrulous.

'I know these parts well,' he informed Mr Haq, waving an expansive hand. 'Some of the best times of my life I spent here at the university. My youth is invested in this place. Many good times . . .'

'Is that so?' At first Mr Haq was a little wary. By the end of the ride though they were cheery acquaintances. For enemies they had a lot in common, gossiping animatedly in Urdu and exchanging cigarettes.

At the dairy they were met by the commandant, Brigadier Ismail, who arranged for the issue of military gumboots. He bristled in a simulated British officer manner and enjoyed a pampered brushed-back moustache. He waved an arm airily. 'The military dairy farms of Pakistan are being maintained under high standards of efficiency,' he announced. 'Every serving soldier is entitled to a daily ration of milk.'

'Just as in India,' Z.M. said blithely. The brigadier looked as if the remark were unduly provocative but chose to ignore it.

121

They squelched through a recently sluiced buffalo shed. A high degree of hygiene was obvious. The buffaloes were arranged in tidy rows at each side of the long shed. They appeared to have been lined up according to height and colouring: at one end were the Ravis and Nilis, at the other the Kundis.

'We are making a strong attempt to maintain breed purity,' said the brigadier. He was a commanding presence, as tall as Cullen, although, not suffering Cullen's present debilitations, appearing a more upright figure. He had a habit of spreading his moustache with the thumb and forefinger of his right hand. It was an aggressive as well as a vain gesture, and showed an element of frustration. Cullen wondered where his career had gone wrong.

'Of course,' announced the brigadier, 'the futile and unproductive argument of buffalo versus cow is posed here as in other parts of Asia. It has even been mooted by the cattle propagandists that the buffalo be replaced as the main milk producer by such cattle breeds as the Sahiwal and the Red Sindhi.' Here he snorted derisively. 'It will not occur while the army is conducting affairs!'

They sat in the brigadier's office drinking tea and nibbling at pastries served by a lance corporal from a triple-layered silver tray. The room was dominated by a handsome engraved yataghan suspended by a purple cord on the wall behind the brigadier's desk. Its double-curved cutting edge caught the light but the heavily etched surface gave off no reflections. He gave the impression—by the sabre's prime position and by little half-turns of his head towards it now and again—of wishing to be seen as a warrior.

But he had an administrator's grasp of detail, reeling off figures, waving sheafs of papers. 'I am turning the faeces into a very big money-spinner,' he declared. 'Forty rupees for a one-ton wagonload, very good price. This is a valuable substance which we are producing in a considerable quantity. Our patties are becoming famous.'

However, the brigadier was happy to turn this discussion to lively tales from the Frontier Corps. Apparently it had been an exciting life in Baluchistan keeping an eye on the cunning Afghans and countering their baseless propaganda. His own resident Baluchs and Pashtoons had also borne some observation, he inferred with a virile wink. He'd watched like a hawk over the Bolan Pass. Snowline manoeuvres presented no more difficulties than desert operations once the men had their goggles on.

He turned towards the yataghan on the wall. 'But now I am needed here.' He shrugged philosophically. His eyes swam in a drinker's rheum. ' "Quetta knows better." It is an old army saying.'

Going back into town there was further banter in Urdu between Z.M. and Mr Haq, and some guffawing. Galash nodded off to sleep. Cullen tried to sleep but the others' cigarette smoke kept him awake.

'Oh my God!' Z.M. laughed suddenly.

'What's that?'

'Mr Haq tells me that when the brigadier was Adjutant-General of the Frontier Corps he was Quetta's most conspicuous supporter of General Yahya Khan.'

'It's a wonder he didn't shoot you for that crack about India.'

'Ha! He's lucky to be in charge of a buffalo dairy.'

Galash was not quite asleep. 'How come we're laughing,' he muttered, 'when it was our *first* choice of careers?'

In the smoke-filled Chevrolet, humming along dusty roads, they laughed, Mr Haq included, all the way back to Karachi. There, in a sort of post-dysentery daze, dull and pallid, Cullen lugged his body along to Mr Haq's other appointments, to the airport, to another link in the Inter-Continental hotel chain in Lahore.

Breathing hard, his clipboard as heavy as a shield, he officially perused small herds of milking buffaloes in Lahore's central business district. Amid decrepit colonial and Moghul grandeur he said, 'Good morning,' and 'Hello there,' to bemused squatting buffalo owners. He patted a crossbred rump here and there. 'What do you feed her? Sorghum? Alfalfa? Turnips? Green oats?' He was looked upon suspiciously. At best nicotine-stained teeth were shyly bared. Children ran from him on grey stick legs. He felt like a sweaty ginger giant. Stains were under his arms. 'Cottonseed cake, yes? Crushed barley?' A disfigurement would catch his bleary eye. Three teats. 'Irregular udder development here, old man. You have to keep the young heifers on a steady nutrition level. OK?' Flies settled on the milk pails. Men spat, out of bravado and confusion. Yashmaked women turned away.

And directly from this activity he went, soiled, the morning's smells in his pores, to lunch at the Gymkhana Club with the local Establishment. Ageing polo players and fussing septuagenarian members of the so-called 'Twenty-two Families', busy parodying English clubmen and retired Sussex colonels, surveyed the buffalo trio with bristly, polite disfavour. Cullen's University Rugby Club tie was not sufficient to open the Visiting Christians' drink locker.

They met not one woman. Galash and Z.M. hung about optimistically that evening waiting for the hotel's cocktail bar to open. Galash had a theory about the role of the cocktail bar in such countries.

'Look at it as the watering hole in the jungle. Open each night for two hours only. For that time all traditional animosities are suspended. Lion drinks with gnu. Leopard drinks with antelope. Come sunset all the shy little does will tiptoe down here for a quiet gin and tonic.'

'Sure. Then lion pounces on antelope and there goes your thesis. Anyway, the antelopes are camels here. You guys are wasting your time.'

Cullen was right. The absence of women in the general environment was, however, making its mark on him as well. With the local shiftless males he found himself idling before lustrous movie posters, restlessly drawn by rare facial nudity. Sulky Anglo-Indian lips. Erotic sloe eyes. Seldom had he been so stimulated. He queued at the Naseem Cinema to see actual female faces on screen. The posters promised

Intriguing Drama,
Spicy Dialogues, Lilting Melodies,

Dazzling Dances, Hilarious Comedy.
WE BET YOU'LL ENJOY EVERY MINUTE OF IT
Complete in Punjabicolor!

Though every row of seats squeaked and shook with his fellow filmgoers' growing appreciation, for him the film was boring and bewildering. Past the pumping fists and twitching knees he sidled gingerly and left the cinema. Rebuffing wall-eyed hashish pedlars he wandered aimlessly down through the night bazaars. Garish stalls leaned in on the narrow alleys. Stacks of cardboard suitcases, cricket bats, racks of raw silk ties ('The Young Men's Passion, The New Age Fashion!'), Japanese pocket calculators, watches, radios, cotton shirts, jewellery, tennis shoes, Afghan rugs, rose in heaps on either side. Insistent youths wobbled on Hondas through the throng, blaring their horns ceaselessly. Men carried sleeping children on their shoulders, dragged shivering reluctant calves on leads, proudly tinkled their bicycle bells. Adolescents squirmed past, advertising the Khyber Insurance Co. and the Paragon Rubber Works on their T-shirts.

A monster snatched at Cullen.

He had turned into a narrow market alley and the creature stood blocking his path. He was a pinhead: short, hunched, with wiry arms dangling. His shaved head sloped upwards to a point. Thick brows sprouted straight across the slanting forehead. Deeply inserted were glittering simian eyes. His colour was light; he looked beyond race or nationality. Like a grotesque Buddhist monk he was standing proprietorially in the centre of the alley in a yellow sleeveless smock. Vigorously he swung a plangent bell. He could have been heralding hecatomb or medieval plague.

Not that Cullen didn't avoid his steady, strangely personal gaze; hurriedly side-stepping him and striding on. But, reacting instinctively it seemed, the pinhead shot out a long arm and grabbed his wrist. And exerted pressure. The small twisted face, tightly concentrated like a fist, gabbled something malignant at him. Urgently Cullen shrugged him off, as

125

he would a spider, and walked on, sweating heavily, his arm tingling with the sensation of the clutching fingers. In the blurring background the bell still clanged.

Cullen composed his mind. The man was obviously a beggar of some sort, exploiting his deformity, or being exploited by others, though what there was to be gained in terrorizing Europeans he couldn't fathom. The market closed in on him again. He browsed through trinkets, bought some jewellery for Margaret, sauntered back along the crowded lanes towards a road where a taxi could be hired. In a similar position at the entrance to this alley another pinhead stood swaying on the balls of his feet, occasionally lunging to one side or the other. The crowd passed him by, oblivious, or giving that impression. It was not the same man. His clothing differed. This one was smaller and his long-sleeved shirt, its buttons all undone, billowed around him. The tight pointed head was similarly shaved; his dark features, clenched together, had the same intense cast. Cullen saw that his expression, like the other man's, wasn't the vacant one of idiocy: on the contrary their angry deformities gave them a look of shrewdness and frustrated evil. They appeared to be seeking retribution for their lot. Their black eyes glinted after a jester's vengeance.

This second pinhead had a whistle on a cord around his neck. Now he blew on it several shrill blasts. He smiled appreciatively at himself doing this, letting the whistle fall from his mouth. He capered and hopped and suddenly spun around on his bare feet. A string of spittle flying from his chin struck Cullen's face as he cautiously edged past him.

11

THE BLACK MANGROVE CRAB, whose claws were as big as a man's fist, haunted the swampy shores, declared Wilson da Silva, the Marxist-Leninist taxi driver, forcing his 1958-model Morris Oxford through Colombo's coastal traffic. Wilson da Silva was an educated young man with a literary turn of phrase. He had a wealth of lurid and bitter information for the foreigner. Right away he volunteered his politics; also, on learning their occupations, plenty of zoological data.

'Sea snakes infest the oozy beds of those shallow lakes,' he told them, swivelling around in the driver's seat and pointing with a skinny arm. 'The fishermen bemoan them and freely express their dread. My grandfather spoke of many varieties clad in beauty. True enough, but it has frequently been proven that some hold agony and a fast death in ready fangs.'

Wilson da Silva had offered his cab and guidance for the duration of their Sri Lankan exercise when their official vehicle failed to materialize. There was a problem with automotive parts, he explained to them. 'It is understandable, thanks to a colonial heritage. Cars are leaving the roads every day owing to a lack of Austin A-40, Ford Anglia and Wolseley components.' Energetic Wilson promised financially competitive rates, access to money changers and bargains in the local sapphires, rubies, moonstones and cats' eyes. On learning that their employer was the world he had shown even political magnanimity.

'I am the original pragmatic idealist,' he announced. 'China is now in the UN. Who am I to oppose this organization?' As well as this loftiness of spirit he provided, between stops, angry intelligence on local politics and social affairs. He had the low-down on prominent personalities. He offered detailed examples of nepotism and pocket-lining. 'Want to know something? Sri Lanka is dying from an overdose of nephews.' One of the leading nephews had been responsible for the loss of influence of the party Wilson supported, the Lanka Sama Samaja Party, and on his head he called down calamities far more severe than sea snake or mangrove crab.

In Colombo the trio felt surprisingly footloose and free. Alcohol was freely available. Women were visible in public places. Perhaps for these reasons, or because it was the last stage of their tour, on their first night they got drunk at their hotel and, on Galash's urging, piled into Wilson's cab.

'To your top brothel,' ordered Galash. The others allowed themselves to be led. The car was full of bravado, chuckling and banter.

Wilson squirmed with apparently conflicting emotions. 'The European still exploits us, I notice.' Then he giggled nervously. 'I mean nothing personal to you fellows. Those girls have to eat.'

As he drove he became increasingly pragmatic, making small pronouncements to fit the situation. 'Today in Lanka the human lives by his wits indeed. Or her wits as the case may be.' Again he giggled anxiously. 'Economic factors make him or her a realist.' As he deposited them outside a wide, low house with vine-covered verandahs, he said, 'Actually, you are the first Europeans to venture here for many a time.'

'That sounds bad,' Galash muttered.

The establishment was called the Sunorama Cabaret. Naturally they were still drunk on arrival, and fatigued from a day spent viewing small sturdy swamp buffaloes with a proud and pure breeding history—descended from the beasts brought by the Sinhala people from northern India in the sixth century B.C. The sensual delights of the Sunorama Cabaret were, even in the trio's condition, obviously meagre.

Geetha, the middle-aged proprietress, offered beer, polite ugly grandmothers and dancing to early Beatles' records. The lavatory walls, Cullen noticed on his first port of call, were overrun with geckos. Laughing Korean seamen competitively attempted to urinate on them. The lizards, presumably attracted by the blowflies and moths jostling for the light over the urinal, seemed fatalistic about this contest. On a verandah by the small dance floor women sat tensely in thigh-high sequined dresses. Some were gaunt and hollow-eyed; others were thick-waisted, with fat neck creases and pocked and doughy skin. They were charming and nicely spoken, however, with an understandable apologetic air about them.

Z.M. was very much at home. He had a respectful way of talking to the women that they appreciated, and he was better able to feign sexual interest. Or perhaps he wasn't pretending, Cullen thought, sipping warm beer which raised gaseous memories of forgotten aromatic curries. Galash, though the initiator, made no pretence—rolling his eyes skywards over his beer glass—that he had done the right thing.

Drink-induced courage and four weeks' libidinous build-up were instantly dissipated, leaving a residue of blurry good manners. They all danced. As usual Cullen felt like Gulliver. Chatting gaily, Z.M. swept around the floor with the grateful Geetha. She was a flash of turquoise and sequins, a tremble of dimpled leg flesh. The zipper of her dress was fastened with a sad safety pin. Z.M.'s skin and teeth shone and his chuckle hung over the verandah.

Shakily, Cullen swayed with a peaky prostitute wearing a sari; a buck-toothed Tamil girl, holding her just inside arm's length. Her small oiled head came to his waist; her delicate lower back, bare in the traditional way, was cool and damp to his hand. Beside them, a strained smile on his face, Galash gyrated self-consciously with a chubby aggressive grandmother to 'Love Me Do'. In the black palms beyond the verandah Koreans stumbled and swore.

'Shall we sit?' the Tamil girl said.

She sat with some reserve beside him and ordered a

Coca-Cola. She was shy; her lips could not close over her teeth, but made the attempt. Soon she lightly touched his wrist with tapering tea-picker's fingers. Generously she pretended interest in the curly ginger hairs. Her fingertips, palms, were rough from labour—possibly involving powerful solvents—and aroused in him only feelings of vague, maudlin goodwill. Naturally her life was unfortunate. Her conversation centred around American groceries. She was proficient at brand names. Her bunny teeth were thin and backed with gold.

The Tamil girl asked him for five rupees to buy curry-flavoured potato crisps 'for my baby'. Her daughter was four, she said, and cared for by her aunt. 'No more children—I had an operation.'

He received this information. 'Is she well?' he asked, anticipating congenital heart disease, leukaemia, at least rickets.

'She is beautiful, a healthy baby.' There was a proud, almost indignant note in her voice. She put the crisps packets in her handbag with a prim gesture.

He was surprised. 'I'm pleased,' he told her.

Abruptly she asked, 'Don't you like me? I am not pretty enough for you?' He felt instantly weary. There was a crash of Koreans in the foliage. Somewhere glass broke and there were shrill male giggles.

Of course he said she was very pretty and that he was old and drunk. No aspect of this trite statement was quite true. He was feeling sober enough now. He considered the absurd chivalry of his age, race and type but a moment later recklessly took her hand and kissed it. She showed neither relief nor unhappiness. Her wrist gave off aromas of patchouli and sandalwood and her homeliness aroused kind and paternal senses.

'May I stay with you instead of the Koreans?' she asked.

'Yes, please. Anyway they're too busy urinating on the geckos.'

She was stunned at this news. Anxiously her lips tried to cover her teeth. 'That is against the *Soonoo Sastere*, the science of lizards!' Her hands shot up to her cheeks in awe. House lizards were great determinants of good and bad fortune, she explained, depending on their colour, the day of the week and their compass position on the wall. From her handbag she unfolded a worn chart, neatly and childishly drawn, for interpreting the omens pronounced by the chirp of the house lizard.

'Were they looking towards the west?' she asked him earnestly.

Thoughtfully he sipped warm beer. Again acrid gases rose in his mouth. 'They were pointing upwards, I think.' Obviously, to escape the range of the Koreans. He could easily have laughed at the picture they presented: the mad pissing Koreans, the all-suffering lizards, the strangely stunned Galash now sharing his beer with his raddled clinging charmer, debonair dancing Z.M. Ali, the toast of the Sunorama Cabaret. More than anyone, himself.

The Tamil girl said, 'North. The lizard on Friday is dark blue. North is bad on a Friday.' Frowning, she perused her chart, darting over it with gracile fingers, shaking her head. Her teeth hung over her lower lip.

'Let me see.'

She quickly folded the chart and put it away.

'That's very ominous,' he commented, laughing. 'It serves the Koreans right.'

'Yes,' she said seriously.

'You are very superstitious.'

She twisted her drink straw in her fingers. Endearing exposed teeth pressed into her lip. Her remark now was right out of *Boys' Own Annual*. 'There is a Tamil proverb,' she said. '"Though one may escape the cast of a stone, one cannot escape the glance of the Evil Eye."'

'Aha, the Evil Eye. Now you're getting into my area.' He mentioned his passing acquaintance, picked up that morning in fact, with the centuries-old Sri Lankan custom of buffalo branding—the individual forms of magical loops, whorls and criss-crosses to ward off the Evil Eye, to guard against illness and theft and to ensure long life. He elaborated on the morning's sightings at Kandakadu: bleached buffalo skulls on poles set up for the same reason; amulets of human hair or from the tail of an elephant; chank-shells, pieces of iron or ivory tied on a buffalo's horns or around a leg. Various other charms dangling from the nose-rope. Metal discs jingling on a chain around the beast's neck.

'My child too wears charmed ash on her forehead,' said the Tamil girl, recommencing to stroke his arm.

Cullen almost surrendered to drowsy sensual feelings. But discussing the superstitious branding of the buffaloes recalled the parallel agrarian procedure they had observed that day in the backblocks. At the time of branding, by a local virtuoso, castration of male working animals was also performed. Nimbly the man clamped the cords with pliers. 'Hoy!' he exhaled, and pounded the testicles with an iron bar. Blood and tissue exploded from the split organs. The visiting advisers, cool professionals, had nevertheless winced. Scrotums tightened. Cullen had made special note of this crude process on his clipboard. *The buffalo is not a vocal animal,* he wrote. *Utterances are usually limited to a querulous, interrogatory or nervous grunt; exactly the sound of a creaking door hinge. But during the drawn-out castration process which my colleagues and I observed, the agonizing pain inflicted by the castrator was expressed in the piteous screams of the victims.* He strongly recommended against it, advocating a proper veterinary service and bloodless techniques.

Showering the Sunorama Cabaret with money they left the alleged debauch shortly after. Cullen gave the Tamil girl fifty rupees to assuage various guilts.

Suddenly bold, she said, 'I would like to go to your country. I could inquire at the Embassy. I would wear a respectable dress.'

He gave a falsely optimistic smile. 'Please do,' he invited.

From the verandah Geetha and all the prostitutes waved warmly and sadly, urging their quick return and regular patronage. As they climbed into Wilson's taxi Koreans were emerging lasciviously from the shrubbery to embrace the women.

Clashing gears, Wilson remarked, 'So my recommendation was favourable, eh?'

'Ha!' Galash said. The others were silent. 'Never liked paying for it,' Galash went on. 'Not when their faces would stop a clock, anyway.'

Wilson sulked all the way back to the hotel. The others slumped silently. In the lobby they separated moodily. Cullen went sluggishly to his room where, undressing, he was struck again by erotic frustration. He lurched and roamed around the room. He ordered room service brandy. His brain flew into scattered fantasies.

But serenity was not as easy to come by as it used to be. He drank the cognac and tried to read magazines. In this part of the world it was even harder to find. For a blind moment he could not remember which country he was in. He snatched at the hotel stationery to find out. Here they provided the traveller with *The Teaching of Buddha* as well as the Gideon Bible. His copy was new, with an eye-catching cover. He flipped through its pages.

'In describing the Buddhist Promoting Foundation,' he read, 'it is necessary to speak of a businessman, and this gentleman is Mr Yehan Numata. He established a company to manufacture precision tools more than thirty years ago. His solid conviction is that the success of an enterprise depends on the harmonious association of Heaven, Earth and Man, and that the perfection of the human mind is attainable only by a well-balanced co-ordination of wisdom, compassion and courage. He is doing everything he can under this conviction towards the technical improvement of tool manufacture and the development of the human mind.'

Mr Numata and his foundation had simplified Buddhism for Western hotel guests. They did not dwell on the doctrine's deep schisms and historic difficulties. Mysticism was played down and monastic asceticism was not unduly stressed. But Mr Numata and the foundation obviously knew their Western hotel guest. Buddha, Cullen quickly noticed, had a great deal to say about lust. Buddha recognized that of the worldly passions lust was the most intense. He had many exotic

133

metaphors, allegories, fables and aphorisms about lust concerning vipers, dogs, wild beasts, bee-hives and crocodiles. Buddha made the point that lust provided the soil in which other passions flourished. Lust was a demon that ate up all the good deeds of the world. Lust poisoned those who came in search only of beauty. Lust was a parasitic vine that climbed a tree and spread over the branches until the tree was strangled. Lust insinuated its tentacles into human emotions and sucked away the good sense of the mind until it withered. Lust was the bait cast by demons: foolish people snapped at it and were dragged down into the depths of the evil world.

Buddha was relentless on lust.

In his Y-fronts Cullen lay on his bed, rebuked and discomforted by these jungle riddles. 'How can you weigh a large elephant?' queried Buddha. 'Load it on a boat and draw a line to mark how deep the boat sinks in the water. Then remove the elephant and load the boat with stones until it sinks to the same depth, and weigh the stones.'

Aswim in brandy, Cullen was not entirely happy with the way Buddha glossed over the getting of the elephant on and off the boat. The fable also did not sit easily with Mr Numata's alleged expertise in the precision tool business.

Buddha had another fable to illustrate 'The Way of Practical Attainment' which was not as pragmatic as it could be. Once there was a young prince named Sattva. One day he and his two elder brothers went into a forest to play. There they saw a famished tigress which was evidently tempted to devour her own seven cubs to satisfy her hunger. The elder brothers ran away in fear but Sattva climbed up a cliff and threw himself off it to the tigress in order to save the lives of the cubs. This spontaneous action by Prince Sattva showed his determination to gain Enlightenment, according to Buddha, not to mention his love of animals. But where, thought Cullen, suddenly drunk again, would such impulsive cliff jumps and tiger feedings, if applied generally, leave the precision tool industry?

On an impulse, in this dazed and silly condition, he rang Margaret. At her end it was 4 a.m. Her voice was faint and tinged with panic, anticipating accidents, jets falling out of the air, not boozy joviality.

'No, nothing's the matter, darling. Just a spontaneous act of love on the spur of the moment,' he told her.

'You gave me a hell of a fright. In Colombo, aren't you? I've been trying to keep track.'

'I am indeed. In the jewel of the Indian Ocean. Serendip. The Resplendent Isle. Tonight I became a convert to Buddhism. It's got all the answers. You should look into it, if you haven't already.'

'What do you mean?' Her voice was weary and wary. 'It sounds as if you've been partying, more like it.'

'Nonsense. I must tell you about a tiger I saw the other day.'

'Go to sleep, Richard.'

Falling alseep on top of the covers, in his state of constriction, it was not difficult to dream wild fantasies of castration involving devices traditional and modern: heavy stones, metal bars, bamboo clamps, the Javanese *pasuran* machine and—made popular on the island of Marajó in the Amazon delta—the application of gradually tightened elastic bands. These implements, wielded by strangers and familiars alike, were demonstrated vividly and enthusiastically. Of course it was not hard to see where this was leading; even in the dream he knew what was coming next, so, panting heavily, he woke himself as the clanking *pasuran* loomed overhead.

A new hangover encroached. He was disappointed that even his subconscious was so blunt and obvious.

Wilson was over his sulks next morning. Driving nervelessly up into the tea hills he filled them with genial propaganda with a zoological link. 'The story is told by an annalist of the exploits of the early Jesuits in Ceylon,' he said, grinning around at them. 'Seven dugongs, male and female, were caught in the Gulf of Mannar and taken to them. On dissecting the dugongs the Jesuits pronounced: "Their internal structure is in all respects conformable to the human." ' Wilson giggled. 'Who would have thought it of them?'

Galash shrugged at Cullen, closed his eyes and drew on a cigarette.

Recklessly reaching across into the glove box, Wilson passed back a bundle of dog-eared political tracts, saying, 'Excuse me, some interesting reading matter for the journey, if you wish.'

Cullen received a Chinese booklet called *Let The Whole Party Mobilize For A Vast Effort To Develop Agriculture and Build Tachai-Type Counties Throughout The Country*. The type skittered before his eyes, his hangover buzzed. There were no pictures. 'Thanks, Wilson,' he said.

'Naturally I had a Catholic upbringing,' Wilson was volunteering. He doubled de-clutched and accelerated around a road-working elephant. (The sight of the beast caused Cullen some childish excitement.) 'What chance did I have, being born on October thirty-first, 1952? That very day Pius XII was speaking on the wireless to the Portuguese at the close of the Jubilee celebrating the Apparitions at Fatima.'

His head shook in wonder. He went on, 'Pius consecrated the world and Russia to the Immaculate Heart of Mary. He and the Blessed Virgin made such a big noise about Russia, who would not gain an interest? I could not see the connection myself. So six times the Blessed Virgin appeared to three Portuguese kids! Lucie, Jacinta and François—I know the story well enough, God knows. The apparitions were marked by extraordinary atmospheric phenomena. OK. On October thirteenth, 1917, seventy thousand people assembled at Fatima witnessed the sun revolving for a quarter of an hour, emitting many coloured rays, and finally seeming to plunge towards the earth. All right, I can accept that, science can accept that.'

Wilson was steering with one arm at this stage and gesticulating with the other. His voice rose shrilly. They were climbing precipitous mountain roads. Trucks laden with produce and clinging windblown peasants hurtled around blind corners at them. Fatal jungle descents loomed by Cullen's window. The back of Wilson's neck quivered with agitation. At close range his brown skin was overlaid with freckles. His hair, swept back in a patent-leather slab, smelled of a musty brilliantine. Dust from the road dulled its sheen.

'So Fatima became the Lourdes of Portugal. Now immense pilgrimages go there, led by bishops and cardinals and attended by the civil authorities. Numerous miracles have been attested to. Ha! My mother in her sixties still saves desperately to go. The Portuguese link is strong with her, the bourgeois vanity of a European ancestor. She will never make it. "Don't waste your efforts," I tell her.'

For a moment he was silent. The muscles of his jaw were clenching. 'Ha! Fatima!' he said eventually. 'On the occasion of the Jubilee—on the day on my birth—Pius sent a wireless message from the Vatican. And next thing we're told the Mother of Mercy backed the Tsars! Well, that is not good enough for me, thank you, Pius XII! Not bloody good enough!'

Angry tears shot from Wilson's eyes. Furiously the Morris surged onward and upward, with many gear changes; Wilson lapsing into an intense silence.

Stunned, they concentrated on their reading matter. Cullen opened his lime-green pamphlet, closed it again. It was greasy with handling; paragraphs were underlined in pencil. Galash and Z.M. at least had tracts with heroic pictures. Cullen peered vacantly out the window. The scenery around the road was equally unattractive. Jungle had given way to bare rocky hillsides. Giant boulders teetered in loose gravel over them; land slides seemed imminent.

He turned back to *Let The Whole Party Mobilize For A Vast Effort*. There was a self-serving tale by one Kuo Feng-lien, secretary of the Communist Party branch of the Tachai Brigade. Kuo turned out to be a buffalo man himself. One day he had taken a water buffalo to market for sale. The animal looked powerful and attracted a crowd of prospective buyers. Some farmers from neighbouring brigades offered sixty yuan for it, others seventy or even eighty. But Kuo refused to sell, explaining patiently that the buffalo had an internal injury that made it useless as a draught animal even though it looked strong. Selling it for the high price offered would be cheating and against the best fraternal inter-collective relationships. So Kuo sold it to the state foodstuffs company for only twenty-seven yuan.

'He's our man,' said Cullen, passing the booklet to Galash. And, he thought, also Buddha's and capitalism's Mr Numata's.

'Right on. Unless that internal problem was haemorrhagic septicaemia,' said Galash a moment later, flicking his cigarette out the window. He grinned. 'In which case, keep an eye on the buffburgers.'

In the tea hills beyond Kandy it was cool, the food was English, the ambience nineteenth-century colonial, the views panoramic. Cullen was at home. The local buffaloes were doing fine. At Nuwara Eliya the trio drank Best Orange Pekoe, dreamily following the complete process from bush to teacup. The fingers of the Tamil girls were a blur of motion.

III THE NAMELESS NIGHTCLUB

1

CULLEN LEFT THE FIELD and headed home. It was easy walking distance; the sports ground lay only four or five hundred yards beyond their rear stormwater channel, just inside the village wall; a former wasteland of rank cogon grass which the Wanderers had transformed into a trim buffer zone between The Fourth Estate and the muddy urban farmlets with their plywood shanties fringing the highway. Now there was a playing field complete with goal posts, a turf wicket, sightscreen, roller, change shed, seats for perhaps a hundred spectators and, with a clear view of the ground, a rectangular open-sided bar. At the edge of the field there was also a scoreboard which declared, at the moment, WANDERERS 21 VISITORS 11, and some playground equipment donated by the social clubs of the various British Commonwealth embassies for the children of sportsmen. As Cullen trudged along the soft clay driveway from the sports ground three shanty children clambered over the wall, dropped to the ground and ran towards the swings.

Jet trails hung in the air. Sweet noxious fumes from the highway. A green army gunship racketed low overhead, dipping away obliquely in the direction of the airport. The toy bodies of the pilot and co-pilot peered from the cockpit and he glimpsed the machine-gunner's legs through the gun-slit in the floor before it veered off. No longer a target, he moved off the clay track on to the macadam of Stop Press

Avenue, padding wearily along in his sneakers, swinging his football boots by their laces.

The television blared in the study. Jabbering growls dispersed through the humid house. On screen the scowling, flamboyantly gesturing figures were blurred by the tropical afternoon light flooding in the study window. They grunted and lunged, screamed maniacally at each other and indulged in mayhem involving swords, *bolos*, daggers, flame-throwers, .38s, hands and feet. Regularly a cleaved limb would fly through the air. Blood fountained in high arcs. Women keened over twitching amputees. Margaret was leaning back against cushions on the divan with a gin and tonic watching a Tagalog adventure-romance called *Cleofatra*—there was that confusion with Ps and Fs again—about a karate-chopping heroine who, in the words of the English voice-over, was 'a dynamic model of the female of today taking a positive role in society'.

A bare muddy knee brushing hers, Cullen sat down heavily and poured beer, back from a Rugby game against the officers and crew of the *Ark Royal*.

'Well, we won,' he offered eventually, '21-11. They had two ring-ins from the Royal Navy team.' There was a tentative note of satisfaction in his voice. 'We sorted them out.'

The beer hit the glass and rose to the rim without a collar of froth. Flat. Frowning, he sipped a little and then topped the glass up from the bottle of San Miguel. 'The girls aren't rinsing the glasses properly,' he complained, getting up and walking into the adjoining bathroom. He tipped the glass into the wash-basin and rinsed it, shook it dry, then returned to the study, re-filled it and drank. 'Whew!' he sighed. 'I've been waiting for that.'

He sat bare-chested, bare-footed, in his football shorts; straight home from the game: no lingering at the bar, no shower even; with grass stains on his palms and grimy shins, making an effort on his first day home.

'Blame me,' she said, sipping her gin. 'It's their day off, remember?'

'Oh, of course.' On Sunday Margaret did the housework.

'It's probably a dud bottle.'

Alongside him her profile was pale and definite. He took a long drink. Sundays depressed him, always had done. Once, no more than nine or ten he had even mock-threatened suicide on a Sunday. A sharp autumn day with long afternoon shadows. He faced Monday trouble at school; the cane seemed imminent; drama-to-come hung over the whole speeding day, disapproval, bad marks, ridicule. Dirge-like church music on the wireless. Assertive American evangelists on the Radio Church of God. Down at the bay with Lindy—she six or seven then, small and healthy in green corduroys—he asked her, 'What would you do if I jumped off the jetty and drowned? On purpose?' Naturally she cried as he strode along. Satisfactorily for the junior sadist.

'Don't do it, Ricky! Oh, please!' He couldn't keep it up for long despite the not unpleasing images of grieving graveside parents, solemn teachers, classmates lined in sad rows, at attention. At the end of the jetty above snappy dark waves she clung to him: 'No! No!' and he cuddled her with sudden sorrow, stood among snowy seagull droppings saying he was only joking; and she herself was drowned eighteen months later. Though accidentally.

In dreams his daughter became her and vice versa, quite gradually and naturally. Strange really, because she and Louise were nothing alike. His sister would be fortyish now, no doubt the usual suburban mother, and they probably would be no more than tepid Christmas friends.

A commercial broke into the programme. It was one which both titillated and annoyed him. A dark beauty with petulant lips mouthed silently into a microphone. A velvety male voice announced: 'Pride is our feeling on RPN of Pilita Corrales. The superstar longstanding in the galaxy. Brilliant as ever the aura of her music. A reflection of a soul rich with musical artistry. Enjoy Pilita tonight. Musical extravaganza with Pilita Corrales and famed guest stars Amado del Paraquay, the Ambivalent Crowd and Lucy Borromeo's Dancers. Remember, join the stellar set on RPN!'

Cleofatra returned, looking vengeful in flared slacks tight around her thighs, and despatched a Doberman with a kick in the throat.

'This is too much,' he said amiably, pouring another glass of beer. Sweat shone over his body; he was vaguely aware of his odour. He held the bottle gingerly because his right thumb was pulped around the nail. One of those Royal Navy forwards may have bitten it, he couldn't remember. He saw he was dripping sweat on the divan and wondered whether she had noticed. For some irritating technical reason the house's wiring could sustain only one electrical appliance per room at a time: it was either the TV or the air-conditioner. In his opinion there was no choice—the air-conditioner every time.

He couldn't be bothered with the local TV programmes, even those in the fractured show-bizzy American-English they spoke here. When they had first arrived they had collected prime examples, repeating them to each other with amazed delight. What a scream—this country gathering up the tacky jargon of beauty contests, public relations men, dubious indoor sports and sharp business practices, and turning it into the language of the élite. Where the briefest, most fatuous Western trend, the nine-day wonder, was legitimized and put to work for the dictatorship.

But there was a touching side to all this: the people were just romantic children, at a cultural crossroad between Asia, America and Europe, in love with love. What a chance for Spain and Hollywood, what a pushover for the Church and the US! Now Margaret no longer seemed to notice these things. She watched *Cleofatra* with the same incurious and inert expression she wore when she shopped and went to parties. Uncritical. Indiscriminately passing the time.

Cullen finished the second bottle, rose from the divan, sighed and left the room to the sounds of gunshots and police sirens. Wearily, he undressed and dumped his football gear in the laundry basket in the bathroom. On the tiles he stood before the mirror amazed at his scarlet face, the effusion of colour spreading from his shoulders and neck upwards to his scalp. A pulse was visible at one temple. Noticing it he believed he could hear it ticking like a clock.

The usual gecko was present—he and the creature both gave a mild start when it appeared from behind a cold-cream jar in the medicine cabinet. He reached in for the antiseptic soap and it opened its mouth gently at him, breathing a timid warning. He left the cabinet ajar so it could get out and stepped into the shower feeling genial towards it and all geckos. Recalling the fortitude of those above the urinal in the far-off Sunorama Cabaret, he smiled, then suffered a sudden guilt about that evening, about having been in the company of prostitutes and ne'er-do-wells. A bad element.

Under the shower he still sweated. The water was never cold enough, nor was it soft enough to work up a lather. It smelled of chemicals. He felt the peculiar glow of his face, pressed his head against the shower to get maximum water pressure on his skin, leaned his forehead on the wall tiles. Chromium and tile were lukewarm to the touch. His muscles were beginning to stiffen; he ached all over. Belching from the beer he rubbed himself with antiseptic soap from scalp to feet. Abrasions smarted on his shins. Water vanished wastefully down the drain—and in the muddy streets a mile or so away women were breaking open fire hydrants for drinking water, tapping pipes to wash clothes. He sighed and belched again, rinsed off the soap and stepped from the shower. Dabbing himself dry, dusting himself with prickly-heat powder, he heard voices: Margaret's laughter and an impression of Galash's accent. Simultaneously, out the open bathroom window, Orosa and his wife were arguing in their garden; with each other or a third person he could not tell.

' . . . and Dick got up, shook his head and brought the guy down. I wouldn't have missed it for the world.' It was Galash.

Next door Orosa's voice rose. He made a savage reference to someone and a chair scraped heavily on the patio.

Margaret laughed again, and the Orosas' back door slammed shut.

'You two always cheer me up,' said Galash, smiling at

145

Margaret. He offered her a cigarette, lit it, lit one for himself with a drinker's ease. His lighter seemed to be snapping all over the place. He would have had several drinks while watching the game, a few at the bar later, Cullen guessed, observing his jolly sheen, his talkativeness. In an open-necked silky shirt, gold bauble dangling against his chest, Galash sipped a beer now next to Margaret and launched into some gossip about the new Assistant Director of the Projects Department, a Finn named Ake Asp.

'Yes, Asp as in serpent,' he said. 'Apparently it's quite a common name. *Flagrante delicto*, anyway, with Boonma Phromyothi's secretary on the divan in the women's comfort room. You can imagine the trouble it's causing.'

'And the jokes,' Margaret laughed. 'The snake in the grass.'

'I hadn't heard,' Cullen said. 'Where do you pick up this sort of information?'

'I guess that makes her a snake charmer,' said Galash, snorting cigarette smoke and laughter. 'I don't like her chances of staying on. It won't do Asp a hell of a lot of good either, the turkey.'

Cullen didn't know the girl, and had seen Asp only once or twice—a shortish thin man with fair receding hair sitting silently behind Phromyothi, his director, at Agricultural Assistance meetings. But immediately he felt he knew him and was surprised at Galash's cynical amusement. Galash especially. He was also surprised at his own sympathy for them, at the entirely different picture he obviously had of the incident. Oddly, he felt ill at ease with his still flushed face, as if it were the glow of embarrassment and guilt. He was identifying with Asp, for God's sake. For no tangible reason other than the secret, well-veiled lust he felt for Miss Fernandez he was struck with hot waves of fright and remorse. It was as if he and Gigi had been the couple caught red-handed. On the job. Chocka—as the old schoolboy expression succinctly put it—chockablock.

Vivid quick images of this nightmare came to him as he sat aching in his hard captain's chair underneath the air-conditioner—now switched on and fanning the back of his neck—facing the others across a table of drinks. There was almost a compulsion to croak out that eternal ludicrous defence plea: 'It's not what it seems!' Nervous tension made him garrulous and busy suddenly, set his foot tapping. He topped up drinks, became louder and more expansive. With cheery *bonhomie* he told anecdotes of his own, painting air pictures with his arms. He made definite, confident statements which allowed no room for disagreement. And during all this, part of him, remaining detached and curiously percipient, heard his father's voice saying similar effusive masking words, saw him twenty, thirty years ago laying down the law at Casuarina Bay in front of the sandstone fireplace in the living room, waving a drink, displaying the same genes.

This was chastening for a moment. Sure the old man must have been a playboy. Even as a kid he'd caught the hints. The quiet verandah chats at parties. The way women regarded him and laughed at his jokes. His casual knockabout charm and outdoor ease went over marvellously. The bedside manner. As if doctors weren't love objects anyway! The brittle socialite role hadn't been such a surprising step then for Dottie, he imagined; her daughter dead and George leading an extra life or two. Parties and the bridge table loomed thankfully ahead. Adjustments were made, relationships reassessed.

Apart from the time of Lindy's death there was only one clear memory of weeping: he was doing school homework on a table in the sunroom overlooking the garden and his mother came in and sat on the couch, snuffling into a handkerchief. She stared out the window pretending to watch a magpie oust currawongs from its territory.

'Oh, Richard, I don't know,' she said at last, and burst into tears. Sun came in the window. A red wasp, frantically buzzing, died slowly on the warm window sill. It curled back on itself in agonies of frustration. He put an embarrassed arm around her, but she patted his hand and blew her nose and left the room, leaving him sad for the wrong reasons, sitting there in oblique adolescent melancholy staring down at his work table. The table had come originally from his father's surgery. It was small and made of oak and he imagined it still smelled of methylated spirits. He sat on a chair originally from the surgery waiting room wondering how many sick and worried people had sat on it over the years, how many damp-palmed patients had clutched its arms, and if any were still alive. His father was a thoracic surgeon; heart and lung disease, not likely! He lifted his arms from the chair's shiny arms thinking, on the subject of his father, how come you're such a cheerful bastard when you're in the death business? And realizing, perhaps for the first time, that he himself was doomed never to fully understand people.

On the coffee table now in the study were six or seven empty San Miguel bottles. Sharp sunlight striking the almost empty Tanqueray gin bottle left a small green spotlight on the table top. Lustful silly Asp was still under discussion. Galash said Finns were dark horses.

'You never know what they're thinking behind those pale eyes.'

'Finns aren't the only ones I have that trouble with,' said Margaret. 'Germans, Indians. And you *never* know what a Japanese is thinking, the men anyway.'

'You know what all the men are probably thinking,' said devilish Galash.

'Oh, Hugh. Don't be absurd.' There was no annoyance in her voice, Cullen thought. Then she added, unnecessarily in his opinion, 'Except for desperadoes like you.'

'Don't encourage him, for God's sake,' he told her, jocularly enough.

Galash chuckled. 'No, getting back to our friend Asp, the snaky Finn.' He wagged a cheeky finger, on his old theme again. 'Never defecate in your own nest. Pardon me, Margaret, but I know of what I speak.'

Cullen, jaded, went down to the refrigerator in the kitchen for more beer and tonic water. He was heavy on the stairs. His head swam a bit and ached behind the right eye.

In the cooler kitchen he sat for a moment at the linoleum-covered table where the house maids ate, pressing

148

an ice block to his temple. On the wall above one of the girls had pinned up an entry form for a soft-drink competition.

ISANG SNAPSHOT BIGLANG JACKPOT!
Basta MIRINDA *Orange ang inumin, it's so easy to win!*
Halos wala kayong gagawin. Simpleng drink MIRINDA
and watch out for sa MIRINDA *roving camera.*
Garantisadong P1,000!
Win up to P20,000!
Araw-araw, WINNERS, WINNERS, WINNERS!

Over the stove, under a patina of grease, Paul Newman surveyed him with eyes of an eerie blue.

The ice gradually melted against his pink face. Poor, nice, optimistic girls, he thought, with their hopeless dreams of wealth and movie stars. They sang lightly through the house. Silently, their bare feet drifted over the parquetry. And not unattractive really, let's face it. Concepción, the younger at eighteen or nineteen, had a sensual mouth, he realized, and a sturdy confidence in the hips. In her shiny hair she wore jaunty coloured clasps that he liked. Beneath her floral shifts her brown bare legs flashed cleverly. And Mina, plainer, eight or ten years older, nonetheless had a certain sexual assurance—perhaps from motherhood—like the mien of the nurse or stewardess. In their absence their images and their trifling trademarks stirred a desire they had never initiated in person. The contest advertisement on the wall and the Hollywood pin-up ceased to be pathetic. They became, like the apron, say, or the tea-towel hanging on a rail beside him, just matter-of-fact impressions of their presence.

But not quite so vivid a reminder as the apron, which, smelling of Concepción's body and cheap perfume, was being pressed experimentally to his face when Margaret came into the kitchen.

'What are you doing?'

A natural question, even he, aberrant and spontaneous, thought. 'Just dabbing some ice on the old head. Got a few knocks today.' The tray of ice cubes was in front of him.

He had a reasonable case. Nevertheless he was hot with foolishness.

'We wondered what had happened to you.' She took the beer and tonic water. 'You could bring up another bottle of gin. I'm almost out.' As she walked out she said, 'There's some codeine in the cupboard if you want it.' Her step was as sure as ever, light but definite, and her carriage as upright as an abbess's.

'Right.'

He hung Concepción's apron on the rail. Following Margaret upstairs a moment later with a bottle of Bombay Dry Gin, he was reciting from the label, announcing heartily, 'I bring you coriander from Morocco, lemon peel from Spain, angelica from Saxony, liquorice from England, orris from Italy, juniper from Germany and almonds from Indo-China!' But his senses were still searching for a more elusive flavour.

They took no notice.

Galash was saying, engagingly, 'What can you do? I mean, what can *one* do? You're human. *One* is only human.' To stress this he touched her lightly on the arm. He gave a smile both shy and naughty. It had the ability to go either way—yet was still not beyond reach of seriousness.

The impression Cullen had was of the world-weary buccaneer in revelatory mood. He placed the gin bottle on the coffee table. 'It's serve-yourself time.' He poured a beer.

'Ha, ha. You can't fight your hormones, the physical side,' Galash said. 'I make no apologies. You need, you know, company from time to time.' He blew cigarette smoke. He made a concession. 'I've got my failings, God knows.' He was leaning forward for emphasis, perched on the edge of the divan. His eyes were set, frank and brave, on Margaret's. He was more rumpled than usual. He still drank enthusiastically. 'Physically, we were wonderful. A knockout, Christina and I.'

Margaret asked, 'Do you hear from Christina?'

Nice steering, Cullen thought, drinking too.

Galash blinked. 'The odd letter. Polite and civilized. It's the end, you know. Kaput.'

'Oh, you never know, Hugh.' Her make-up looked fresh. Her profile was sympathetically defined in the softening light. 'You could easily get together again.'

'Oh, sure.' The steam seemed suddenly to have gone out of him. 'She's happily back on the culture trail: 57th Street, uptown galleries. All that *élan* and panache and the hub of civilization. She wrote me one letter, three or four pages, just on some artist she'd seen. Larry Poons—ever heard of him? Nothing about us, just the typical critics' bullshit about his torrents of colour, his forest deeps, his cathedral glooms. His astral shimmerings. Jesus! Astral shimmerings!'

'Will you go back?'

He shrugged. 'We've all painted ourselves into this little corner, haven't we? We're an integral part of this particular *opéra bouffe*.'

Abruptly Cullen raised his glass in a mock toast. 'Let's drink to forest deeps and astral shimmerings.'

Galash reached for the Bombay Dry Gin. 'This is just too colonial for words. Queen Victoria and all that.'

'To the American Raj.'

'To the brave *Bubalus bubalis*.'

They subsided. The room was becoming dim. The whir of the air-conditioner became noticeable. From next door came the rapid staccato of drums.

'Bong Bong,' Margaret said resignedly.

'The natives sure are restless,' Galash said.

Shortly the drumming stopped. The sun disappeared under the ilang-ilang.

'Anyone hungry?' Margaret asked, rising unsteadily to draw the curtains.

In the dark Galash announced, 'She had an orgasm every time. Never missed.'

Garantisadong! thought Cullen, deep in Sunday melancholy. *Araw-araw. Winners, winnners, winners!*

'Whatever else, I'll always be grateful for our beautiful children,' Margaret said obscurely, standing in the doorway as bright savage light flooded the room.

151

2

AS CULLEN HEAVED against the palm tree next morning Orosa leaned over the wall and suggested lunch.

'I'd like to welcome you back, Dick. We don't get together enough.'

Strange, Cullen thought. He was panting too hard to make an excuse: he'd lost condition on the tour. They agreed to meet at Pete's Steakhouse, popular among the upwardly mobile local businessmen for its uptown, American ambience and for its seeping steaks which this clientele would order, pick at, redistribute on their plates and leave virtually uneaten. Cullen suspected that the ritual there was important—the ordering of the expensive masculine food of white businessmen. Only in the privacy of their homes or in the company of old friends would they relax over *relleno* or *adobo* or perhaps a surreptitious handful of dried fish—the familiar tasty food of maids and peasants.

Orosa was there before him giggling and mingling. Lunchers clapped him on the back. He made a fuss of Cullen, shaking hands as if they were old friends parted for years. He motioned him to a key table in a quiet but prominent corner. He hissed, 'Tssst!' for the drink waiter.

'Well, how is Asia? I want to know all about your adventures. Give me a full briefing, as we say.'

'I've got nothing very newsworthy, I'm sure.'

'Oh, you would be surprised. I am interested in the overview, the overall picture.' Turning aside, he waved suddenly towards the door as if struck by extrasensory perception. Henry Beaumont was limping into the restaurant. 'Poor Hank,' Orosa said, shaking his head. 'I feel responsible for his accident. He hurt his back enjoying himself at my home. I sent him some nice bourbon and a card. "Get well Hank", it said. It was the least I could do. Wild Turkey. He sent me an amusing thank-you note from "the clumsy Yank who fell on his ass". His very words.'

He tittered, his eyes shooting beyond Cullen. 'Hank and Florence are very dear friends of ours, very close.' Modestly he adjusted his cufflinks, heavy silver inlaid with stones the deep colour of claret. Presumably they were rubies. His head was half turned to the table where Beaumont was now loudly settling himself, greeting his companions and guffawing stoically at their repartee. Orosa could barely restrain himself on his chair, stricken, it seemed, by conflicting desires. He wore a small keen smile, open to any opportunity. 'Well,' he said eventually. 'What's the situation? I like to keep in touch.'

'Oh, states of emergency everywhere,' Cullen said provocatively. 'Martial law, constitutional authoritarianism, the usual thing.'

Orosa gave a little giggle. 'How do we compare?'

'Very well. The food's better here.' He spread a bread roll with white butter.

'You rascal!' Orosa patted at his hand. 'Ha, ha!' His eyes still strayed enviously to the Beaumont table. 'Any Bhutto feeling left? What's the score in Bangladesh? We look pretty damn good, huh! Gaddafi and China on side. Who would have guessed it?'

The steaks arrived, exuding a high smell of recent slaughter. Idaho potatoes. Californian red wine. Orosa focused on his meal, shovelling it in, chewing noisily. Flesh fibres showed between his teeth during the small-talk. He was frowning with concentration. All at once he took an aggressive mouthful of wine. As he held it in his mouth, swilling it around inside as if deciding what to do with it, his dilated nostrils loomed up at Cullen like caves.

Cullen also bore down on his meal. There had to be a purpose behind it, presumably some political snooping, but he was too jaded to care. Most of his attention was going to a big praying mantis, green as a leaf, climbing the wall only a foot or two behind Orosa's head. It was a difficult climb, slippery, and its legs found it hard to get a grip. Nevertheless, by poking out its hooked front claws warily before it and then laboriously experimenting with its middle legs—stretching them out tentatively wide at its sides—it was able to inch up the wall toward the mesh screen covering the air-conditioner.

It was hypnotic, watching the insect's progress. Chewing his gamy steak Cullen contemplated its spindly rocking gait and thought of a drunken mountain climber. But its head had a weird inter-galactic look about it, swivelling like a Martian's. Part of the fascination of course lay in whether it would lose its grip and fall on Orosa. Cullen almost held his breath.

Orosa had another drink of wine. 'Very good,' he commented seriously, dabbing at his mouth with a napkin. Then he took a conversational tone, smiling amiably. 'You know, as an outsider it amazes me sometimes how trusting your people are, how good-hearted. They must be aware here if not in New York of the occasional stormy petrel.' Again he sipped, more gingerly. He raised a quizzical brow. Then he winked. 'These guys must stretch their forbearance, eh? The lone wolf subversive element?'

'Which guys? What's on your mind?'

Orosa smiled tightly. He seemed to be waiting for some explanation.

'That's nonsense.' It sounded lame. Orosa was still smiling, waiting. Cullen would have wished for the praying mantis to drop on him exactly now, but it reached the screen, climbed still upward and, as the cold draught of the air-conditioner struck it, stopped as if paralysed.

Orosa quickly filled the air space with chatter.

'Have some more wine,' he said expansively, abruptly shifting expressions. 'You catch me in a happy mood. I cleaned up at the casino last night. Very lucky.'

'Baccarat?'

'Pai kiu. I prefer the Chinese form of baccarat. Number nineteen wins as well as nine. The stakes are not so high, but I find the house is not so fortunate.' He laughed, briefly but loudly, then dabbed at his mouth again with the napkin. 'Very lucky,' he repeated.

Cullen caught a hint of embarrassment. The praying mantis had begun moving again, jerkily tip-toeing from the air stream. Orosa was now out of range. Jolly banter came from the Beaumont table, the deep timbre of Beaumont's voice and a fricative European accent dominated the conversation, but Orosa's attention no longer wandered there.

He gave another soft giggle. 'On the deck of the casino ship out there,' he gestured vaguely in the direction of the bay, 'I was walking last night in the air, in the cool. I had won twenty thousand pesos at Pai kiu. I had a Scotch in my hand. Twelve-year-old Chivas Regal. Over the intercom they were calling out the winning keno numbers. There was relaxing band music coming from the cocktail lounge and,' he giggled again, 'wonderful looking girls, tourists and rich mistresses with curvaceous figures, strolling the deck. People spoke several languages and behaved with charm to each other. I thought of myself doing what I was doing. Watched myself from on high like a veritable god. Fun times. The choice of various different games of chance. Roulette, craps, blackjack, keno, cusek. I could see the lights from the cathedral, lit for Sunday, and next to it, Fort Santiago.'

He paused dramatically. *Fort Santiago*. His little mouth was set firm. The first time they met Orosa had recounted the ferocious death of his father in the fort in 1945. Orosa senior had been one of six hundred partisans locked in a dungeon called the Powder Magazine. Before the Japanese retreated they had poured gasoline in through the windows and set fire to the packed prisoners. Orosa had noticed the impact this story had had on him but asked him now, 'Are you aware of Fort Santiago? Do you know it, my friend?'

'Of course, Ted.' Orosa knew he did. He was holding it

over him like some moral lesson. This was an uncharacteristic and arrogant act for him, though he was speaking quietly and his face was placid.

'Naturally you do. You have visited it as a sightseer, had refreshments at the café. Perhaps watched a cultural performance. Relaxed in an atmosphere of peace and leisure.' He smiled thinly. His gums were grey. Even his sarcasm was oblique. 'It is a fascinating place.'

'Indeed. A shrine, wouldn't you say?'

Orosa appeared not to hear. 'You know it is where the Spanish imprisoned Doctor José Rizal before they shot him? It is where he wrote *Mi Ultimo Adiós*.'

'Sure, he smuggled the manuscript out in the base of an oil lamp,' said Cullen, reaching for a toothpick. 'They've got MacArthur's staff car there now—a sixteen-cylinder 1935 Cadillac. And the bullet-riddled car in which Quezon's wife was ambushed by the Huks.'

Orosa blinked. 'A heroine, Mrs Aurora A. Quezon. A wonderful lady.' He sighed and pushed his plate from him.

'I heard the Japanese had another trick as well as the gasoline. A deeper dungeon connected by pipes to the river. Apparently the roof was below high tide level and prisoners put there drowned within six hours.'

Orosa gave him a questioning look, then shrugged. 'That is all forgotten now. Life must go on.' He sighed. 'I am a very philosophical writer—that is the essence of my type of creative mind. I am a poet really.'

'Of course. The "Lord Byronist".'

'To you I am a hard-bitten newsman, right? Getting scoops. Influencing affairs. It is understandable.' Again he shrugged. 'It is my living. It buys the swimming pool and the Mercedes. But underneath my on-the-ball exterior is a poet's heart. Soul, as the Negroes call it.' He made a curious egotistical gesture, expansive, with much hand fluttering. 'I am *makahija* like the sensitive plant, you know, the bashful mimosa.'

Cullen kept a straight face during all this, watching the tight brown features opposite twitching with self-possession.

Orosa's mahogany eyes were darting again, settling nowhere, and he began crisply folding his napkin in front of him as he chattered. When it was a small square he patted his lips with it, and his eyes.

He said, 'I was considering this while standing on the deck of the casino with my pocket full of Pai kiu winnings. Fort Santiago. My father killed there, the Bataan march, all those terrible happenings. The voice of history spoke to me.'

'Quite so,' said Cullen sympathetically. The little man was giving off light waves of perfumed hair tonic, an air of glossy dignity like a well-buffed wooden figurine. They had had a bloody time of it all right.

'I saw the lights. The wind blew night smells from the city. The cathedral bells rang over the bay and I thought, boy oh boy, I thank God for the New Society.'

Cullen finished his wine, nodding slightly.

'I have *mucha suerte*, no kidding,' Orosa snorted humourless laughter. 'I could be living in a cardboard house now in some Ilocano *barrio* eating dog casserole. No dice!'

'I thought it was supposed to be a delicacy.'

'It's not *that* much of a delicacy.' His eyes were on the move once more, cooler, appraising. 'Though naturally I could be at home there at once, perfectly happy and at ease with the people. I am a simple man. I love the boondocks.'

'You should go into politics,' Cullen said, draining his coffee cup. The glance Orosa gave him set him back for a moment. He looked at his watch. The Beaumont table was in a huddle. The praying mantis tip-toed past Orosa's ear. 'Fort Santiago,' he said eventually. 'I like to imagine the Spanish galleons sailing from Fort Santiago in the sixteenth, seventeenth and eighteenth centuries. Carrying fine porcelain from Peking, silks from Shanghai and Benares, diamonds and damask from Golconda, pearls from the East Indies, spices from the Moluccas. Gold, silver and ivory from every corner of the Orient—all bound for Mexico.'

'Brilliant traders,' said Orosa seriously, nodding his head. 'Amazing merchants.'

'If the tough English seadogs didn't get them first.'

'Interestingly, an early victory for British propaganda. They captured only four galleons in two hundred years.'

'I know that Cavendish took the 610-ton *Santa Anna* with his tiny 120-tonner, *Desire*, and only eighteen guns. What a pirate!'

Orosa began tapping his fingers agitatedly on the table. Blood rushed to his neat square forehead. Maybe the Spanish side of him made him sensitive. *Makahija*! Cullen wished he'd kept this schoolboy historical material to himself, considering his expression now. But Orosa took a deep breath and grinned and offered one of his giant Tabacaleras. Blowing acrid smoke across the table he murmured, 'Friends must keep a weather eye open at all times for attempts to sour up the atmosphere. There is a lesson for us in this.'

'Not stressing the "negative realities", you mean?'

Orosa sighed and tilted his chair back. 'Camaraderie is paramount in our circles of similar attitudes. You are aware there is a constant fear of infiltration of subversives determined to create a revolutionary situation.' He shook his head wearily as if at the stupidity of such an attempt. Or perhaps at the naïvety of his companion. He drew on his cigar, inhaled, swept it from his mouth and threw back his head so his nostrils loomed once more. They were meshed with black hairs. Blue smoke suddenly poured from them.

'Not much chance of that, is there? The President has things pretty well sewn up.'

'Hmm. We always need the help of our friends.'

'Understandable.' Time to bow out. Politics really bored him, Cullen thought for the umpteenth time, excusing himself and stepping out into the enveloping humidity.

Orosa stayed behind and joined Beaumont's table. Beaumont's black Batmobile loitered at the curb in a no-parking zone. Its radio said, 'Eagle Eight, this is Eagle One, do you read me? Come in Eagle Eight!' The driver continued to read his comic, Beaumont being Eagle Six.

3

MOROSELY GIGI FERNANDEZ typed Cullen's field notes from the Asian circuit. Presently she was transcribing 'A Note on the Hair Whorls of the Murrah Buffalo'. She had just completed typing 'Some Observations on the Measurements of Female Buffalo Genitalia' and was not sorry. She disliked writing the words vulva, vagina, cervix, ovary, uterus and fallopian tube. She had never uttered one of these words and never would. The compilation of figures relating to these organs she considered eccentric and unnecessary. Science could get along without them. It was with some force and relief that her vermilion-tipped fingers had typed in capitals ENTIRE GENITALIA WEIGHT—577.81 grams on the last line. She would never be able to look at a *carabao* cow the same way again.

Gigi was a city girl, the daughter of a travel executive. She had been taught by the nuns of the Sacred Heart Convent and by religious academics at Our Lady of Fatima College where she obtained her MA in fine arts. In her *dégagé* fashion she had studied *Death of a Salesman*: Miller, Arthur (one-time husband of Marilyn Monroe!); *A la Recherche du Temps Perdu*: Proust, Marcel; and *Metamorphosis*: Kafka, Franz. The last author, a Czech with a slight resemblance to Peter Lorre, seemed to have some sort of preoccupation with the similarity between people and creatures and Gigi thought he might have something there. In flights of fancy she could imagine herself as a deer, a gazelle, something graceful of that nature. In *Horizons* she had read the amusing references to her boss as a 'buffaloing' footballer. Rather than struggling to see him as some movie star look-alike she enjoyed the image of him as a big and weathered buffalo, roan-coloured, thick in the neck and shoulders, strong and docile. Her personal office *carabao*.

Subconsciously, perhaps this was the reason she found the genitalia report so distasteful. Or, more likely, it may simply have been that her mind veered away from these clinical yet emotion-charged words. Gigi was in favour of romance. She liked the idea of sweethearts, glamour, fashionable parties and dancing at the Hilton's discotheque with rich boys. She was twenty-one and, though she scoffed at the chaperone system under which her cousins in Cebu still suffered, she was still, technically, a virgin. The most frightening thing she had heard in her life was a Cebuano curse uttered by her cousins' driver, Vicente. '*Bilat siyang yawa*!' he had shouted at an overtaking jeepney. '*Cunt of the devil.*' Vicente had wide facial pores and mysterious red eyes. Sometimes at night she re-heard the saying and shuddered.

Although she was momentarily huffy at him for her heavy workload, she thought of Mr Richard Cullen as a novelty and hence cute. Since lunchtime he had been fussing over her desk, anxious to finish the tour reports and collate them for inclusion in *The Poor Man's Tractor*. They had worked for two hours beyond finishing time. This was a rare happening. She was becoming tired and making typing errors.

He was hanging over her again, biting his lip, as she smote her way through the paper on hair whorls. 'Gigi, that's enough for today,' he said suddenly. 'Let me buy you a drink.' The abruptness of the invitation surprised her. His eyes were more tentative and inquiring than his voice, however. Rather worried and weary.

She agreed. His breathing was amusing, the sound it made in his lumpy nose.

Concise visions of Asp's comfort-room contretemps had his

heart pounding all the way down in the elevator. Neverthe-less he performed the necessary entrance and departure manoeuvres with a sort of fatalistic chivalry, standing aside for Gigi, pressing buttons, sweeping her in and out with a flair that surprised himself, given her proximity, terrifying svelte daintiness and light but exotic odour. In the bare foyer her heels rang like gunshots. His own pile-driver feet thud-ding on the marble seemed to be broadcasting intentions far more urgent than his. At the after-hours exit two loitering guards watched them approach, muttered to each other and smirked faintly over their machine guns. Despite the failing light one man wore sunglasses. He held the door open for them, saying emphatically, 'Goodnight, sir,' as they left.

A sunset was fading over the bay. The turbid air caused green and grey tinges in the sky; it was filled with electricity and the racket of engines. Aircraft landing lights flickered as troop transports thundered overhead. Motor vehicles hooted in the boulevard; pop music blared from car radios. Cullen could have suddenly laughed with highly charged emotion.

'Here we are, here we are,' he said, steering her into the Eden. Her back responded instinctively to his fingertip con-trol. A faint smile up at him started his adolescent nervous gabbling. Otherwise he could have eaten her there and then.

'*Mabuhay*!' He read from a large sign in the lobby. '*The Eden Hotel says Welcome to all Overseas Visitors! Coach leaves for Doctor Tony's Healing Residence Sun.-Fri. 9 a.m. and 2 p.m. Juan Placido's Faith Medical Centre Tues.-Sat. 8.30 a.m. and 1.30 p.m. Tonight in the Jungle Bar Fantastic Nick Diaz and The Emotionals. Mabuhay!*'

'Ssh!' she whispered, and lightly smacked his hand.

He hadn't been inside the Jungle Bar for months. Even in his present hectic state he saw that extensive redecorating had taken place: amazing layout changes and decor dramatiza-tion. A forest of potted palms had been introduced. Sharks' jaws, a wild boar's head and various extra antlers were fixed to the walls. Now there was a tank of live turtles, one of sinister striped sea snakes and another containing two lethargic iguanas. A mossy reptilian reek hung over this part of the bar, but as they walked across the room to sit down other layers of smells intermingled: a whiff of cooking fat and the mustiness of dead hair and claw. Taxidermized moulting pelts. Protruding from a wall was a tree full of civet cats, shrews and flying lemurs, all simulating life and potential action, and several dangling bats. A solitary stuffed pangolin stood on one end of the bar. As they passed, a blonde woman sitting at the bar was patting its imbricated horny scales and muttering into her drink.

As well as the old tables and chairs there were new fur-lined shadowy recesses. His heart beating, Cullen led her to a furry cave.

'It's a real jungle, huh?' Gigi remarked, stroking the seat behind her. 'Very clever idea.'

A grinning waiter came for their drink orders. 'You want to eat, sir, we got the works,' he said. 'Make you dangerous to be with.' He winked lasciviously. 'Real aphrodisiac food!' He pronounced it 'appro-deezac'. 'Turtle soup, iguana, King Arthur's pish lips, venison. Also exotic mermaid *lapu-lapu*, humble lobster, oyster, glass of real Guinness stout no charge.'

Gigi giggled behind her hand.

'Maybe *balut*, genuine two-hundred-year-old duck egg. Baby still inside, great delicacy.'

'No thanks.'

'All long-time performance libido menu. Also regular dishes—teriyaki, chicken and so on.'

'He is ignorant saying "pish lips",' she whispered. 'He means "fish lips".'

The waiter blinked. He was a short round-faced man with a tricky gold tooth. '*Biga*!' he murmured to himself. Taking their drink orders, he said to Cullen, 'You're the boss. Stick around anyway. Later we got a great new combo and Nick Diaz, the Roving Troubador.'

Momentarily the zoological sights took some of the attention Cullen would have focused on her. And he was compelled to peer nonchalantly around the room for familiar faces. He saw none. The animal heads looked down on several lounging foreign invalids: a young man with home-scissored hair and careless cheap clothing sat in a wheelchair sucking some yellow drink through a straw; a dark middle-aged woman, her neck thickened by goitre, flicked peanuts into her mouth.

In a furred alcove nearby a local businessman in a shining sepia suit ate sticks of teriyaki and drank beer. With dabbing restive movements he patted the hand of the girl opposite him drinking Coke. His appearance was sharply canine, like an anxious dog protecting a bone. The girl had a flat, passive face, accustomed to excesses, and dull knowing eyes casually covering the room. A trickle of brown juice ran down her boyfriend's chin. Wordlessly she wiped his face with a paper napkin. He looked nervously at his watch, grunted something, drained the last of his San Miguel and they left, followed by invalids' eyes.

A creature clattered against the side of its tank. Perhaps the iguanas scraping. From somewhere near there was a deep sigh, animal or human Cullen couldn't tell. They began drinking and conducting conversation. Gigi spoke brightly to him in a manner flattering and coquettish.

He fell into a state. Sipping beer he became calmer, mesmerized by her presence. He heard her say, 'I read that you are a football player—even, still these days. . . .' She giggled like a child. Once more he was thrilled by the moist fresh appearance of her lips and gums. The way she used her hands, her sensual innocent gestures, also delighted him. They fluttered from her drink to her face. She would touch a long coloured nail to her mouth in a practised pensive movement that fascinated him for the same reason he sensed it would irritate any woman who saw it. He knew Margaret would hate everything about her: her cutie-pie name, her subjective Eastern femininity and elegant young sexy looks, her personal way of addressing men, her potential for guile—all the attributes that made her a knockout, a match-winner.

' . . . a *buffaloing* football player.' Again she giggled. Boldly, she said, 'I can see why the buffalo part,' and she hunched her shoulders in childish imitation of him and made a comically grim expression with her mouth and eyes.

Amazingly he felt not mocked but again flattered. The old buffalo reference could have got under his skin but this peach made him feel ten feet tall, the prototype for attractive masculinity. She hung on his words. They talked about football, of all things. He mentioned the inroads Rugby was making worldwide. Look out soccer! Rugby was on the move in Fiji, Japan, Tonga, Argentina, Canada. Also the USA, if they could settle their domestic differences. The Soviet Union, likewise, seemed to be more than nibbling at the game.

Once he had had these sorts of animated chats with Margaret. She too had listened avidly. But these days any overt enthusiasm or animation on his part seemed to make her suspicious. She was at home with the stalemate, the Cold War, the Demilitarized Zone of the emotions. Further from simple happiness, but also less far to fall.

Across from him Gigi savoured her white rum and Coke at the tip of her tongue.

Kicking his microphone cord savagely, Nick Diaz, the Roving Troubador, stepped around the turtle tank muttering '*Puneta*!' and began singing 'Arrivederci Roma'. The Emotionals' piano-accordionist almost drowned him out. The cord snagged on jungle furnishings. Nick Diaz disappeared behind a leafy palm. As his pomaded head reappeared, crooning unhappily, Cullen, holding back laughter, raised his glass in salute.

Apart from the comedy of the singer's troubles the song had good-humoured connotations for him. The last time he'd heard it was in the Big Joy Club in Kyoto, sung by Howard Oates of the World Health Organization. It was the night before they had left for Peking, via Osaka. The whole UN agencies' team was dispersed around the city's night-spots. Ahead lay the great mystery of Chinese animal husbandry, agriculture and human health. Three weeks of decorous behaviour, banquets, cowsheds and acupuncture exhibitions. A hot ball of tempura, beer and *sake* sat high in his chest.

Again he was a giant Asian novelty. They were drinking Suntory whisky with their shoes off. Businesslike pretty hostesses topped up their glasses from individual bottles. Voices rose, there was waggish laughter, and Western male innuendo was soon initiated. The girls were coy but steely and kept the Suntory flowing, all the time their voices tinkling like ice in a glass. Apple-cheeked with drink, a Japanese businessman lurched among them, chummy and aggressive. 'You sin a son!' he demanded, and amiable gaunt Oates from North Carolina padded over to the pianist in his socks and launched into 'Arrivederci Roma' in a lilting tenor. When they finished applauding they saw the businessman was crying from alcohol and his own peculiar joy. Flushed spots glowed on each cheek. He kissed Oates on the ear, sobbing, 'Best son lon time,' scattered around his business cards and vanished into the Kyoto night. 'Old Howie's scored!' they teased, drank more whisky and stumbled, still laughing, up on to the street. And in Peking twelve hours later the standard tumultuous airport welcome—the massed drums and cymbals, the orchestrated shrilling children, the threshing red and gold and purple flags and banners—had been so fantastically unapt a greeting for twenty off-colour internationalists, so exactly wrong, that it had driven away their hangovers as it would evil capitalist spirits.

Nick Diaz finished the number, flicked the microphone cord from him with greater poise now, and bowed his head modestly. There was a smattering of applause. Cullen and Gigi clapped, Cullen ironically. The youth in the wheelchair thumped apathetically on his armrest. The blonde woman sitting by the pangolin called out, 'More, more,' and beat her hands together.

Cullen glanced at his watch. It was nine o'clock, neither early nor late. He was becoming more distracted as the evening progressed, he realized. He did not know which direction it would take, or which he really wanted it to take. But it would need some sort of decision shortly. He noticed his foot was tapping. Gigi was humming softly along with the music. Her expression had a passive but knowing beauty. He sipped his beer and mentioned things that might interest her: office trivia, gossipy anecdotes. Again she was a good listener. The Asp affair was still on his mind but he didn't introduce it. Among the palms and animal tanks the waiter rustled.

'Tell me Mr Hugh Galash's marriage situation,' she said suddenly. 'He is a funny man.'

Surprising how this wily interest inflicted some sharp emotional damage. Of course, with women 'amusing' was a euphemism for sexually attractive. In his youth he'd longed to be witty in female company like his father. Humour was as much an aphrodisiac as power, he believed, then and now. In those days, straining on his Don Athaldo Chest Expander before the bathroom mirror, he'd paid heed to the muscles theory too, only to realize, sadly, that broad shoulders came a long way back in the field. Only men persisted in the belief that physique was a turn-on—and what did they know? *Vide* bantam Galash, thin as string and the scourge of the tropics.

'Oh, Hugh's a bit of a rascal,' he said. 'His wife went back home a while ago and he's been burning the candle at both ends.' Why was his instinct all at once to present the least attractive picture possible of Galash? To knife him to shreds? Only office protocol prevented him from damning him with fainter praise. And notice how he had said his wife 'went back home' rather than 'left him', which might have given Galash a freer, more available image. These ridiculous semantics skimmed through his head while at the same time self-preservation cautioned him not to appear a sour knifing bastard. He could put himself in an unattractive position if he weren't careful. This was the fine line you walked as a jealous cuntstruck adolescent. *Stupid*! he thought, gripping his beer glass.

Meanwhile her eyes shone across the table. She was positioned delicately and erotically on a sleek furry backdrop. Still she hummed softly, like a child. Above her breasts hung a small cross.

'Actually,' he went on, grabbing at a straw of comfort, 'I'm surprised he's not here tonight with one of his girls.' Only the last vestige of honour stopped him from saying 'call-girls'.

Enigmatically she fiddled with her drink, arching a brow but showing no other reaction.

He imagined making love to her, and began to sweat at explicit carnal visions. 'And what's your situation, romantically?' he asked her, smiling like an uncle. The question cost him a little more composure. He was edging out on a limb here. Also generation and cultural gaps loomed. The correct jargon eluded him. Surprisingly, a coaster was tattered in his sausage fingers. Beyond her, to one side, the waiter fed something to the iguanas and then moved toward the sea snakes. At this distance, in the low light, their venom was secret. Their slow green and blue curves meandered serenely. A turtle snorted as he hung on her reply.

She blushed and smiled, showing that fine flesh thread which joined her gums and lip. The effect on him was agonizing. 'I date several boys, but I am not going steady at the moment.' She giggled self-consciously. 'I have many interests. I am footloose and fancy free.'

Going steady. He smiled at the American teenage charm of it all. He had never met anyone who went on 'dates'. He was in another world, an Oriental, high-school time warp of bobby-soxers and double malteds.

'One last drink,' he said, taking control of circumstances. The waiter was still feeding the reptiles, clicking his tongue at them, flipping fish heads into the turtle tank. Cullen got up and walked through the marine smells to the bar.

The woman sitting by the pangolin jerked her head up at him. 'You American?'

'Australian.'

'Never mind. What exactly *is* this sidekick of mine?' She patted the scaly back. 'Never seen one of these doohickeys before.' Grey roots grew out of her scalp; otherwise her hair was lemon. Shadows lay under her eyes. Her bare upper arms were thin but loose.

'A pangolin.'

'Some sort of ant-eater, huh? Reminds me of an armadillo I saw one time in New Mexico. Before I got divorced.'

He nodded vaguely. There was no sign of the barman,

though he could hear a low rapid conversation in Tagalog going on in the kitchen. He tapped a coin on the bar. The woman was eyeing him, rocky on her stool. He had the impression the staff were ignoring her, hiding in the kitchen to avoid serving her.

'What's *your* trouble?' she asked.

'Nothing at all. Some service would be fine.' He wished to be intimately alone with Gigi, and paradoxically for the evening to be over and to be safely home in bed with no demerits registered and a clear conscience.

'Excuse me.' She smiled oddly, slack-mouthed but brisk. 'Me, I got a pituitary tumour. I got cell deterioration. I got sight in my right eye only. Now you tell me something as a matter of academic interest. Do I go see Juan Placido up in the mountains and have him regress it, or do I go for conventional surgery back home where I can expect to lose my sense of taste and smell and possibly other abilities and be doped up forever with continuous medication?'

Oh, God! He shook his head sympathetically. 'That's a big problem.'

Again the loose smile. 'No kidding? I'm still a young woman. I was once a looker. Juan's a long shot. I realize that Juan is a long shot.' Her voice rose. 'I want you to appreciate that I am not a believer in magic. Do you appreciate that?'

His fingers drummed on the bar. 'Sure.' The barman still chattered in the kitchen. Someone was banging pots around carelessly. Back in their plush nook Gigi sat alone, creamy and wan. 'Tssst!' he hissed for the barman.

'You are not talking to a complete idiot.' She raised her empty glass to her mouth and shrugged. 'But who am I to question paranormal processes?' Now she winked sadly and confidingly. 'Don't worry, I've got a scrapbook this thick on faith healing. There's this West German homoeopath, Mrs Sigrun Puthaff, Buthoff, something like that, who has personally observed more than two thousand psychic surgeries, including one in which Juan relieved her own serious heart condition. This lady—this *professional* person—swears by him.' Again she raised her empty glass and frowned. 'No one opens up my body in any old way—knife, magic fingertips, magnetic passes, whatever, without them having my fullest trust. Do I make myself understood?'

'Perfectly.' He could not tell which eye was the blind one.

'No one passes a pig membrane off on Maureen Decker.'

'Right.'

'So tomorrow there I go, large as life, up to the mountains where Juan will somehow penetrate the bone structure of my head with those mystical fingers to get at my pituitary.'

'God!' he exclaimed. Eating a hard-boiled egg, the barman peeped around the corner of the kitchen. As Cullen signalled him for drinks the woman began weeping.

'The lady should go to bed,' the barman said, and giggled, flecking his shirt with egg white.

When Cullen was able to return with the drinks he was surprised and not delighted to see Gigi now accompanied by Galash and Z.M. Both men were velvety with alcohol and self-assurance. Their hormones gave off an unlimited potential for debauched mysteries. This chemical charm seemed to have distracted Gigi. She was blushing and fidgety. He did not acknowledge Galash's broad wink.

'Mind if we join you, Dick?' Z.M. asked.

'Working back late, huh?' Naturally Galash couldn't resist this. His eyes glinted with mischief.

Z.M. smiled faintly.

The woman by the pangolin began an argument with the barman.

Cullen crunched peanuts. 'We have been.' He was polite and proper. Conversationally, he pointed out that the noisy woman had a pituitary tumour. Perhaps he was crazily optimistic that Galash would instantly rush this novelty. Galash gave her the briefest glance and hissed for the waiter, who came instantly, referred to Galash by name and was very servile. Beers materialized annoyingly swiftly. Galash and Z.M. drank, stretched out their legs and relaxed. They twinkled, thought Cullen, like bloody stars.

'Quite a little den of iniquity, this place,' Galash remarked happily.

'It reminds me of a bar in Kowloon frequented by corrupt policemen,' Z.M. said. 'Except for the absence of bare-breasted waitresses. Amazing ladies. Fine examples of the silicon surgeon's artistry.'

Galash shook his head thoughtfully. 'I don't go for it in Asian girls. It's false, man; a denial of their unique charms.'

Gigi appeared nonplussed. Her demeanour reverted to that of the office. To Cullen she became immediately crisp and controlled. Primly she sipped her drink. She shied from the conversation, assuming a stenographer's fealty. Gone was the sportive languor in the eyes, the teasing moist curve of the lips. Sitting up rigidly, she adjusted her neckline and brushed motes from her dress.

He sensed it coming.

'It is ten-thirty. Late for me,' she announced. 'My parents worry unless they know my date.'

He could have smacked Galash's glib cheeks for him, Z.M.'s into the bargain.

Galash winked again. 'Good night, kids.'

'Oh, I drive my own car,' she said, with the clarity of a pronouncement. At this the air was full of amusement. Cullen stood up, pushing with his neck and shoulders against the weight of disappointment and self-loathing.

'I'll see you to the car park,' he said. Erotic events would occur without him, as they always did. Once again a patina of sensual anticipation and certain enjoyment shone on everyone but him. The familiar stupidity of his size, the unbalanced nature of his position, struck him deeply. Out of kilter once more. He mourned his lack of tropical guile, his missing manipulative ability. What had gone wrong with his genetic inheritance, he'd wondered more than once before, that he'd missed out on George and Dottie's cleverness?

He walked her from the Jungle Bar, through the provocative shrubbery and aromas of spiced foodstuffs and rank animals. In the doorway they passed the sepia-suited businessman and his girlfriend, returning from upstairs. The man's face was smug enough to hit; the girl's as expressionless as before. Gigi sniffed snobbishly. Her skittishness was gone but her luxuriousness almost choked him, now that it was fast escaping. Her cooling manner was in inverse proportion to his growing lust, but naturally his perverse character prevented him from touching her, from encircling her with a thick persuasive arm. The car park was a microsecond away and blindingly lit. Of course her yellow Toyota and his car were only yards apart, and unmasked by shadows. José was awake and watching, ostensibly reading a magazine. Polyestered young men loitered nearby, anyway—pimping, selling black market cigarettes, promoting sexual exhibitions, planning larcenies. Their transistors blared pop music. She actually spent their ebbing moments humming along.

Cullen slanted sadly above her, inhaling her suddenly unique scent. Bravely he gripped her arm. 'Goodnight,' he breathed over her.

'Thank you very much for the drink,' she said, patting his hand almost patronizingly. She giggled. 'Isn't Mr Hugh Galash bad?'

Moping home in the car he wondered obscurely whether it had counted as a date.

4

MARGARET, STRAIGHT-BACKED, flicked through *Time*. She could make newspapers crackle like sound-effects thunder, magazines explode like fireworks. Her glance was intense but enigmatic as he loomed through the door sighing with fatigue and tension, a peppermint only recently dissolved under his tongue. His shoes reverberated on the parquetry. Why were they so noisy tonight, his guilty feet?

'Whew!' He wrenched off his tie. 'I had a lot to catch up on.'

A salvo of pages sounded from her lap. Her expression, headachy and studious, did not waver as he came up to her, passed her with a tight smile and retreated to the kitchen. There, perched on the table, he munched leftover pork as dry as string and swilled a glass of calamansi juice so cold and sweet it made him gag. Bile and meat fibres rose in his gullet. He felt acidic through and through: stomach, brain, heart, all sour and gaseous. Paul Newman smiled arctically from above the stove. Against Cullen's wishes an eyelid began to twitch. Patches of prickly heat danced over his back and chest. Scratching, breathing hard, simultaneously crunching pork crackling, gristle, fat, with a savage determination, he fought back his gorge and itches, seeking a posture of nonchalant ordinariness.

The advertisement for the soft-drink competition was gone from the wall. He pulled up a chair and sat down, reaching

172

aimlessly for a paperback lying on the table. *Sensible Fasting*. He flipped through it. Here was her Professor Flehret condemning protein grossness, welcoming instead the daily enema, abrasive bran and sauerkraut. And confidently drawing on such mucus-free sources as Immanuel Kant, Jean Jacques Rousseau and J. C. F. von Schiller—who also liked to dip his feet in cold water while thinking. It turned out that Pythagoras was a faster, also the clear-spittled Nietzsche and other greats.

But he and the professor weren't entirely at loggerheads. As it happened, Flehret was a ruminant fancier. 'Man is the sickest animal on earth,' he had written, 'in that no other animal has violated the laws of eating as much as man. Oh, if he could learn the eating habits of the humble grass eater.' While the fast was all-important for the mucus-free life, tyros should not at first go beyond two or three days. The professor himself often fasted for months at a time, he alleged, before finally breaking it with a meal of cherries, grapes and stewed prunes. Cullen laughed despite himself. Riveting reading. 'While sojourning in Italy many years ago,' wrote the professor, 'I drank about two quarts of fresh grape juice after such a fast and immediately experienced a vast intestinal explosion. Almost directly I had a feeling of such unusual vitality that I easily performed my knee bending and arm stretching exercises 326 times.' He called this procedure 'Nature's operating table'.

Grinning anxiously he sauntered over to Margaret clutching the book and a bottle of San Miguel. An affable strain in his voice, he said, 'How about Flehret's fitness scheme?' and began to recite, '" While sojourning in Italy . . ."'

She rose stiffly from her chair in an arrangement of sharp angles and physical hollows. Her weight loss surprised him, its extent and the awkwardness rather than vulnerability it gave her. She had no make-up on, and a shift patterned in bright ethnic embroidery emphasized her pallor. The formerly gold lights in her hair seemed as lemony as those of the sick woman in the bar.

'I'm not interested,' she said, and left the room.

So he drank the beer alone in the kitchen, and another bottle, and around midnight, noticing their lights blazing, sallied from the house—clutching a bottle of Courvoisier like a club—into the Orosas' domain.

At the door Orosa was surprised to see him. Dancing an indecisive semi-circle on the doorstep, he said, 'Why, hello again! Twice in one day I have the honour.' They milled on the threshold for moments until Orosa could summon his usual familiarity. 'Dick, come in. A nightcap on your mind? Sure.' However, his skittish feet, pattering in black leather moccasins as tiny as a child's, made Cullen suddenly diffident.

'Sorry to bother you,' he mumbled. 'It's late, I realize.'

'No, no.' Black hornrims were removed and pocketed fussily. He waved away the cognac offering. 'Oho! What sort of host do you think I am? When you're in my home you drink my liquor.'

Cullen followed him across the cool polished vestibule. Again his shoes rang uncomfortably. He was at risk of slipping on slick surfaces. He gripped his bottle foolishly, swung it nonchalantly like a racquet, but still felt a deranged intruder. The logistics seemed vaguely changed since his last visit. He would have veered left instead of right to find the den, but Orosa steered him down a smooth passage, past closed doors and open, over-furnished rooms, in one of which, Bong Bong, in red pyjamas and headphones, gyrated plumply to secret music. They arrived in the den. But perhaps it wasn't the same room. The bar and Olde English decor appeared the same, but this room had a pool table and appurtenances, dart board, backgammon table and a chess table with big fancy crystal pieces.

Orosa fussed abstractedly at the bar. He produced cognacs in warmed glasses. As the brandy fumes rose in Cullen's nose Hazel materialized in a silken house-gown and Chinese slippers. She took a cognac and drew a chair up beside him, saying cheerily, 'Out on the tiles, eh? You boys give yourselves a belt.'

'Just socializing. Sorry to intrude so late.' She had the ability, he realized dimly, to make him feel boyish and gauche. The older woman, the bawdy aunt. Her hair had subsided and, losing its lacquered stature, made her seem more defenceless. She was out of uniform. Less tightly dressed, her body relaxed; it no longer oozed over constrictions. She was showing an expanse of pulpy white chest, faintly scored with paler striae in the cleavage. Tugging at the edges of her kimono, she had an older-womanish way of simultaneously concealing and drawing attention to her secrets.

'Always glad to see an old mate,' she said, patting his hand.

Imperceptibly Orosa excused himself and left the room, closing the door.

Cullen got to his feet, a little unsteadily. 'The changing of the guard,' he remarked. 'Look, Hazel, I won't keep you.' His body hung heavy and stale above her chair. Already the night seemed days long but he did not want it to end.

'Nonsense. Sit down. A bit of domestic trouble?'

A gossip-conscious glint in her eye? He considered this warily. But in his low mood he quickly succumbed to sentimental gratitude. This woman was a sport, a concomitant, he thought tenderly. 'The old, old story,' he said, gulping brandy. He was dizzily comforted, he was surprised to discover, by her attention. The receptive over-scented flesh began to suggest powdered pleasures.

'Talk about it, love, if you like,' she suggested, jouncing her chest.

He recognized this old ploy but even the devious drag of her lips on her glass rim couldn't dull his appreciation. He imagined a touch of gallantry in his maudlin smile. 'What to say?' he shrugged. He rolled up his sleeves, ran a hand through his hair. Like dwarfs, Johnnie Walker figurines marched in order of descending size along the bar, reproducing themselves in the mirror. Hazel poured them another cognac. Fumes shot into his head. Beyond, the den doors opened and closed and there was a low discussion between two or three male voices.

Over these murmurs Hazel said, 'I live from day to day myself, darl. Who doesn't?'

A tentative forefinger prod would be interesting, right in the soft chest mass. Merely a childlike exploration.

'Asian men!' she exclaimed. 'After four or five years I'd had a gutful of wearing flatties.'

Suddenly sharp, he caught her looking at his crotch.

A door closed and then Orosa entered the den, smoking one of his Tabacaleras. 'Busy, busy,' he announced, blowing smoke. He sighed and grinned tensely, showing his grey gums. 'There's no more I can do,' he muttered.

Behind Orosa's line of vision Hazel winked. Stealthily Cullen increased the air space between their bodies. 'Did you get a scoop?' he asked.

The columnist's face was ageless and taut with pride, though he waved a nugatory hand; as smug and close-lipped as a politician's.

'Congratulations.' Cullen raised his brandy glass. 'Has the President decided on World War III?'

A perfunctory giggle. Though showing strain, this little bantam was preening in front of his Guinness mirror while pouring himself a cognac. 'Of course there are embargoes in this tough old profession of mine. The protection of valued contacts is paramount.' The twin ranks of Johnnie Walkers strode blithely onward.

'Professional ethics,' Cullen pronounced. 'Ha!' He drank some more.

Orosa said, 'Naturally. The weighing up of the greater good.' The mouthpiece seemed asquirm with *sub rosa* delights. The pleasures of the grapevine, of sources and go-betweens, had him a little distracted. But he gave Cullen a steady glance for a moment and said, 'Naturally it is easy to satirize us Third World buffoons, nothing simpler. All corrupt vulgar animals and so on. Swiss banks. Hollywood starlets.'

Huffy, Cullen reeled. 'I won't embarrass you by talking on the subject further.'

'No, no. I must unwind. I'm a hyperkinetic guy. Jordan Loeb of *Time* once told me that.' He savoured the word. '*Hyperkinetic*. He did great work on Watergate, Jordan. We did the town one night in LA.'

Softly, Hazel said, 'Christ!' and adjusted her gown. The antipathetic lowering of her eyelids revealed them as tired and crêpey.

'What's the story then?' Cullen asked drunkenly.

Shaking his head, Orosa began pacing the room, swigging brandy, pausing to flick dust off the baize of the pool table, suddenly swishing a cue like a sword, and all Cullen heard were snatches of words—'national security' and 'developing nation' and 'historical circumstances'. Striding around in his glossy little slippers Orosa said something like 'the democratic luxury' and 'countering agitprop'—all these phrases swimming round in Cullen's head like paramecia, and each of these particular protozoans had its own complex parasitic life system and capacity for harm to man and beast.

Bold with drink, he said airily, 'Words, words.'

Hazel sighed, but did not join in.

'You understand my position,' Orosa said. Suddenly he adjusted and tightened his body into a stiff self-righteous posture. 'Jesus and the Holy Mother guide my instincts in the right direction,' he said loudly. It was not clear whether this was a prayer or a statement of fact.

Standing to leave Cullen noticed, for some reason, that Orosa's front garden, normally drenched in light, was dark. 'Must go,' he muttered.

'Of course,' Orosa said, inspecting his watch. 'It's after curfew.'

'It's only next door,' Cullen said stupidly.

'Yes.'

Showing him out, as her husband walked ahead, Hazel goosed him.

A car engine started up as he reached his gate. An abrupt instinct anticipated a Batmobile. Half-turning, he saw instead a white Mercedes edge slowly past. From the front seat a strong light beam played on him for a moment. No words were exchanged.

5

Z.M. DID NOT ARRIVE at work next morning. It took several hours for the gossip that he had been expelled from the country to be substantiated. The expulsion was unique, his being in one sense a member of all countries—or one hundred and thirty-two, anyway—and in another of none. The government made no announcement. The President made no immediate political capital of the incident. The Organization kept silent, too, while reporting it to the Economic and Social Council, which referred it as a matter of course to the Secretariat. While New York cogitated on the expulsion Batmobiles came and went all day, their radios crackling with exasperation, engines humming overtly in parking spaces normally reserved for heads of Operations, Administration and Internal Auditing.

Jogging earlier that morning Cullen had had an inkling of something of the sort. Heaving himself around the estate, his head palpitating with pain, he saw imaginary official silhouettes on the bright shrubbery. He thought of Orosa and the Mercedes at the gate as his rubber soles slapped heavily, dead on the ear. Sibilant dawn birds and insects sizzled above his thud and thump. Their reconnaissance opened other avenues of tropical inquiry further on. Oozy sweet plants seemed to cringe from him, like Orosa's bashful mimosa, or droop deliberately on his face and shoulders, leaving their sticky residue or an ant or two.

But he and Galash, bandying about their vague suspicions in Cullen's office some hours later, could not come up with anything. Except Orosa, and Cullen kept this blurry theory to himself.

Galash said, 'They've locked his office under orders of the Regional General Counsel.'

'After they've gone over it with a fine-tooth comb, I bet.'

'Do you really think Z.M. was some sort of spy?'

'Scapegoat more likely. A sacrificial lamb to keep foreign critics in line.'

'What critics? Amnesty International? The occasional blow-in from the *Guardian* or the *Washington Post*? Jesus, why bother? I reckon it's the Muslim thing. They thought he was mixed up with the MNLF.'

'Maybe his own people wanted him back. There seemed to be no love lost there.' Cullen saw the sly eyes of the Minister over the brown fish and 7-Up.

'Who knows? They're ripe for a coup, I'd say. Maybe he'll go back as a heavy. Christ, who would have guessed this last night? Z.M. was in great form. After we saw you we met a couple of socialites at the Hilton and had a grand time. He was full of Polo Club scuttlebutt. Funny, with those women he always lays on the Oxford bit, the tweedy accent. Francie Osmena, the judge's wife, calls him James Mason.'

'You live dangerously, don't you? No wonder he's gone down the mine. God, judges' wives! Can't you stick to pineapple millionairesses? These establishment guys have got private *armies*.'

'The President knocked them off. This is a peaceful, controlled environment, Dick.'

'Well, hit men, anyway. Jesus, any cab driver would do it for fifty bucks.'

'You've been watching too many Kung Fu movies. Don't worry, in this Byzantine joint sex is the least complex problem. No, if he's been deported it's for politics, not sex. As if you can talk, anyway. How did you go last night? I thought Miss Fernandez looked particularly winsome despite the low-rent scene you chose for your concubinage.'

Cullen was too overtaxed to react to this flippancy. The teasing, whether malicious or cheery, got his heart beating guiltily, however. Perhaps that was Galash's intention. They all seemed to read him like an open book, whereas the reverse was never true. He never guessed their secrets. Even the patently obvious Ted Orosa had him conned. His hangover throbbed with the irony of things: the harmless Gigi episode and the continuing lone misery of his night-time bunk.

'Don't be silly,' he said eventually.

'Remember the tragic Asp.' Galash wagged an admonitory finger. 'How would Margaret take it? Badly, I'd say.'

The unanswerable staggering injustice had him speechless. Suddenly it was all turned back on *him*—Margaret's polar silences, the Asian ethical malaise, the whole state of contemporary morality. The story of his misunderstood and patronized life. Years of unfair treatment welled up in him. Breath came thick through his nose. He pushed himself up behind his desk, feeling his size, his pounding head, the blood-rush to the shoulders and arms. He leaned on his clenched fists, balanced threateningly on the brink. He fought for words. 'Up yours, Yank!' was all he could shout. The bellow hung over the office. He suspected he had saliva on his chin.

Immediately he felt grossly stupid.

'Never lose your cool,' Galash advised, leaving the room.

He felt silly—hickish and whispered about—when he emerged into the outer secretarial office. The girls looked up as his door opened. Gigi was perched on the edge of another secretary's desk, confidingly close in his opinion, also tellingly pink-cheeked. He was about to speak, however, to mutter any fraternal trivia, when the telephone rang. Gigi answered it, stretching breezily from the desk top.

'The front desk says there is a lady on her way up to see you,' she announced pertly. 'Chinese or something.' Naturally a plucked eyebrow was raised.

A lady? 'Please show her in when she arrives.'

As he closed his door there was the impression of stifled giggling.

The woman was Jenny Loh, Z.M.'s rarely glimpsed girl-friend. 'May I have a word with you?' she asked. A nice-looking girl, young, with the voice of an English education, waist-length glowing hair, stylish clothes.

He thought of it, oddly, as a way of getting even. He looked at his watch. Twelve-thirty. 'Certainly,' he said, regaining a little poise. 'How about lunch?' He had come to this: banal office game-playing, trite vengeance.

Beneath a mako's serrated teeth Miss Loh nibbled sticks of teriyaki and told of the night's happenings. Four soldiers with M16 automatic rifles had been waiting at the condominium when Z.M. returned home at about 2 a.m. She had spotted two plainclothesmen watching the apartment for several hours beforehand. When Z.M. arrived, these two, Special Branch heavyweights, had leaped in behind him waving some sort of warrant covered in official signatures and had begun rifling through his work desk and bookshelves.

'Zulfikar kept his temper. He was amazingly placid for him, quite amused, really.' She too was surprisingly unruffled, nimbly finishing her lunch, napkinning her lips and fingers, rotating a swizzle stick in her gin and tonic. 'Poor Zulfikar.'

Zulfikar? This did make him sound like a Middle Eastern cloak-and-dagger man. Cullen wondered, 'But why did it happen? What did they say? Where has he gone?' Asian mysteries crowded in again.

She shrugged. 'I hope for his sake, New York. He's not popular at home. His ways annoy them, I suppose.' She giggled lightly. 'He was expecting me to chastise him for his bad bachelor behaviour, but soldiers and security men waiting up for him too—this he didn't expect.'

'I bet.'

'Back again, huh? Sir is a real regular customer.' The brash waiter of the previous night wheeled past with a tray of beers. He eyed Miss Loh, then gave Cullen a wink.

'They took stacks of books, files, letters—also some reports he was working on for you. He said to tell you. Specifically

181

something on Mindanao, I believe. There was great excitement at the map, also at some graphs and tables. They were very pleased with themselves.'

'The classic cop confiscation. Subversive *buxtonella sulcata* cysts in Mindanaoan buffalo guts.'

'Zulfikar wondered if you would see the wry side of it. He said, "This is going to get Dick's goat." ' Again she twirled her swizzle stick.

'It has. That stuff is important.' He swallowed some beer. His temples were pounding once more. A whole section of *The Poor Man's Tractor* down the drain. A sharp acidic pain zig-zagged along his own alimentary tract as Miss Loh regarded him with dainty amusement. He drew a steadying breath and looked around the bar. There were fewer foreign invalids today; either they were late risers or the current consignment had taken the morning coaches up to the faith healers. The pangolin stood alone on the bar. Dull light fell on its scales and fake eyes; the earth-tunnelling claws were varnished black. By day the assorted animal heads and skins gave the room more the atmosphere of a run-down museum than any jungle. Dust motes floated in thin sun streams. Some lobsters clashed softly in their tank, a turtle moved sluggishly, but the other creatures could have been living or dead.

'Isn't this a wonderfully kitsch pub?' said Miss Loh in her pukka accent. 'I love sordid dives.'

'Did Z.M. take you to plenty?' She was beginning to get his goat, too. Sometimes he yearned after one of these casual unemotional girls—young, international, good looking, able to stroll away from disaster. Paradoxically, he associated such tranquillity with extreme passion, whereas the excitable ones quickly went to pieces and consumed themselves, leaving nothing for you but scraps of cooling shell. But this modern sang-froid was disconcerting in a platonic sense. Lessening your self-image somehow. Jenny Loh's imperturbability about Z.M.'s fate in a curious way reflected on *him*. He felt like saying, '*Don't be so lackadaisical about us men, girlie.*' Mentally, he cracked his knuckles.

Over her gin glass she glanced at him calmly. 'Don't you

pry? Actually, we saw the occasional exhibition. They're quite popular here as I'm sure you would know. Some tourists expect it—the hushed arrangements, the conspiracy with the cab driver, all sitting around sniggering in some sleazy motel room while a couple of Asians have it off.'

Mildly shocked, he sipped his drink then said breezily, 'Vice is not what it used to be.'

'Really?' There was a prim superiority in her expression and gestures. 'Are you an authority?'

In lieu of conversation they both looked about them. The Jungle Bar was filling with lunchers. Cullen recognized a few harmless lower echelon Organization faces. The noise level rose, and the fur-covered booths were quickly occupied by men and girls. As he peered around the room, Cullen felt the infringement of others' stares. Abruptly a solid European man, middle-aged, in a sports shirt, shorts and long socks, detached himself from a table of men at the far side of the bar and with a strange inevitability threaded his way through the tables to them, grinning broadly.

'Pardon me,' the stranger said loudly, presenting his hand. 'Dick Cullen? Gordon Ingersole from Sydney. Small world. Many's the time I saw you on the old Cricket Ground.' Now, turning from Cullen's lame smile, he addressed himself to Jenny Loh while transferring this fatherly right hand to Cullen's shoulder. 'One of the best second-rowers in the business, this feller,' he told her jovially. 'A real work-horse, always had great control of the scrum. No kidding, I've seen this bloke pack down with his face only eight inches from the ground.' He laughed, revealing chummy short teeth. 'Of course, none of us is getting any younger.'

'Is that so?' Obviously she regarded this person as deranged. For a moment she almost appeared disconcerted.

Cullen muttered, 'Pleased to meet you.' Oddly he found himself blushing.

Ingersole still stood by their table, beaming. He seemed to be waiting to be asked to sit down. 'What do you think of this place, eh? Not a bad country. A few of us are doing the town, mixing business with pleasure.' He laughed again and nudged

Cullen with his elbow. 'Tax deductible,' he said merrily.

On Cullen's shoulder his hand began a series of vigorous pats which, fading in intensity, indicated that if, as seemed disappointingly likely, they were not to become a threesome, he might soon be on his way. 'Well,' he said eventually, 'you'd do us an honour, Dick, if you and the young lady would join our table.' He waved airily across the room. 'I know you'd enjoy it.'

As Cullen begged off Ingersole's smile was brave and proud.

'Pleasure to meet you anyway. Very sorry to take up your time. All the very best.' He shook hands once more, formally, nodded to Jenny Loh and left them. In his retiring back there was a hint of umbrage, though his chunky pink legs had the spring of good fellowship and healthy self-regard as they passed through the crowd.

'So you're an Australian?' From behind her glass she asked this question almost accusingly, as if he'd been hiding some contagion from her.

'Yes, why not?' Why was his laugh self-conscious?

'I should have guessed. They're everywhere these days. Unusual people.' She smiled. Her little teeth were as clever and white as cultured pearls. 'Did you know there is a colony of Australians in Rome who play cricket in the Janiculum Hills?'

'Oh, have you seen them?'

She raised an eyebrow. 'No, I don't think it was the season.'

He said, 'I haven't heard of them.' It annoyed him that he felt like apologizing. 'Where are *you* from, as a matter of interest?'

'Hong Kong, naturally,' she said, with surprise in her eyes. 'In my generation, anyway.' A mainland dynasty going back thousands of years should be presumed.

Cullen was vaguely surprised at his lack of resolve with this girl. He was uncharacteristically prepared to sit there apathetically tearing drink coasters into strips while she exerted any subtle forms of gamesmanship she wanted. Surreptitiously eyeing his watch he was allowing their meeting to fizzle out into increasingly wider silences. So it was with a slight jolt that he saw the ebullient waiter arriving with more drinks for them. 'What's this?' he asked, but knew even before he looked across the room he would meet Ingersole's smug glance and convivial upraised glass.

'From the gentlemen over there—those friends of yours,' said the waiter. All four men at Ingersole's table were now either raising their beer glasses or saluting him with easy-mannered waves of the hand. Over the alien hubbub their matey cries rang out.

'How peculiar,' said Jenny Loh.

Patronized on all sides, Cullen nevertheless toasted the men back and ordered the waiter to take them a return round. The unforgivable sin of his nationality: unsociability. 'It's very pleasant of them, really,' he mumbled. He'd defend them against this condescending girl, but their gesture and his response filled him with a strange despair. It was as if he were now inextricably linked to these countrymen of his, across seas, in different climatic zones, forever. He could never get away—and immediately this impression astonished him. On what date had he ceased being the most clubbable of men, a true sportsman for God's sake, pally to all and sundry? How and when had this changed? Forget about Z.M. Ali—when had Dick Cullen become a stateless person?

He was considering this, the current picture of himself as a big sweating anchorite, gingerly pouring tonic water into Jenny Loh's gin, leaning morosely towards her delicate body, when, turning at some terrible telepathic signal, he saw his wife, a hand to her white face, staring at them from the bar.

6

SHE HAD HEARD HIM GET UP, walk from the study into the
bathroom, go to the lavatory. She had heard the cistern flush
and the erratic plumbing knock in laboured stages all along
the length and depth of the house as usual, and the bathroom
tap flowing briefly. He had coughed twice. There was a dull
fumbling while he changed into his jogging gear. Then she
heard his rubber soles pad past the bedroom, and his weight
on the stairs, and the stealthy opening and closing of the front
door. She had anticipated all these sounds, and when the last
one—the front gate clattering shut—occurred, she released a
deep breath and fell asleep at last. But seemingly only seconds
later, the gate creaked again, waking her, and she knew he
was back below her puffing in the garden.

Her head seemed to balloon with fatigue as she sat up. Her
stomach, also as anticipated, began throbbing as she got to
her feet. Steadying herself on the edge of the dressing-table,
avoiding her dank white image in the mirror, she peeked out
through the bamboo blinds. He was doing pushups on the
moist grass. His neck and face were red. His hair was stuck
down with sweat in the front, though at the pink crown,
where it was thinning, ginger strands were still awry from
sleep. Veins bulged at his neck. Dispassionately, she said to
herself, *His thighs are like hams.* Several times she repeated
this phrase in her head before discarding it. Now he got
wearily to his feet, almost shakily, and peered down vacantly

at the garden bed as if he were about to be sick. The right knee had a zig-zagging pale slash from an old cartilage operation. He did not vomit, however. Panting, he stood upright and began touching his toes, up and down, again and again. His Wanderers T-shirt was grey with sweat. Spray flew from his forehead. The glazed look was in his eyes each time his head flew up. His disoriented face had only an acquaintance's familiarity as he flung it up to her.

Looking down at him from behind the blinds she managed a rare objectivity, as if viewing the antics of some relative from the vague past—an older brother or cousin. Of their own accord her hands were smoothing her night-dress down over her nagging stomach, rubbing over the curved swelling, as she stared down at the performance in the garden. It was when he shuffled up to the palm tree, packed down against it with his shoulder and began pushing, that his grunting, faint, peculiarly personal exhalations, sent her detachment flying, aroused suddenly a confused emotion so bound up in mingled memories of him making love to her, of him once or twice lying in pain on the football field, of the sounds of his sleep, of that occasional semi-comic vulnerability, that a spasm rooted in her abdomen flashed through her chest and thighs, branched out into the limbs and forced her back to bed.

When she heard José reverse the car into the street, then the gate clang shut, she rose. She showered, dressed and packed a small bag. She put another dress in the bag and a change of underwear. Downstairs she drank a glass of calamansi juice and a cup of coffee. In front of the girls she was poised, pleasant, reserved. Absorbed in the newspaper, frowning over the headlines, she absently rubbed a hand over her stomach.

Today's top news items concerned the arrival of the Miss Universe contestants for the quest at the new Cultural Centre and the war with the Muslims in the south. Hostilities had resumed, it seemed, though the Defence Undersecretary 'scotched reports' that this was so. The government would continue to honour the ceasefire agreement with the MNLF, he insisted in an indirect quotation, but only if the isolated guerilla bands—which might or might not be members of the MNLF—ceased their ambuscades and harassments. Meanwhile, in Tripoli, the First Lady was in lengthy conversation with high Libyan officials. Correspondents travelling with her were optimistic that she and President Gaddafi would be able to negotiate a peaceful settlement in the south: talks so far had been frank and fruitful.

Coincidentally, the First Lady also figured indirectly in the other central news story. She had been responsible for the construction of the multi-million dollar Cultural Centre on landfill in the bay. She herself was a former beauty queen—initially coming second until the judges reversed their decision overnight. The Cultural Centre had a museum consisting exclusively of gowns she had worn on state occasions.

Margaret turned to 'As I See It'. Inevitably, in every paragraph of his column, in each snappy, convoluted phrase, she saw Orosa himself. She imagined his busy little hands smiting the typewriter; the wrinkled brow of concentration; the self-congratulatory smirk at the punch line. The column this morning lamented the fact that police had not seen fit to charge or identify a youth who had shot a man dead in an argument during a girls' volleyball game a week before. Orosa, identifying him only as 'the son of a top army colonel', called for 'plenty of action on this tragic matter to avoid scandals in high places and ugly tastes in the mouth'.

Ted the crusader, Margaret thought wryly. These political and social realities jolted her lately. She was as weary of her own cynicism at them as of the broader corruption of life. There was never peace, never order, never a sense of bliss and tranquillity. *All that we know is sorrow and conflict*, she thought, breathing deeply to steady herself. As usual she could find relevance in Rajamurti, however. He always came through. It was Rajamurti who said, *We are a battlefield from the moment we are born until the moment we die.*

She took her coffee into the living room and, reclining on a padded rattan chair with a collection of Rajamurti's talks and dialogues, tried to accomplish a state approximating philosophical serenity. Especially today she wanted to be free of the so-called petty sorrows, like loneliness and the fear of death and of not being a particularly creative person. She agreed with Rajamurti that self-knowledge was behind everything, but definitely not self-knowledge as interpreted by Jung or Freud, that crowd. The psychologists and analysts ('infantile', Rajamurti called them) were no better, because if you learned according to their lights you learned what *they* were, sure enough, but not about yourself (certainly nothing palatable, anyway). Rajamurti said, *To learn about oneself there must be no moment of accumulation from which one learns; no previous conclusions about oneself. Oneself is a constant movement of yesterday through to today and tomorrow, a single movement, endless.*

Richard could not see that when you listened to thunder, say, if you listened and if there was space between the listener and the thing listened to, you didn't hear the thunder. But if you listened without any idea, directly, then you were the thunder, because there was no space between you and that. 'Bullshit!' he'd snorted. 'Oriental rubbish.' He talked about oneself as a product of genes and environment. That was the only level on which he understood life. The breeding and nutrition angle.

This browsing engaged Margaret for an hour. Then she went up to the study and wrote her chatty affectionate weekly letters to Mark and Louise. She didn't weep as she sometimes did when writing to them. While she worked at the desk Concepción entered the room to make up Richard's bunk, not looking at her and humming in a subdued and polite manner in place of conversation. The smell of his existence surrounded them. They were both aware of it and self-consciously kept their heads down. Three of his smudgy footprints, imprinted in prickly-heat powder, were on the parquetry. Concepción rubbed them away, these impressions, with her mop.

José had returned and was flicking a chamois half-heartedly over the car. Margaret had him drive her to the post office where she posted the letters, and to the bank where she withdrew five thousand pesos from the joint account. Then, with a calmness that pleasantly surprised her, she instructed José to drive into the city. The traffic flowed eccentrically as usual, though it was lighter, and they made good time. A warm breeze swept away the vehicle fumes. She kept her window down and instead of chemicals smelled people, food and the ripe organic combustion of the farmlets and weedy verges. The car's radio aerial sizzled in the breeze. On the radio the US Air Force station played country and western requests. An announcer said, 'Hi there, from the home of the jungle air force, the Fighting Thirteenth.' José's fingers tapped in time on the wheel.

At the edge of the bay they pulled up just beyond the monolithic Organization building. As she got out of the car with her bag Margaret looked up at the rows of windows in the vicinity of Richard's office. Third World HQ. The building, only five years old, had rusty stains mysteriously seeping down its cement façade. Seeing his professional whereabouts, his other life, reminded her of him panting in the garden, fighting his own strange battle with mortality, and she felt a surge of tender fatalism. More confident than she had expected, she entered the lobby of the Eden Hotel where she was booked on the 1.30 p.m. coach to Juan Placido's Faith Medical Centre. Before legitimate surgery, she remembered, eating was not advisable; presumably the same applied. But she could do with a drink.

7

'WAIT!' Cullen was immediately expostulating with his wife even while he got to his feet, almost cannoned into tables and animal tanks, and pushed towards the bar. She fled from the room. He moved in her wake. Curious drinkers and diners frowned at this unapt momentum. There was a risk of being trampled underfoot by the huge *Mang*. In his path was the buttery waiter; he palmed him away as the man, spinning, saved his tray saying, 'Big hurry. Another one, huh?' By the time he reached the lobby she was gone.

Jenny Loh was applying make-up when he returned. She said nothing, briskly dabbing at her harmonious little features with lipstick and mascara brush. The lashes fluttered experimentally over the canny Asian eyes as he collapsed into his seat.

'Excuse me,' he muttered, desperate and baffled. At this absurd moment his spirit and stride were as good as broken. His heart thudded under his damp shirt, guilty and faultless at once; how long could it stand up to this crazy pressure? Her glossy lips did not move. Normally this sort of silence would drive him to explanations, but, regarding his charge across the bar, he could say nothing. Simply, it was now beyond him to communicate events.

She stood up, smoothing her dress. 'I must go.'

'Goodbye.'

'You fellows lead exciting lives for bureaucrats.'

'Hah!'

'Please pass on any word of Zulfikar.'

'Of course.'

Her hair fell straight in a silken drop; she was petite, symmetrical, pretty. Her passage through the crowd was meandering, the motion of her body was absolutely confident. The slim hips dummied, feinted around obstacles and implicit glances. Dully watching her, heart-sick, he thought he should have asked her what was going on.

Keeping his head down he drank alone, slowly finishing the beer Ingersole had bought, until the gradual departure of the lunchers drew his attention to the time—1.55. He became aware that the drift of people was correlative. There was a choreography, a patterned coming and going through the door of the bar. As the businessmen and minor bureaucrats and typists finished their meals and left for their offices, the afternoon shift—the foreign invalids and prostitutes—took their places. The youth in the wheelchair was steered in by a young woman, and the dark woman who had had the thyroid swelling, her neck now wound around with a dangerous-looking bandage, followed them. Cullen glanced around for the blonde American woman, half expecting her to be positioned near the pangolin, but she was not in the bar.

The young man's white face was as blank as a cement slab. His feet lolled on their footrest in shiny new cowboy boots, yellow and elaborately embossed. 'Double bourbon,' he ordered the waiter in a loud bossy voice. 'Speed it up.' The woman with him slumped in her chair, abject, drinking nothing.

Cullen presumed that a coach had just returned with a faith healer's morning clientele. He got up from the table, not wishing to think of the tantalization of those cowboy boots and of people's blighted expectations.

But on his way out there was a peremptory call from Ingersole's table. 'Dick, over here!' Wearily, he came across to them, four men in their late forties grinning sheepishly in their Antipodean casualwear. At once he was struck by their meaty male odour: the rare smell of carnivorous Celts and

Anglo-Saxons. They were pink with alcohol, heat and excitement. Though the temperature had activated their after-shave, the mingled fragrances did not stifle the smell of their bodies. Little sickly clouds of chemicals hovered around their faces, but at table level there was only the smell of beer and hot flesh.

One man said loudly, 'Pour the man a drink!'

'Give the man a chair!' ordered another.

With insistent good humour they catered for him, laughing in harsh accents at his protests. All the time winning flashes of dental work were turned on him. A call brought the waiter with more drinks.

'Great little drop, this,' one man insisted conversationally, tapping a San Miguel bottle with a fingernail.

'Not as good as Swan,' another man pronounced.

At this opinion they all began swearing amiably and barracking for various brands of beer.

'Carlton every time,' said Ingersole sagely. 'And I speak as a Sydneysider, mind you.'

'What about Cooper's?' This comment, treated with derisive laughter, brought the topic to an end.

Cullen took the opportunity to make his farewells. Ingersole, however, retained possession, clasping his forearm confidentially.

'You must know the ropes, Dick.' He smiled anxiously. 'A local feller was going to set it up for us, but he hasn't fronted. What do you advise?' This anxiety was that of the suburban bargain hunter. He could have been inquiring after a superior make of radial tyre or lawnmower. He wanted quality, a good finish and value for money. The others obviously recognized this Rotarian organizational ability in Ingersole because they suddenly began behaving as if his conversation with Cullen were not occurring, commenting animatedly among themselves on the decor, the heat and the local exchange rate. Until Ingersole asked, patting him on the back, 'Perhaps you'd like to join us, Dick? On us, of course.'

'Yes, be in it,' the others chorused.

'Sorry.'

'Be a sport.'

Gripped, pinned. Marine noises came from one of the other tanks: snorts and the slap of flipper on water. He had forgotten how to slip free from these particular scrummages, forgotten, in fact, the emotional weight they supported. The containment, the holding action, the pincer movement. The national scrum of mateship.

'Well, where is it then? Where's the action?' Where had he heard that question before? There was a hint of petulance, of time being wasted, in their queries now. Obviously they had got him wrong, said their envious cynical glances: not one of the boys; a spoilsport and probably a snob. A Rugby player, after all. Old school tie. A bloody 'Rah-rah'.

'Right here!' He waved an arm recklessly. He heard the sharp rise in his voice. 'Here!' Standing in the Jungle Bar, whose clientele were now beginning to cast apathetic looks towards the cause of the disturbance, he had the impression that his eyes were starting from his head, that his face was inflamed and that of all the customers he was by far the most graceless and formless. Just an amorphous mass.

'Ask the waiter,' he went on, lowering his voice. Feeling giddy, he steadied himself on the back of a chair. 'He'll fix it.'

The aggressive touch had mollified them. Now they took him seriously, relaxed and smiled at each other.

'Well then,' Ingersole said, patting his hair.

'We'd better get into these then,' advised the Swan Lager fancier, offering around a small bottle. He shook it and its contents rattled like peanuts. 'Penicillin,' he announced genially to Cullen. 'Can't take a dose home to Mum.'

He returned to the office. He learned that the Organization would not be registering any protest regarding the expulsion from the country of Z.M. Ali of the Animal Health and Production Section. It would not be asking for the confiscated reports on buffalo diseases to be returned. The Regional General Counsel advised against this end and no one pushed for it, anyway, it being such a minor matter. The Regional General Counsel was aged sixty-four and a cautious man. A former corporation lawyer in Tokyo, he was rumoured to be looking forward to a career in Japanese politics.

It was decided instead—though on a much lower level—that Cullen and Galash should travel down to Mindanao soon, to go over the same ground.

8

THE COACH FOR THE FAITH MEDICAL CENTRE was named Cecilia the Beautiful. The name was painted in gold along both sides and across the hood. Every seat in the coach was full as it pulled out on to the boulevard and into the streams of early afternoon traffic. In a window seat Margaret turned from the other passengers and stared numbly out across the muddy landfill to the bay where a couple of Japanese freighters rode at anchor near the gambling casino. The windows were shut, the air-conditioner had not yet begun to work and the stale oppressive atmosphere drew moisture from her. The upholstery stuck to her thighs and back. She took small shallow breaths, inhaling odours of plastic seat covers and hot European bodies. She wondered why sick women always over-scented themselves, and clasped her hands across her stomach. The pain was dull, intermittent, with an occasional hot twinge that eased only when she pressed against it tightly. She repeated to herself: Wait until later. Wait, wait.

A woman beside her gave an eerie loose smile. 'Nice day for it, anyway,' she said wryly.

Margaret nodded. The effort to speak was too great. This woman was awash with cologne. Waves of it swept into Margaret's head; she could pass out. She determined: I'm not fainting here, and concentrated on wiggling her toes in her sandals. Then the air-conditioner began to work and the false cold air bringing waves of stale vinyl also brought the sur-

196

roundings into clearer focus. She blinked and took deep steadying breaths and held her stomach.

'Maureen Decker from Stockton, California. Formerly of Albuquerque,' the woman announced, fixing her eyes on her. They were light in the irises, dark-circled and brimming with rheum. Edgily, she brushed a limp strand of pale hair from her forehead. 'I've got great vibes about today, honey,' she said, and in a sudden intimate gesture took one of Margaret's hands and squeezed it. She sighed, still gripping her hand. 'Goodbye pituitary tumour, that's my attitude.'

'Margaret Cullen,' Margaret said unwillingly sliding her hand carefully away. She didn't speak further, managing, by a half-turn of the head, to retain some privacy while not removing herself entirely from the woman's ambit. She declined a cigarette, then sat there placidly, impassive, as the woman, in a flurry of swivelling movements, tapped on neighbouring shoulders, tugged sleeves, asking adjoining invalids in a dry loud voice, 'Would my smoking offend you?'

Eventually she lit up, inhaled deeply, and said to Margaret, 'Rest easy, hon.'

'Of course.' She straightened her dress and was momentarily busy fluffing out the damp patches of material on her back and legs. 'It's the only way.'

The Decker woman said with emphasis, 'I'm in complete agreement. Look, originally I was scheduled for surgery at the University of California Medical Centre in San Francisco. Then I heard of this Juan Placido. It was a long shot, I realized that. I'm no believer in magic, believe me. I'm the last girl in the world to go for any hocus-pocus. I went into it thoroughly and I'm of the opinion that Juan has a gift.' She exhaled smoke and nodded vigorously. 'A genuine gift from God. I've got a scrapbook this thick on Juan's successes. He's been written up in *Fate* magazine. You know the common thread in all the stories? Witnesses say something paranormal happens. It's true. Take the abdomen. Now Juan's fingers appear to penetrate the surface of the belly, open it right up. Wow! Now I'm a cynic. I won't say it definitely opens in the normal sense because some people say there is a materialization on top of the skin and I'm not going to sit here and argue the technicalities of *opening* versus *materialization*. Either of them is pretty good for my money. But on top of the skin or in the apparently open area of the belly where the flesh is parted, my sources say you can see *tissue*. You can see peristaltic *movement*. You can see *blood*.'

'Please!'

'Then, as you watch, the whole thing closes up and disappears.' Maureen Decker snapped her fingers.

The pulse in her stomach ticked like a bomb. Margaret hugged this sensation in her flesh and turned half away once more. The reflection in the window was faint but recognizably hers. Her deep eyepits loomed out of the glass whenever the background was in shadow—wide, dark and strange. Conversations occurred over and around her, some of them involving the woman next to her who was now engaging fellow Americans in geographical banter. Names of towns were exchanged, travellers' coincidences bandied about. There was dry, nervous laughter and Margaret identified the states of New Mexico and Oregon. An old man with a balding crewcut and a black string tie fastened in a steer's head clasp turned around and said vehemently, 'My opinion, nothing's all black or white. A thousand shades of grey.' He spoke out of the corner of his mouth and his voice was thick. 'One thousand shades!'

Margaret nodded politely at his remarks, but distractedly she thought again: Wait, wait. She concentrated carefully on his close-cropped head, the pink crown coming up through the sea of short hairs like a bare desert island, the network of crisscrossing neck creases. She felt a vague nausea. She had no camaraderie for these people, she realized: they were all sick, old, losers. She would keep a disciplined grip on herself. She thought: Soon. Take things in stages. She glanced out the window. The coach was passing the Wack Wack Golf and Country Club. The fairways, dotted with brightly clad figures, were lush in the humidity; the greens were verdant almost beyond belief.

The old man turned again, enunciating with effort and

anger. 'I told them that. I wrote them. I wrote my Congressman.' His voice was thick. Bubbles hung in the corner of his mouth. This side of his face seemed to be battling paralysis. 'You try fighting the Federal Trade Commission! I said, we're voters too, boy. We're not dead yet. You say it's a hoax, you better prove it, I said, before you withdraw those charter flights. Back they come with their pebbles story. Not real kidney stones, ordinary pebbles off the ground, they say. Sheep guts instead of tumours, sleight of hand, a nice little racket. You talk spiritists to those Washington guys, psychic surgery, they think you're a loony.'

She nodded again and turned away. She kept her mind channelled. The greens were smooth as baize. On the fairways businessmen, swinging clubs in the heat, would be clinching deals entailing huge foreign borrowings. Margaret wondered fleetingly if the President was playing today. His handicap was down to four, according to Ted Orosa. 'A wonderful sportsman,' she'd heard Orosa remark ten or twenty times, his fanclub adoration transforming his shrewd eyes.

But of course the subject of sport was also charged with danger. She tried to shy from it. It brought back painful scenes: Richard, young and fit, grinning awkwardly at her during a lull on the field; hands on hips, getting his breath, pink with exertion and joy. From the sidelines she would catch his eye, and inside her coat, sweater, scarf, she would hug his quick self-conscious smile to her secretly. Safe, warm and happy in the chilled afternoon, as if his actual size and athleticism encompassed her with a medieval security. The football mêlées couldn't neutralize his physical and psychic impact on her. Even on the dark muddy field his ginger hair, spiky from the scrums, marked his individual position, his uniqueness. Their minds ran alongside.

Such memories, coming to her in a faith healer's coach heading for the mountains a world and a generation away, remained so poignant and sharp that she could feel the comforting weight of the duffel coat on her shoulders—even the silver brandy flask in the pocket. She smelled mud, grass and men's pungent sweat. The wind stung her cheeks.

Then she was in the Jungle Bar and her mind almost screamed aloud: Not yet! Wait, wait.

The coach driver had a row of magnetized religious statuettes stuck to the dashboard: Jesus as a child and man, the Virgin Mary and the former Saint Christopher, all chromium plated. Despite his recent papal demotion, Christopher was in a prominent position. He must have had an internal klaxon, because the driver pressed him once or twice and he honked, causing several passengers in the front seats to chuckle, a couple to click their tongues in vague disapproval.

Margaret made no judgement on this curio: bad taste was part of the complete picture. Everything was a mockery. She looked out the window. The city was disappearing into urban farmlets and sterile expanses of cogon grass. Small padi fields and vegetable gardens lay behind big billboards proclaiming the New Society. On some of these family workings, buffaloes trudged, overseen by small children. Margaret said to herself: They are always in the landscape here. They were as ubiquitous as the palm tree, but she didn't care if she never saw another one again. Little wooden, tin and palm-leaf huts stood in the dust of the highway among Coke and San Miguel signs, and on doorsteps thin pretty children squatted on their bare buttocks. Chickens and pariah dogs picked through garbage heaps. Margaret surveyed this Asian scenario with a curious inattention, rubbing her stomach, soothing it like a baby. With hardly any effort she focused her thoughts intently on the line of Rajamurti's, *Oneself is a constant movement of yesterday through to today and tomorrow, a single movement, endless.*

Beside her, her cigarette still alight in her hand, Maureen Decker was asleep.

In the mountains it grew cooler and pines grew thickly on the hillsides. A thin mist slid along the valleys. Occasionally a scar in the forest revealed a copper or silver mine. Margaret applied make-up to her face and combed her hair. Those passengers who had been sleeping stretched and began murmuring again. The women inspected their faces, using large amounts of cosmetics—where this was necessary—in an effort to achieve normality. Men coughed, grumbled and began the geographical banter again, gingerly prodding their afflictions as they talked.

The coach's changing momentum woke Maureen Decker. On the upward grades the driver was experimenting with many crafty gear changes; the coach's lurching sent her head banging against Margaret's shoulder. She was more subdued now. Making adjustments to her features, she said quietly, 'Soon as this thing's over I'm doing the town. Boy, am I going to tie one on.' Her top lip was creased with tension as she powdered her nose. 'What about you, hon?'

'I'd like a drink now,' Margaret said. The sound of her voice, high and tremulous, catching slightly, surprised her. 'Right now,' she repeated firmly, to correct any wrong impression.

'You bet. Incidentally, excuse me for asking, are you an Australian?'

She nodded. Again she had no wish to talk. To risk that shaky foreign accent.

'Nice country,' said Maureen Decker.

The coach's brakes hissed. The driver turned off the highway on to a narrow side road, now travelling downhill through high pines, temperate European vegetation, riding the brakes. His jerky decelerations and the twists in the road buffeted the passengers against each other. A gaunt woman exclaimed, 'Ooh!' and giggled nervously as her handbag spilled open on the floor.

Soon, Margaret thought.

Again the brakes hissed and the coach stopped in a gravel parking lot before a small cement-block bungalow set back from the road. Dust rose around them and the air was sharp. Chattering nervously, clutching handbags, cameras and walking sticks, two of them manhandled into wheelchairs, they assembled on the bungalow verandah, these vulnerable and motley tourists, and were immediately arranged alphabetically on high-backed chairs by a smiling woman in a soiled white coat.

Margaret was riveted by the coat's rusty smears, its burgundy butcher's whorls. She kept a hand on her stomach, stroking and smoothing.

'*Mabuhay*,' announced the woman, as chirpy as a tour guide, when they were settled. She was small and brown with a vivacious gold tooth. She waved an enthusiastic general hello. 'Welcome to the Faith Medical Centre. Please remain seated. The Reverend Doctor Juan S. Placido will be with you in a jiffy.'

Supporting himself on a three-legged walking aid, the old man with the cowboy string tie got to his feet grumbling at her, 'I got seniority. No waiting for me. I got me my appointment six months ago. I been held up by bureaucrats. Check your files. Name of Turpie.'

The woman ignored him and disappeared on slapping rubber sandals.

Outwardly calm, Margaret sat and waited. Observers would have seen a blonde pale frowning woman sitting with folded arms and staring straight ahead with an air of boredom and self-possession. She was only one seat from the head of the queue. Once more the Decker woman was next to her, smoking and chattering aimlessly and brushing ash from her dress. To a non-European observer they could have been sisters. Near the end of the queue the old man muttered angrily.

There were no magazines, no pictures on the unpainted cement-block walls, only the line of rattan chairs side by side facing the gravel parking lot where the dust was settling again and the driver now dozed in the front of the coach. At least if it had offered a few *National Geographics* or *Reader's Digests* like every other waiting room in the world, Margaret thought, there was a chance she could have read about the mysterious faith healers of South-East Asia. Momentarily this fantasy preoccupied her. She contemplated seeing photographs of herself reading the *National Geographic* while waiting to see a mysterious faith healer and seeing photographs of herself reading and waiting to see a mysterious faith healer and so on until she was a microscopic dot. Was this the same as infinity, this endless progression? *A single movement, endless*—that was oneself. But she confused infinity with geometric terms, something to do with never-meeting parallel lines. How did you describe this ever-diminishing boundlessness? Willie Weeties on her childhood cereal packets had been a genius at it. Holding aloft a Weeties packet showing himself holding aloft a Weeties packet showing . . .

The woman in the coat appeared and beckoned to the first patient, a small man with a goitre stretched tight like a pink golf ball above his collar. He followed her into a doorway off the verandah. She closed the door behind him.

There was a shuffling and coughing along the row of chairs. Invalids straightened anxiously and looked expectantly at the closed door. Margaret's heart raced. She imagined she smelled blood, chemicals and surgical spirits. Perhaps a whiff had escaped through the surgery door. She thought again of the stained coat. Somehow she had been under the impression that the wound of a faith healer's patient barely seeped. Just a delicate incision as fine as a hair, less gory than the faintest shaving nick. And instantly healed by a pass of the supernatural fingertips. But of course this would be magic! He was right. How could she have swallowed such Oriental rubbish?

Blowing smoke nervously, Maureen Decker said, 'I met an Australian last night in the Eden Hotel. The Jungle Bar, what a joint! Big fellow, red hair, perhaps you know him? Not interested in a pass from this old broad, though. Not with a slick local chickie like the one he had in tow.'

She rose stiffly at the woman's beckoning, followed her through the door into the surgery. It was also bare, of similar unpainted cement blocks. Surprisingly there was no smell. Her brain registered this. Her sandals clicked quietly on the scratched parquetry. She was receptive to the sound. Perhaps there was a couch, yes, against the wall covered with a sheet, and a grey metal filing cabinet, and a desk, and a couple of wooden chairs. Nothing else, apart from a yellow plastic bowl on the filing cabinet and a small bluish statuette of the Virgin on the desk and, on one wall, a calendar from the Asia Pacific Real Estate Corp.

The woman said, 'Sit.' From the plastic bowl she took some rubber gloves and put them on.

At the far end of the room a door opened and the Reverend Doctor appeared. He was a neat, stocky little figure in short-sleeved sports shirt and tight slacks. His shoes seemed to make no sound. A gold belt buckle caught Margaret's eye. Oddly, she thought, Gucci copy, a fake. As he moved towards her he nodded but did not speak. His short bare arms showed well-defined muscles. They were hairless, ageless; his skin was a neutral beige shade, representing no particular race, and as he stood in front of her, rubbing his hands together with a slight force, his triceps moved and expanded. Then, without using a light, he stretched her eyelids apart and looked into her eyes. Vaguely she wondered what diseases or madness he read in them.

Maybe he was thirty-five or forty. There was no curiosity in his expression, no frown, no creases on the round face. She was busy watching the hands as they motioned her to the couch. They were square, fleshy, with stubby fingers, more those of a golfer than a surgeon, except that the nails were lacquered. He clasped his hands together again, gripped them and did the rippling trick with his triceps once more. His body gave off a whiff of pomade and stale perspiration. The woman came from behind her as she lay on the couch anticipating this very action and unbuttoned her dress and lifted away her underclothes.

The Reverend Doctor hovered over her flesh. She perceived this perfectly from the vantage point of a third, or fourth, person. Suddenly but subtly she had become a hyper-perceptive onlooker. She watched the soft white abdomen contract under his fingers, the flattened pubic hair. She saw the probing of the stomach. She saw this person, herself, screw her face into a concentrated red ball, as if in birth agonies, and was both astonished and embarrassed to watch this naked body heaving and arching. To hear the demented cries, to observe and experience the convulsive bouncing of the breasts and the threshing legs was a wonder to her. Despite all this wild bucking activity, the sweating and fighting, from her unique position she was able to inform herself: *Now! Now!* hear herself shriek these very words, and watch herself—under the bewildered restraining hands of Placido and his white-eyed nurse—sob with the relief of having reached the edge and toppled over.

9

CLATTERING SOUTH ABOVE THE JUNGLE Cullen was struck by
the paradoxical peace of gun-ship travel. There were no
take-off and landing tensions. The ground was safely acces-
sible. Moreover, in his flimsy emotional state the fierce din of
the rotors fortunately made deep thinking difficult. Right
now he welcomed the racket and the diversion of the
experience, and the scenery—its new dimension—in any case
adequately filled the mind.

Through the gun-slit in the floor the foliage below, richly
green and within reach, had a novel force: no longer the
mundane trunks and branches of ground level nor the remote
dark patches in the general earth-quilt but an ocean sweep of
cambers and parabolas undulating in the helicopter's draught
and billowing away at either side. This lush sinuosity was
itself full of life: streams of birds—white storks and several
varieties of parrots—rose at their approach, and once a cloud
of black butterflies. In the safe zones the helicopter flew so
low that several times, seeing shapes in the crooks of branches, he thought he saw crouching cats, monkeys and lemurs.
Possibly he imagined these.

The machine-gunner, an angular young sergeant with a
gold canine tooth, swivelled in his seat. One hand resting
possessively on his gun, he peered back at Cullen and mimed
the act of smoking with the other.

'Sorry!' He could barely hear his own shout. He shrugged

elaborately and shook his head.

The sergeant grimaced, then gave the same questioning look and made exaggerated chewing motions.

Cullen shook his head again. 'No candy!' he shouted. 'No gum!' He shrugged apologetically.

The sergeant turned morosely back to his machine gun, his flat eyes on the jungle.

Behind the machine-gunner, strapped in tightly to the last notch in his webbing seat belt, Cullen, also shut in behind dark glasses, was actually feeling, after forty minutes in the air, his most tranquil for days. Below him, within the gun-slit, thin lines of pale smoke rising from the treetops became a faint haze through which the helicopter alternately rose and dipped. Bolstered by military appurtenances, experiencing the fatalism of exhaustion, he could finally say to himself: so she has gone.

Events carried him on beyond desolation.

In the cockpit, sitting behind and at right angles to the pilot—a Captain Acoca, F.X. according to his pocket flash—Galash was concentrating on some by-play between the captain and the co-pilot. Apparently an inside joke: the co-pilot's helmet and shoulders shook with hilarity. But Captain Acoca half-turned and included Galash in the anecdote. Cullen saw Galash's eyes sparkle. He watched him zoom one of his palms through the air like a child imitating a jet plane, while his lips and teeth expressed a series of smiles. The officers laughed. Captain Acoca passed around a packet of cigarettes.

The gun-ship ride, their ferrying south by this army patrol, had come at short notice. This time the day before they had been booked on a regular Fokker flight to General Santos City. Arrangements had been made for one of the field workers to pick them up and drive them around the various *barrio* stations. The collating of the relevant disease data was expected to take no more than two or three days, less time than seconding a local officer to the task. But a sweeping offer of co-operation had come suddenly from the Government. It appeared that the Government and the Regional General

Counsel had been engaged in discussions since the morning of the Z.M. Ali affair, that the Government and the Organization had taken the opportunity of the incident to re-think and consolidate their whole relationship. As a beginning the Government had expressed itself willing to help wherever possible in matters of transport and communication, especially in the emergent zones. The Regional General Counsel's advice to local Organization staff was to accept such offers.

A curious affair, thought Cullen, pondering it for the first time since the chaotic day of Z.M.'s expulsion. Other events had intervened, as it were. The turmoil surrounding Margaret's departure had kept him away from the office for two days. And then the Orosa fracas had blown up.

A week ago life had been very different. With the usual stupid hindsight he saw it to have been extraordinarily peaceful. Above his head the rotors drummed. They were flying over a thin khaki beach. The pale sea lapped languidly; even from the air it looked tepid and soupy. It was Orosa's nerve that astounded him. Ted would have expected his column on the uncharged assailant to touch a raw spot, the youth's uncle being the President. Hazel had outlined the drama of this scoop with characteristic equanimity before leaving herself for California.

'Right from the night when they appeared with the first edition in their hot little hands he was waiting. The suspense got to him. The censors' visit, the rumours of the secret police. Finally he went to see the First Lady's cousin. He took Ted to see the President at the end of a golf game when he's usually in a good mood. "Sir, I've apprehended Orosa," the cousin said. The President cocked his fist as if to hit Ted. Ted threw his hands up in front of his face. Then the President laughed, made a joke about it, and Ted left. Next day he was sent away by his paper. The bastards tell me nothing.' She had grimaced, standing there on her doorstep, a pile of gowns clasped in the pulpy white arms. ' "Absent," they say. "On sabbatical, Mrs Orosa." '

When he'd called next day to inquire after further news she and Bong Bong were gone. Jaime, their driver, was swimming in the pool. He was drunk and made no sense. At night someone played Bong Bong's drums and there was laughter.

Moro vintas were drawn up on the sand above the high water mark, covered by dry palm fronds. From a height they appeared impossibly frail without their masts and high Oriental sails, their outriggers as thin as matchsticks. As they passed over, shirring the surface of the shallows, some naked children ran out of the palms, waving.

The gun-ship canted inland, flying across hillsides of cogon grass, then padi fields, brown irrigation canals, fields of pineapple and cane. In the padis buffaloes plodded their circular time-honoured routes. Cullen was touched by the ancient spectacle; their simple, honourable silhouettes.

'Straight out of the third millennium B.C.,' he said suddenly to the sergeant, pointing below.

Frowning, the sergeant peered down through the gun-slit. Suspiciously he surveyed greenery and swamp.

'*Carabao*,' Cullen said.

The sergeant looked at him, then shrugged.

Unchanged from their representations on Mesopotamian vases, seals from the Indus Valley, Cullen thought. Same temperament, same dreamy physiognomy, identical crescentic horns: the truth of the mould and cast. An image of hard work, serenity; indeed, of the whole continent. The embodiment of the Third World he now observed in the rectangular frame of the gun-slit, like a giant postcard.

They descended over peasants' huts, farmlets, dusty roads, the outskirts of a town. A tricycle chugged below, heading for the town. Its passengers, two women, held on to their hats, anticipating the helicopter's down-draught. The tricycle's oily exhaust trailed behind it, a streamer hanging in the air. Then, below, was a flat commercial area of single- and two-storeyed buildings, a market square of stalls overlaid with pieces of hessian, palm fronds or galvanized iron. The helicopter stirred up puffs of dust and beside a school, in a playing field, it landed. Unclipping his seat belt, Cullen noticed three old bullet holes as wide as a finger in the floor by his feet.

Immediately children swarmed around them. They poured out of the school in a chirping wave of blue shirts and tunics and flooded the field, followed by three tiny brown nuns blowing whistles. He and Galash were as good as film stars. Precocious charming kids asked for autographs in their exercise books and called them 'Sir'. They wanted his home address to initiate long and mutually educational correspondences. Even the nuns wished to be pen-pals. Cullen was snowed by this happy tumult. He attracted surreptitious astonished glances, too; wide eyes at his novel size and colouring. His accent brought on fits of the giggles. This sideshow attention could have gone on for hours if Captain Acoca hadn't indicated an army jeep waiting at the edge of the field.

He said, 'To work, to work,' and clapped his hands at the children. Over the hubbub he hissed for the jeep driver.

'The universal "Tsst!",' Galash said. 'These guys have got ears like dogs.'

Cullen mumbled, 'A rude bloody sound.'

But it seemed to work as usual. The jeep shot across the grass to them and braked flashily. A corporal with a dark and pitted southern face saluted casually from the driver's seat: an approximate US salute to match his mock American uniform.

'Give him your itinerary,' the captain said. 'He is your man for the duration. Twenty-four hours a day, OK?'

Galash said, 'That's real service.'

Acoca gave a wide white smile. 'We aim to please.'

The corporal revved the engine. He was a solid man, rounded, and his uniform gripped the contours of his body. Cullen noticed that he wore sidearms. The gunbelt was tight round his belly.

'Is the corporal a safety precaution?'

'He is just your personal chauffeur and general factotum.' The captain laughed and slapped Cullen on the back. 'Relax, champ. You will not be heading into any risky areas.'

Galash said, 'He'll keep the MNLF off with that pistol, will he? Wonderful.'

210

Now the captain, still grinning, gave Galash a wink. 'Corporal Panglinang is armed to the teeth. The very teeth.' He took a step over to the jeep and patted the throbbing hood. 'Corporal, you are under these gentlemen's orders. Top VIPs, understand?' He also spoke in Tagalog. As they climbed into the jeep he gave the hood a farewell pat. He seemed to be restraining further amusement. 'Leave no buffalo unturned,' he said.

That afternoon they called on one field station twenty miles south of the town, in the middle of the padi belt in the inner lowlands. There were no problems: the parasitic disease statistics were available for the south and south-east of the island. But Jesús Licaros, the young local superintendent, apologized for the age of the data.

'We have not been able to update since Mr Ali last called on us. Even here the Muslim business is a worry. They are a minority but their farmers no longer co-operate. They take us for an arm of the Government, you know how it is.' Simultaneously he frowned and giggled. 'A love-hate relationship.'

They sat under a coconut-frond sun shelter on the front lawn of the station. Some time earlier Licaros' staff had placed a plastic bin full of ice and bottles of Coca-Cola under the shelter, but by the time the guests went to take refreshment the ice had melted and the drinks were submerged in warm water. A maid brought plates of nutty rice cookies. A line of ants moved constantly up one of the shelter's supports and disappeared into the palm leaves.

Masking a belch, Galash said, 'Tell them you're above politics, that you only want to improve their stock. Christ, read them the charter!'

'They're naturally conservative, and very mistrustful these days. They make it hard for the surveyors, highway engineers—even the sanitary inspectors—because of their reticence and pride.'

Cullen barely listened. Beside him on the seat his briefcase was full of Jesús Licaros' statistics. Grisly varieties of snail, hookworm, lungworm, roundworm, leech, tick, mite, mosquito, louse and fly were represented. A lush savage range of tropical bloodsuckers depended on *Bubalus bubalis*. One or more species seemed to tunnel into every buffalo orifice and organ; the hide, the horns, even the hoofs. There was a moth with a saw-like proboscis that fed nocturnally, voraciously, on its eyes. There was a fluke which slid into the liver, its sucker gripping the bile duct. Yet the host prevailed.

The feeling of security it gave Cullen to again possess at least part of the confiscated data outweighed any misgivings about its slight datedness. He could afford to be philosophical: after all, they were dealing with age-old infestations and infections. During the war hadn't their Vietnamese information been severely restricted? And the complete buffalo situation in China had remained a mystery for decades. But work went on. Projects came to fruition. Gradually circumstances improved. You made the best of it.

He put down the tepid half-finished drink, smiling at Licaros. 'Well, we've relied on intelligent guesswork before now. This is what we came for.' He patted the briefcase. His fingers were sticky. 'It will get us off the hook.' If Licaros had had any other Christian name he would have used it now. But finding it difficult to say, he called him nothing.

Licaros smoked busily, frowning. 'Equipment disappears. Things fall down in the night. Triangulation towers, electricity pylons.'

'Moros?' Galash asked.

'I don't know. Plenty of troublemakers on the other side. Always one power struggle or another going on in the *barrios*. Local smart guys. Some political, some plain gangsters. The PC patrol sticks its nose in, gun-happy soldiers; there is a shoot-out. More kudos in despatching one sort of terrorist than the other.' He grinned wryly. 'It's more complicated living in the safe zones. You wonder, who's doing this to me?'

'Exciting times,' Galash said airily. 'Don't think we don't live dangerously in the capital. My secret unexpurgated copy of *Newsweek* yesterday said they'd arrested the Queen of the Pacific for subversion.'

'A beauty queen!' Cullen snorted. 'I thought they were sacrosanct.'

'So did this little chick apparently.' Galash was breezy. An eye gleamed provocatively. 'Mind you, they're the intellectuals in this country.'

Cullen did not laugh, merely smiled cautiously. He avoided Licaros' eyes. 'You'd better watch it then,' he said to Galash.

'Oh, I'm only to be seen with the daughters of papal knights and leaders of industry. Sacred Heart girls.' Galash was beginning to twist the knife for some reason. 'By the way, Dick, did you check out those little nuns back at the school?'

Licaros said abruptly, 'Well, you have all you need.' He stood up and made as if to leave them, taking a couple of sideways steps in the direction of his office. The sun was low over the shelter. The others also stood. Corporal Panglinang was squatting nonchalantly on the office steps, like a pro golfer lining up a putt. He was chatting to the maid and occasionally raising a Coke to his lips. His cap was folded neatly under an epaulette. The ants had begun to carry cookie crumbs up the shelter pole into the coconut fronds.

Licaros turned back to them.

'My curiosity is aroused about Mr Ali,' he declared in an offended sarcastic voice. 'Everything being above politics, et cetera.'

'Yes, well . . . ' Cullen said.

Galash hissed, 'Tsst!' for Corporal Panglinang.

10

NIBBLING PORK RINDS GALASH SAID, 'I knew it. I could see it coming a mile off.'

'Indeed? You're very perceptive.'

'Sure. It's an atmosphere. I can pick it. That Sunday I recognized all the signs. Boy, I can if anyone can. A couple of very discontented unhappy individuals. All overlaid with the tropical malaise. You're speaking to the expert, man. One adroit glance around a patio, a half-hour at a dinner party and I'll give you chapter and verse on that particular relationship. I'm sitting up there in your study having a few casual drinks and you're coming and going in and out of the room and Margaret's in a trance, staring out the window, and I think, oh, oh, there they go.'

Cullen bridled but said nothing, pouring himself another glass of beer.

'And when they allude to their sex life—I'm talking generally here—nothing flagrant, mind you, more-in-sorrow-than-anger sort of stuff. . . .'

He had felt an immediate pang at the first remarks, at their brusque smug delivery. And he was hurt that their state—even misapprehended, misrepresented—had attracted notice. He still held a romantic public view of their marriage. Sentimentally, he wished to defend her against vague insinuations and cordial malice. Also against generalizations and hackneyed behaviour patterns and the jaundiced impressions of this smart aleck. The sexual inference he could also do without. Innuendo bothered him. It was an injury ever anticipated, like knees or collarbones, but you never carried enough padding.

Galash must have sensed his annoyance. His attitude became soothing, comradely, now. 'I know you're cut up about it, Dick. You're not Robinson Crusoe. I've been over that route, I know how you feel. Christ, how many other guys do you know in the same boat?'

Delivering this nostrum, Galash leaned back in his chair in the Fiesta Lounge of the Hotel President in General Ramón Tortosa City, his hand delving into a bowl of miniature dried fish, nuts and pork crackling, scooping up a handful, filtering it so the fish fell back into the bowl and fingering the remaining morsels delicately into his mouth. The greedy muffled voice speaking through the food, the neat expressive hands darting from the bowl to his mouth, gave him an air so amiable and patronizing Cullen could have knocked his head off.

'One point I want to make to you, Dick. Don't feel guilty. Guilt can drive you insane. Believe me, never get locked into a guilt situation.'

Cullen was busy drinking, handling all the appurtenances of drinking: bottle, glass, coaster, nifty Styrofoam insulated bottle-cooler; sipping, pouring, blotting, arranging for low temperatures to be maintained. During all this activity he said, 'Hugh, do you mind? I can do without the jargon.' He thumped his glass on the table, half accidentally.

'Fine. OK.' Briskly Galash put another handful of savouries into his mouth. He licked the salt from his fingers. For a moment neither spoke. Then Galash carefully selected a rigid tiny fish from the bowl and held it up to the light, transparent, close to his face. 'Dehydrated but intact,' he said. 'Eyes, scales, bones, gizzard, the lot. *Pescao seco.* Ubiquitous little devils. Everywhere you go they're munching them by the thousands. Maids and socialites alike. Fish and rice, fish and rice, that's the whole picture.'

'Protein. Bloody second-class protein.'

'As soon as you go into a store, kitchen, anywhere, you smell them. That dry stale Asiatic fish stink. Christ, I'm sick of it.'

Suddenly Galash popped the fish into his mouth, crunched, swallowed. 'Tastes appalling. I knew it would. I've been avoiding them for years.'

Galash had introduced the subject of Margaret after they had been drinking in the Fiesta Lounge for three or four hours, ever since their return from Licaros' field station. There was no other entertainment, nowhere to go in this small dull town. The corporal had vanished in the jeep, saying nothing. They drank quietly, chatted desultorily, and scanned the other drinkers from time to time as a diversion from each other. The only females in the lounge seemed to be the wives and daughters of some perky provincial businessmen. These women gossiped behind long fruit-encrusted drinks and once or twice flung cursory glances in their direction. Fathers, husbands, brothers, however, sleek in barongs or open-necked shirts, hovered over them possessively, smoking cigars, laughing and whispering *risqué* anecdotes to each other.

'Family night,' Galash had said. 'Mistresses tomorrow night.' Then, barely drawing breath, 'Is Margaret well?'

Cullen could have gasped at the crass conjunction. He did glare at him but Galash, an innocent, steady expression in his eyes, said seriously, 'I thought she looked quite ill—you know, not exactly in touch.'

Obviously he had heard something on the grapevine. Or did he just imagine Galash's audacity? He could never satisfactorily fathom whether he was being obvious or subtle. It was as though his thick-skinned extroverted blatancy was a form of super-subtlety. The nuances of his language and body-English were different, and implicit in them was the knowledge that in any misunderstanding or confusion his particular style would prevail. This was just one advantage of being the representative of the master culture: he had all the leeway.

Eventually Cullen had said, 'Yes, she's been sick. She went

home three days ago. I put her on the plane and off she flew.'
He added nothing more.

Now, a little later, he was aware that Galash's present state
was, for him, unusual. His impulsive devouring of the dried
fish had been uncharacteristic, almost a fatalistic act. He was
gingerly sipping beer, presumably to drown the taste, with an
attitude of karmic resignation; staring impassively across the
lounge toward the door.

He said 'I'm sorry. Very sorry.' His eyes were full of
sympathy. His sincerity was clear. Taking a deeper swig from
his glass as if to bolster himself, he murmured, 'You were the
last. You two were the last, you realize. There's none left
now. It's all downhill.'

The maudlin words, depressed and depressing, struck
Cullen as alcohol-induced. A drinker's fake guilelessness. But
he was articulating clearly and seemed otherwise as self-
possessed as ever.

'I had a lot of faith in you, brother.'

Cullen squirmed with guilt and annoyance. Misery was
weighing in swiftly. There was little to say. As usual he was
left offside. He drank some more and muttered, 'Nothing's
final.'

The air in the Fiesta Lounge was too cold. His bare ginger
forearms, dipped in freckles, also prickled with goose-flesh.
Gusts of laughter came from the nearest family group. One of
the young men was standing and mock-crooning into his
glass/microphone, imitating some popular singer, and the
women were clapping their hands, their bright nails and rings
flashing, tittering and regarding him admiringly. An older
man, short and pudgy, with bristly grey hair, stood slapping
his side with conspicuous amusement. Then, breezily reaching into his wallet, he plucked out a handful of notes and
pushed them ostentatiously into the youth's shirt pocket. The
others clapped his action appreciatively and with respect. The
benefactor patted the boy on the back, still beaming at him,
and with an authoritative wave ordered more drinks. Silently,
the boy sat down. Close attention was paid the older man
and he began to regale everyone with a yarn.

Galash was saying reflectively, 'I don't suppose it was anything like our split. You couldn't imagine the drama. Up till then everything was rosy.' He laughed bitterly. 'Apart from Asia, I mean.' He belched softly.

What was this, a new side to him? He had never imagined him a sufferer. 'You've always given the impression everything was hunky-dory. Especially after she left.'

'I'll tell you something. For the life of me I can't figure what got into me. We were a top act. Our only bad scene was when she caught me once fantasizing in the john with a copy of *Penthouse*. She hit the roof. She's got very little understanding of the male psyche, Christina. She wanted to own my soul. She wanted my fucking daydreams!'

Where was the suavity, the style, the Yankee *élan*? Cullen couldn't help himself. 'Maybe she just wanted to use the toilet.'

'You may well laugh.' Rarely had Galash looked so strained. A glazed look had taken hold. The drink was obviously taking over because he was talking with an unusual animation. 'Want to know why she split? You've never heard anything like this tacky little number. It almost makes *me* laugh. Remember that wind-up tour I did of Cambodia and Laos? Naturally I made a welter of it. In Tonlé Sap I got mixed up with an absolute princess. A peach. At the end of ten days I could hardly bring myself to leave with my Dakota load of files and bunsen burners. I considered tossing everything in, braving the Reds and becoming the idiosyncratic merchant prince of the Mekong. Viva romance! That sort of effect she had on me. I wasn't myself.'

Nor was he now. This tale had given him a haggard, apologetic look that was new to Cullen. The air of superiority was not noticeable. This was an *event*.

'Anyway, after tearful farewells I left and two days later I'm in Bangkok having a restorative bath before flying home and the little girl with me says, "Oho, what this thing?" She jumps out in disgust and throws in the sponge and as the old mama-san's tossing me out and I'm trying to dress I look and there's this ominous pimple on the head of the old fella. So much for my pristine Cambodian! And what do I do? I panic. To this day I can't figure why I acted like this. Sure, any analyst would say I wanted discovery and punishment. Ha! But I rang Christina and told her. You can imagine the phone call. My behaviour was peculiar. I was crying drunk, distracted. See, I didn't want to have to explain to her face-to-face why I couldn't even kiss her hello, touch her hands, much less have our usual welcome home.'

Cullen sighed and took a mouthful of beer, feeling, for several moments, strangely and selfishly elated. He signalled for fresh bottles, arranging the empties neatly at the end of the table. This smug feeling dissipated gradually. On re-appraisal he was again surprised and melancholic at the unusual lack of sophistication as much as anything.

'But, that's not the end of it. Here's the dénouement. So I get on the plane and there's no one at the other end to meet me, naturally. I go straight from the airport to one of those VD and circumcision wizards that thrive here. This bastard examines my growth, looks stern, snips off a sample and says he'll let me know. Picture the abject traveller arriving home. I'm in pain for a start. The house is full of packing cases and piles of ironed dresses. Christina naturally ignores me. She's booked on a New York flight leaving next day. I spend the worst night of my life sitting up drinking and contemplating cutting it off. In the morning I sit twitching by the phone. An hour before she's due to leave Doctor slimy Perez rings. "That pimple on your private organ that is causing concern," he says. "Yes?" I say, almost weeping. "You're right," he says. "It is a pimple," and the bastard giggles. "It's just a pimple!" I call out to Christina. "Bully for you," she says, and leaves for the airport.'

Galash grinned bleakly and tossed savouries into his mouth. Cullen could imagine the scene. Christina was an intense dark woman with self-reliant, wide hips; he could see her making excellent dramatic departures, a quick East Side quip on the lips. A lot of his sympathy went out to his companion, newly and badly flawed. Offered this rare glimpse of vulnerability what could he do but sympathize?

Hugh had been through the ropes.

And, all things considered, the tawdriness of the confession did please him. It marked a subtle shift in their relationship. Now it was all silly boys together. The condescension had disappeared. 'True story?' Cullen asked, pouring him a beer.

'Ha!'

They were still drinking when Corporal Panglinang strode, grinning broadly, into the lounge. He wore civilian clothes: a red knit shirt, denims and high heeled boots: dressed like a street cowboy except for his service haircut—shaved exaggeratedly high at the back and sides—and the military dog-tag showing at the neck. Marching across the room with a look of keen amusement he managed to glance approvingly yet menacingly at two of the businessmen's daughters from behind their parents' backs, gave Cullen and Galash a jaunty salute and sat down at their table.

'Hi, hi,' he said.

Galash said, 'At ease, Corporal,' with a wry smirk.

Panglinang ate some savouries, dipping a quick rapacious hand into the bowl. He pushed the fish, nuts and pork rinds between his lips and chewed with his mouth open. He hissed for beer. A smell of alcohol already came off him, and of the sweet grease which kept his hair upright. As well as the dog-tag he wore a gold crucifix at the neck. He tapped his feet and a light tremor of energy and anticipation flicked over his skin.

'What have you been up to, Corporal?' asked Cullen.

He giggled.

'Come on, man. Where's the fun and games? Nightclubs, girls, dancing?' Galash was persuasive in several dialects. '*Pampams*? *Putas*? *Tuway* in the dark?' To Cullen, he said, 'Tropical Rule Number One—the military always knows.' On the table his fingers drummed with impatience.

Why not? Cullen considered. Why on earth not? Tentatively but optimistically, he said loudly, 'Spill the beans, Corporal.'

Panglinang muttered, 'I know a nightclub.' He drank his beer, leering first at Galash, then Cullen, over the rim of his glass. A pock mark stretched into an embarrassed dimple. Then he shook his head and laughed, 'No, girls a bit wild there, boy!'

'Really? We're on our way,' said Galash. 'Bring your American Express card.'

Passing by the partying family group on their way out, Cullen saw that the young amateur crooner was taking no further part in the frivolity, nor had he transferred the money to a more secure place. The notes stayed poking precariously from his shirt pocket while he drank, aloof from the others, and eyed them watchfully.

11

ON THE SHEEN OF THE ROAD a magenta reflection of the Hotel President's neon sign, the only one in the vicinity, glistened for some distance. Rain had fallen while they were drinking in the Fiesta Lounge, apparently heavily, for sheets of water still lay in the depressions of the road and in the headlights the clay verges appeared eroded on the rising ground and boggy in every hollow. Corporal Panglinang, one clever hand on the wheel, impelled the jeep along the slick macadam, through the oily puddles and erosion ruts, using the horn to browbeat any adventurous tricycle proprietor with a chance of crossing his path.

Though the rain had stopped, the corporal's aggressive driving technique was throwing an occasional stream of spray over Cullen, sitting in the back seat. He was glad then when the jeep suddenly decelerated and turned off the macadam on to an unlit and deeply rutted side-road of clay and rock fragments which cut into the dark walls of high dripping foliage. It curved randomly for three miles or so until it reached a collection of shanties set out more or less in the formation of a village.

Around these wood and tin huts among the wet buri palms and jackfruit trees there was a sweet rich smell of animality and organic luxuriance. This moist fusion of faeces, food remains and vegetation struck Cullen as soon as they got out of the jeep and, with the corporal leading them, picked their way through the mud up to a well-lit wooden hall half way up a slight hill. Raucous music, ten or fifteen-year-old Western pop tunes, came from the hall. Outside, groups of short dark men with weathered faces stood smoking and chatting. As they approached, some shuffled out of their way with mildly curious expressions on their faces. Others, similarly dressed in coloured sports shirts, denims and basketball sneakers, staggered out of the shadows zipping up their flies or lighting fresh cigarettes.

Corporal Panglinang, assuming the same swagger he had used in the Fiesta Lounge, pushed through the clumps of men loitering in the open doorway and with an insouciant jerk of his head, motioned them to follow him into the hall.

The old directive against taking firearms inside was tacked to the wall. Beneath the notice, sitting on a flimsy chair with a cashbox on her lap, an old, exhausted looking woman sold admission tickets at five pesos each. A look of recognition crossed her face on seeing Panglinang but she didn't speak. By the time Cullen and Galash had their tickets, the corporal, hissing and clapping, then holding up three fingers and speaking loudly in dialect, had obtained a table and ordered beer.

'So,' said Panglinang. 'So, here you are, sirs.' As a host he was both coy and proud. 'Not a very terrific nightclub, but in the *barrios* . . .' He shrugged. 'Only a jukebox and girls. I'm a big city boy myself.'

'We all are, Corporal. We all are,' Galash said, lighting a cigarette, looking about him casually but keenly; establishing a beach-head.

At the moment the space in front of the tables which presumably served as a stage was bare except for men walking across it on their way to a room at the back and for skittish girls running to put coins in the jukebox or to simply hover around it in giggling conversation. Another record began. Petula Clark singing 'Downtown'. Several men and women around the room joined in the chorus. A couple with dark Malay faces got up and danced, the man making the audience laugh by wiggling his hips comically.

Some of the drinkers at adjoining tables began stealing glances at Cullen and Galash to see whether they found the man's antics amusing. Ignoring his partner, he was bumping and grinding his skinny hips in drunken imitation of a stripper or perhaps a hula dancer. There was a guarded though strangely childish interest in their reaction to this silly performance and Cullen found himself forced to respond to it, smiling foolishly, playing the genial guest. This seemed to be greatly appreciated. Several people now openly looked at them, one or two nodding good-naturedly. When the record finished and the dancer stopped his gyrations Cullen felt a further responsibility to clap him. Other tables followed his example and the man, grinning hugely, a dull gold tooth prominent, sat down to whistling and table thumping.

The corporal was poker-faced. He leaned back in his chair aloofly fingering his dog-tag. 'That's nothing. There is more to come.'

Galash and Cullen exchanged glances. Cullen refilled their glasses. 'What the hell,' he said.

An atmosphere of frivolity, of contagious high jinks, had been created around them. There was a rush to the jukebox. Showing off, a small man with a farmworker's burnt walnut face and a cigarette hanging from his mouth crept up on all fours behind the former hip wiggler and pinched his buttocks. Laughter grew. High pitched giggles. Cullen could feel the strain of his smile. From his hands-and-knees position on the muddy, ash-covered floor the pincher looked up at Cullen for approval and winked.

'*Sioke*,' he said, indicating the man he had pinched, who was taking it cheerfully. He wiggled his own hips and giggled again, then discovered his cigarette had gone out. 'Oh! Oh!' he called in a small demented voice from the floor. He got up to a squatting position and reached for Galash's lighter. With a resigned gesture Galash lit his cigarette. 'Americans?' the man asked.

'Sure,' Galash said. 'There you go, brother.'

Still the man squatted there, wobbling slightly, unwilling to break the contact. He seemed to want to offer something, to impress, but could bring forth nothing, not even conversation. His frowning eyes were losing their hope, becoming inert. He was fixed on the spot, rocking gently on his toes, leaning on his knees surrounded by the grime and betel sputum. He may have been humming. The reactivated jukebox drowned his susurrations, however, the suggestion of murmuring, and the undercurrent of voices, laughter, the clink of glass, the movement of feet over the thin springy floorboards, carried them away. His head was at Cullen's waist level, his nodding presence was becoming more obeisant and embarrassing by the second.

By degrees they turned away from him, initiating new conversations.

'What's your Christian name, Corporal?' Cullen asked. 'It seems silly to keep calling you corporal when we're all out on the booze together.' He evinced some interest in the reply.

Barely inches away, the man still squatted beside them—intimately, as if presuming years of friendship. His eyes had given up but he remained there, an amiable mute parasite. Cullen was becoming uncomfortable at the infringement of his personal air space. Smoke rising from the man's cigarette—fixed in his mouth—wafted over them. Its ash lengthened and fell on his shirt.

After a pause Panglinang said, 'Luz. My name is Luz.'

'Is that a regional name, then?' Their heads were turned completely from the squatting man yet his presence dominated the table. 'An abbreviation of Luzon?'

'Luz,' Panglinang said. 'L-U-Z, Luz.' Morosely he raised his glass to his mouth.

'Carmelo!' they were calling the interloper now. Hissing him and calling his name. '*Carmelo!*' A woman clicked her tongue in disgust. Carmelo squatted on his haunches regardless. Another record began on the jukebox, there was a sudden hubbub and a young man walked up and slapped Carmelo's face, caught him under the arms, and another man helped lift him to his feet and lead him away.

'*Mierda!*' one of them said.

This small fracas was just registering in Cullen's awareness when he saw a naked girl unfolding her body in the space before the tables. She had been the cause of the commotion. Rotating to the music, a strange insistent local pop song, she was spiralling and unfurling her flesh like a flag opening in a wind.

'See. Much better,' Panglinang said. A smile came again on his heavy pitted face. He sat up and leaned forward over the table. 'This girl . . . ,' he said. 'This girl. . . .' He broke off and giggled.

Her pubis was shaved. An initial impression was therefore of childish vulnerability. Long black hair reeled behind her and twisted damply across her face. She was slight, brown-skinned, but with neat mestiza features, and the polite expression playing over her mouth and eyes was neither overtly carnal—genuinely or falsely—nor one of satiric maidenhood. She was not playing a role, neither was her tensile whirling and uncoiling actually a performance in the sense of an act or show. She did not strip—being naked from the beginning—or wiggle or tease. She had no props and moved on a bare wooden floor. It was simply a display, like gymnastics or calisthenics.

Woman as exhibit.

Not that whistles and clever cat-calls didn't follow her every undulation. Backwards she arched now, presenting her pudenda to the front tables. An amused male cry went up. A general eye-contact occurred around the room, men winking at each other across the tables. There seemed a common desire to appear nonchalant but rakish, to show a playful interest for the sake of fellowship and the social circle.

Through his teeth Galash remarked, 'Showing the pink, boy.' He raised an eyebrow. 'Gynaecology to music.' However, his attention did not wander.

Panglinang was hissing softly with delight, whistling into his cupped hands. 'Only a young girl . . . fifteen, sixteen. Not a city whore.'

In the smoky humidity of the hall, amongst the sweating audience and the sly pervasive smell of the tropical life-cycle coming in waves through the door and windows, even on the soles of the crowd's basketball sneakers, Cullen, too, was not immune. Far from it. Shutting out the surroundings, the general drunkenness, his own near-drunkenness, the repetitious banal music, his febrile senses were nevertheless perfectly tuned to this ever-uncoiling flesh.

The youthful resilience was a wonder: that amazing soft elasticity. The shade of her skin was brown. Not exactly brown—he was alert to its precise foreign highlights—creamy fawn, and especially to the pearly pubescence of her belly and breasts. Under a film of moisture they were as canescent as frosty leaves. The nipples could have been silvered.

'*Querida*!' howled a voice from the back of the hall. 'Darling! *O, o!*'

A man sitting at the front reached out and ran his hand up between her thighs. Leering, he lingered there. He grinned at the crowd and rolled his eyes. The girl did not move. Her face was placid. Cullen's heart fell at the offence, but above all at her bland courtesy. Subjectively, this was treachery. Appreciative laughter burst out. The molester, as if he were an integral part of the entertainment, got to his feet and burlesquely sniffed his fingers, running them one by one backwards and forwards under his nose.

The audience roared its delight. '*O, o!*' Some of the men made mock-masturbatory gestures.

Again detached, Galash could be wry once more. 'A traditional folk dance of these parts.'

But Cullen's throat ached with misery and dehydration. He poured the rest of the beer into his glass. How easy for his ego, his Anglo-Saxon naïvety, to be betrayed. This suddenly amazed him: his ability to have regarded this girl as an amorous possibility. His search for the exotic princess never faltered, reaching into the farthest equatorial dungheap for its jewels. Why? Implicit in it was an unpleasant but, he was convinced, not untrue self-image: I am the biggest, strongest man in this room. I am white and have money and brains enough. This is irrefutable. Therefore, why don't you see this and act accordingly? Why don't you want me? Let me put it this way. Why aren't you flocking to give me the chance to consider your possibilities? Even to discard you?

Simply, this was the state of affairs. Why did even he think it unreasonable?

The music stopped. Simultaneously the girl quivered and with a flick of her pelvis slid abruptly to the floor, legs divided: the splits. Her body finally opened for the crowd on the clotted floorboards.

Whistles, hoots and foot stamping, partly ironic, greeted the finale.

'Beware of splinters!' Galash murmured. 'Well, what did you think of that little effort?'

Cullen shrugged. Sadly he still watched the girl, mannerly to the end, spring to her feet, smile and run lightly to the back room. Her buttocks were smeared with dirt; on her calves small scars from tropical sores were like shiny coins.

'That creep who got the handful is following her,' said Galash. 'Mister Stinkfinger.'

'Is her husband,' Panglinang muttered. 'Same seat every night.'

Drunkenness was not coming fast enough. Cullen wanted to help it along. Strategically then, picking their marks, three women came out of the crowd with fresh beer bottles and topped up their glasses, saying 'Good evening, sir,' to each in turn, sitting themselves on their laps with unusual subtlety, and, in thirty or forty seconds, with a similar politeness and seemingly at a pre-arranged signal, inevitably, commenced to pluck casually at their genitals.

12

RAIN PELTED ON THE ROOF, thudded on the soft ground outside, driving back into the hall the gossiping clumps of men who had overflowed it. Stamping the mud from their feet, their shirts sticking to their bodies, they came in giggling like children and milled around the space in front of the tables. The roof had several old leaks; dark fresh patches in the fibreboard ceiling traced over their outlines of mould. Over the tables the humidity rose. One of the drenched men, his hair plastered flat, put coins in the jukebox. Petula Clark resumed singing 'Downtown'. Small steaming men flashed gold teeth, ran combs through their wet hair and drank from bottles.

Absently, the woman's fingers stroked on. At intervals they would reach for her glass of Coca-Cola or cigarette, then drift back lightly to his trousers. His anticipation of their return was keen. Above the table, however, he registered only a sociable smile, a humorous eyebrow, perhaps an imperceptible flicker of the cheek during the pause between the setting down of her glass and the resumption of activity. Occasionally he or Galash would laugh sharply at something either had said and heads would turn to look at them.

He had not caught her name. She had repeated it—a short pinging sound—and he had nodded, but he had not heard it properly. Her whole conversation was like that; stilted but pleasant: trivial jokes interrupted by occasional asides to her two friends in a mixture of English and dialect and muffled by the loud music and raucous chattering voices, but at all times courteous, almost like that of an attentive stranger on a long train trip. In no way did the two activities, the conversing and fondling of him, appear to bear any relation to each other. Certainly nothing he said or did was bridging the disparity between the two procedures.

So in a way it was like a dream. She was nameless. She was a face in the crowd. Other-worldliness interlaced it all. Now and then his consciousness seemed to hover over the table, the soggy crowd in the nightclub, floating up against the stained mouldy ceiling noting these vaguely bizarre proceedings. His superego was undecided whether any guilt was necessary. After all, his life was in abeyance. Normal restrictions no longer applied. Coming down to earth though he was sorry she was not an exotic princess. Surreptitious glances caught no hint of that mysterious foreign lubricity. His passion was not fascinated by the slant of her eyes, her tongue tip, a shred of damp membrane here or there, the shape of her mouth, other clues. Her hands were work-worn and displayed a wedding ring. She wore a bright cheap dress of frictional synthetic material that caught on the cloth of his trousers and rode up constantly. But he didn't throb for nothing under the table. He could persuade himself she was almost pretty. She was pleasant featured and, though plump for her race, on his knees her weight was negligible.

Strangely objective for the moment, he presumed by the way she had made a beeline for him that she would deliberately select the biggest man in any group: to set her size off to best advantage. Of the other girls the better looking—the prettiest of the three, he noted ironically—had chosen Corporal Panglinang. Of course—the regular customer! Galash's girl was the plainest, surprisingly, but younger, livelier; now squirming happily on her chair, knees ajar, while her partner, swinging into the recklessly engaging side of his personality, whispered into her hair, made her giggle, and idiotically tip-toed his fingers up her brown legs.

This arrangement had probably been settled between them

beforehand. They had been divided up like spoils. He had a good idea what this presupposed and foreshadowed, but then portents weren't always what they seemed in Asia. Clinging servile hostesses had a habit of turning into remote ice-maidens at closing time. Only Galash seemed to be able to interpret the nocturnal writing on the wall.

He led them from the table now.

Cullen allowed Galash's standing up and stretching, his canny observation on the late hour, to serve as a decision for them all.

'We're with you,' he said adventurously. A joint statement.

He was content to be swept along by events once more, specifically by this well-organized girl with the tinkling name. The drink, the exhibition by the unfurling dethroned princess, his partner's efficient proximity, had made him eager, spunky as a pup. In the mêlée of swaying, wet men crowding forward for the next sexual exhibition he was a little unsteady, but holding her soft upper arm in his hand he surged behind Galash through the audience, clearing a wider path to the door.

The rain had stopped. A new wave of vegetal and faecal smells came in on the cleaner air. By the door the old cashier was hunched over her cash box winding rubber bands around rolls of five- and ten-peso notes and passing the rolls to a wiry youth with a canvas bag. He looked up smiling at the three women. The old woman held up an erect forefinger and giggled. Cullen noticed with a peculiar clarity that she wore running shoes with holes cut out for each little toe.

'Goodnight,' said the young man loudly, addressing the girls by their ding-dong names.

The girl with Galash said good night, and then something in dialect which amused them. The cashier slapped the cash-box with the flat of her hand. To one side Corporal Pangli-nang whispered to his girl and fingered his dog-tag.

Galash bowed from the waist. 'Thank you for your hospitality,' he told the couple. 'Great little show. Next stop Broadway, eh?' He winked at Cullen, sidled rakishly up alongside. 'What do you think of that story I told you?' he asked. He nudged him with an elbow. 'No princess. No pimple. All bullshit, my man.'

He could only blink. The air through the doorway was as pungent as a compost heap.

'Goodnight, sirs.' The couple beamed happily on them, the young man showing matching chipped front teeth. 'Welcome back any time,' he said. He milled about between them and the door, one hand clutching the canvas bag, and then proceeded to shake their hands. 'Next time guests of the management.' His hand in Cullen's was small and hard. Something about the handshake was slightly tricky, a withdrawal of some of the fingers perhaps. It was like one of those secret, coterie handshakes, but obliquely so: a small teasing gesture of odd familiarity. 'Regular customers, no trouble.' His final grin, the short sharp teeth, recalled some cub yawning.

Outside moths beat at a caged electric bulb lighting the muddy yard. Galash and the girls were still laughing and talking in riddles. It dawned on Cullen, instructing the others to wait while he set off for the lavatory behind the hall, that he had not once tonight considered the word 'prostitute'.

He trod just as delicately through the mud and animal droppings, lurching only once or twice as he followed the extreme smell of the latrine. Cheers came from inside the hall, a scream: *Wheeeeeiiii* and amorphous laughter. Reaching the tin cupboard, he kicked open the door but could not enter. It was filthy and awash. In the thin light coming through the door something half-scuttled, half-swam, and he shuddered and let the door fall shut. Standing instead in the cupboard's shadow, visible to half the yard, he was reminded of the stoic lizards in the distant Sunorama Cabaret. The memory of that innocent sad dive was nostalgically rosy. What had become of the Tamil girl, he wondered? The wrong race in the wrong place at the wrong time. A dignified victim, an offering to the famished tigress. From there he could easily go on to other more painful considerations. He kept them out of his mind with effort and trudged back through the mud.

A bottle landed near him, perhaps thrown from inside the

hall, but plopped in the mud and did not break.

Under the light stood the girl, flapping a loose hand at the moths. As he walked up to her she called out something into the doorway and came and took his arm. In this new perspective she was smaller, even more of a stranger.

'Where are the others?'

She giggled and raised a stiff forefinger, like the old woman's gesture. The jeep was still there, he noticed.

So the night had taken its inevitable course. The suspense was over. Determinist Cullen reeled down the hill with the girl. His legs seemed to be free-wheeling; loose-jointed and mechanistic. With reckless good humour he swung her over ditches and puddles, reconnoitred the black path ahead for boggy hazards while she clung insistently to his arm humming 'Downtown' and occasionally breaking into little burbles of song. The childish sound, together with her size, put him in mind of Louise for a subversive moment. Ruthlessly he urged his senses back on the track: his elbow nudged a breast, his leg bumped against her hip; he maintained the resistless urge of the evening; his blood was still up. In the high stands of wet trees along the path tree frogs chirruped. It was cooler now and dark except for faint moonlit reflections in the puddles on the clay. Her skin released a cheap high scent in the area of her neck and armpit; at the same time his own meaty sweat came to him like a stranger's.

Ten or fifteen minutes along this convoluted path they came to the silhouette of a hut in a clearing before some palms.

'OK, here,' she murmured, and drew him by the sleeve around to the *batalan* at the back of the hut: a roofless outhouse of bamboo and tin.

Damp laundry swung in his face. Something dank and slippery, like a chamois, touched his cheek. The warmth of the house seeped out through the kitchen door: the seminal smell of boiled rice, a rancid hint of pork fat. Gradually he heard someone breathing heavily inside the kitchen. His own breathing was tentative and unsteady at this surprise.

She said it was her son. 'He sleeps,' she said. In the dark he couldn't see the expression on her face. He imagined it would be calm and enigmatic.

Stooping awkwardly under the lines of washing he could feel the erotic momentum ebbing rapidly away. Her movements around the *batalan* were quick and definite but their arrival at the hut had created a hiatus. Once more he was forced to think. The wrong images flooded in—sentiment and sadness. Where he had sought salacious beauty, jungle women, the exotica showered on sultans and caliphs, he was subjected to the mundane emotions of a household: the affecting domestic milieu of a *barrio* prostitute, a Third World struggler: even to that final damper—the introduction of a sleeping child.

'He sleeps,' she had said, translated as: 'He usually doesn't bother me when I bring home a drunken man every night from the nameless nightclub.' A mouth breather to boot. He was full of conflicting feelings, annoyed and aching at once.

Plucking at his sleeve she brought him across to the bamboo wall. A small table was against it and on the table she indicated the dim shape of a basin of water and a towel next to it.

'Wash your body first,' she directed. 'Soap and wash clean, very clean.'

He hovered over the table, every limb weighty and phlegmatic. Clearly he anticipated her using the basin afterwards, squatting like some Stone Age aborigine. Vigorously sluicing. She vanished inside the hut, quiet and brisk as a nurse, and he heard the rustling of clothing. In the dark he leaned over the basin and dipped a hand in the cold water. In a dream he sprinkled water on his face. He began to undo his clothes. Inside the hut the child murmured in its sleep and the sound finished him. Wiping his face on the towel, he stooped under the washing and crept from the *batalan*. In the yard he paused, his heart leaping as a bat broke screeching from the palms, then strode quickly away from the hut, not looking back, sloshing through the mud towards the track, moved by an urgency stronger than any of the evening. Simply to get away was his instinct.

Thus impelled he hurried along the dark slippery track. Twice in his haste he slipped, and rose swearing from his hands and knees. More often than not the track faded away in the mud and crumbly gravel of the hillside, but remembering the downhill journey to the hut he continued to trudge uphill, aiming for the nightclub again and Corporal Panglinang's jeep.

Alone, of course, the night seemed blacker. Monsoon clouds and high vegetation hid the moon for long stretches. His head ached behind the right eye: souvenir of the Tongan tour, wasn't it? He heard his breathing becoming laboured, and the exertion and humidity gave him a feverish giddiness. He stopped to urinate and gather his scattered wits. Look at me, he thought, and began to take all this with a half-amused resignation, even to gain a little self-satisfaction from his retreat, in doing the right thing. One more tropical adventure! Mosquitoes, too. When they began biting, he thought, *What else can happen*? And when he slipped again to his knees in the clay, he laughed out loud.

He imagined himself almost approaching the village, with only several more turns of the path ahead. He was moving more or less evenly now, in his second wind, his shoes and trousers wrecked, actually clumping along in thick overshoes of clay. A light unfamiliar breeze started to blow, cooling him down and discouraging the mosquitoes. Each step made a distinctive double sound in the slush—squelch-suck—the pulpy assimilation of one foot, the reluctant egression of the other. To this ponderous rhythm he was reciting in his mind his priorities back in his room at the President: Show-er-drink. Show-er-drink. To one side of him a dim shape moved out of the trees, lightly, unencumbered.

'Hi, hi,' said a male voice.

'For Christ's sake!'

'Your friend here, sir.' The shape became a discernible figure moving along the side of the track against the wall of vines and protruding tree roots. 'After curfew, huh? *Juramentados* about. PC patrols.'

His scalp still contracted with surprise, Cullen grunted and resumed walking. The man was keeping to the grass and palm leaves of the impossibly narrow verge, skipping nimbly away from the mud. His size was hard to estimate. From the corner of his eye Cullen also squinted anxiously after possible companions. In the thicket nothing else moved: tree trunks remained stable; overgrown bends in the path provided no ultimatum.

'What do you want? I must warn you I've got a gun.' Schoolboyish, precious, this sounded, as he knew it would. How could a gunless threat sound otherwise? But the blood was racing to his arms, his fists hung loosely. He shuffled onward, half-turning toward the figure blurred against the vegetal mass. He grunted again and assumed what he hoped was a threatening outline.

'No trouble, sir. Our countries pals. I may be of help. You lost, huh?'

'No, not lost. Walking back to my friends—soldiers—in their jeep. Very near here.'

'Sure. You come to the nightclub, huh? Meet pretty girls, break curfew. Very bad.' He giggled and sprang over a ditch. His sneakers made hardly a sound. Cullen made out that he was slight, probably young. He could not see his hands.

'Sir, you married, got kids eh, at home?'

'Yes.' On he trudged, his fists hanging uncomfortably. There was something unwarranted in that question. On top of everything his mind struggled with detribalization and forfeiture. All three together, probably at Casuarina Bay; Margaret recovering, the kids happier than before. Leading simpler lives, with him the only complication.

'Your wife a pretty woman I bet you, sir.'

He tried to keep sharp. There was a sly jaundice about this; a servile intrusive note that was suspicious. How much further to the jeep, he wondered, simultaneously gauging the distance between the man and himself—about eight or nine feet and his legs were leaden.

'What colour hair? Blonde? Redhead? Good figure?' His chuckle came from the shrubbery.

'Blonde. Now get lost.'

Suddenly the tone was confiding. 'You make love to our girls, eh?' The man's breathing was light but now noticeable, a faint whistle through the nose.

So that was it. 'No, not me.' Of course. 'Not me, son.'

'You fucked Emeng Bancheng many times!' There was a quiet definition in his phrasing. It was a formal proclamation of dogma.

Ignoring him, Cullen walked on, his arms dragging against his sides. Around another bend he saw a light in the distance: the electric bulb burning outside the nightclub. Filling his vision, it threw everything else into blackness.

'Two, three times,' the man said mildly. His statement was flattering, almost wheedling, around and beside Cullen. 'Fifty pesos each. One hundred for a long-time, all the way through curfew. Bargain till 5 a.m.'

'Not even once, if you want the truth.'

'Huh! You make her do things, eh? In her own house?'

'Not a thing.' Stamping mud from his feet he strode toward the light. He could see at last the hall and the fainter shapes of some other huts in the settlement. His companion, however, was still in the jungle shadows, muttering, running lightly beside him, three or four arm lengths from him. Abruptly he came almost within reach, apparently struck by a thought of immense import.

'Why you didn't pay Emeng Bancheng one hundred pesos?' His voice was a bitter hiss.

'What?' More vividly than in reality he saw the chipped enamel douche basin in the dark outhouse, the shabby washing, heard the wheezing child. The path was ooze under his feet. Ahead the beacon gleamed, filling his vision. He was night-blind and overwhelmed by the seminal smells of nocturnal flowers.

'Fifty pesos even? Seven dollars US? Why you didn't fuck Emeng Bancheng?' the man howled, angry and incredulous, and darted in and stabbed him because of this irregularity.

The wound hardly hurt, but despite presentiments old and recent the shock was great. The thin body of his attacker had little impact but Cullen still fell into the mud, clumsily, on his back. He was massively affronted at the unfittingness of the attack. A space near a lower rib was numb and cold, that was all. The man lunged at him again; he slithered out of the way and the knife cut his left arm.

'Give me money for Emeng Bancheng!' the man screeched, spinning in the mud. He swore in dialect and sliced ineffectually at the air.

Now that it was happening Cullen felt clear and definite. If inevitable events had occurred, anything further, said sweet reason, was finally in his hands. He was within his rights. Acting by nature's and man's laws. He got to the verge of the track, inhaled deeply and faced the knife, crouched low as if to make a tackle. Inexorably the man lunged at him again with a thin muscular arm, the arm of the hand-shaking nightclub tout, but Cullen feinted and stiff-armed him in the face. He went with his body's guile and heavy momentum and crushed him to the ground. He hadn't used all his strength for maybe twenty years. This tackle took some of it. With what he had left he pinned the small body beneath him while his right fist pounded the head, the face, the little animal teeth, repeatedly, like a pestle in a mortar, until the grunts and moans became one sound.

Their noise ebbed away into the moist darkness. Eventually, panting, he crawled off the nightclub tout and managed to get shakily to his feet. Immediately he fell. He was weaker than he had thought. On the verge of the track he rested for several minutes, a bird or fruit bat screaming nearby making no impact on him. Under the torn mud-caked shirt the wound near his rib had an icy ache. The cut in his arm was more painful, surprisingly, and other pains were now nagging in his sides and back. He was surprised to find the knuckles of his right hand ripped open. By his feet the nightclub tout was pressed into the mud, almost flush with the surface of the track, alive or dead.

Sucking his knuckles like a child Cullen stood and hobbled toward the light outside the nightclub. In its glare moths and gnats still swirled. The jeep was gone, the customers; the nightclub was deserted and locked. He rattled on its door, banged and called for Galash and the corporal. Slumping on its wooden step he called their names again many times but no one came. Gradually he fell silent on seeing the blood swamping his clothes. Running into a terrible pool on the step it reminded him, oddly, of childhood; of cut feet, broken glass at the beach; of tender ministrations by his mother, soothing bandages and applications of Dettol and Mercurochrome. He was close to crying for Dottie now, actually; only an invigorating fury at Galash and Panglinang prevented him.

He cursed them both, especially Galash, constant in his undependability. What on earth was he doing in this godforsaken hole? *The Poor Man's Tractor*! Z.M! The trouble Z.M. had caused him! The subtle indirect influence on his life! On the edge of the step was a discarded San Miguel bottle, half full. Suddenly dehydrated, he reached for it, involuntarily wiping the top with his caked hand before taking a swig. Germs! In case of germs! Dirty foreign mouths! He almost laughed, crusted in mud and blood, taking a deep swallow until the flat beer was finished. He let the bottle slip from his fingers to the soft ground, which absorbed it. Above him the light bulb buzzed and crackled with electricity, or perhaps it was the insects. The glare hurt his head and he rested his eyes.

For seconds he dozed, then awoke with a painful start. Struggling to stay conscious he exercised his mind on the last chapter he and Z.M. had prepared together, 'Conservation, Use and Management', sub-heading 'Methods of Slaughter', which was rather more semi-delirium than mind-exercise.

Hmm. . . . *Animals killed ritually wherever a large Muslim population. Usual throughout Asia for slaughtermen to be Muslims, whatever predominant religion of country. Muslim method of killing known as 'halal' may be conducted by any adult male without previous training . . . animal must be bled to death, and this generally achieved, where buffaloes are concerned, by almost complete severing of head from body. . . .*

And he had brief sharp dreams, all concerned with blood,

woke again and thought of moving off but considered himself safer under the light, in the only public place. For the first time in his life there was a unique fear of being too weak to cope. Of fainting away in the dark, in the shrubbery; of being set upon by the tout's cohorts. And he had to wait for the jeep.

It seemed important to be accurate in his recollection. He forced himself to elaborate as the noise of the insects swelled over and around his head.

. . . As so may buffaloes slaughtered by 'halal', wise to consider method in some detail. Davies? no, Davidson (1969) noted that the animal is thrown to ground, and at moment of cutting the throat slaughterer is reminded of seriousness of his action by the pronunciation of the name of God. . . . Main Koranic requirement of 'halal' is that meat for Muslim consumption should be bled as thoroughly as possible, and it is assumed, wrongly assumed [Z.M. got a kick out of this bit] *that because the meat of animals bled to death looks paler than those killed by other means, this is because the meat contains less blood. Wrong. Davidson, quoting Rossman (1958), states the demonstrable fact that there's actually more blood left in the flesh of ritually killed animals than in those made unconscious before bleeding . . . paler colour of ritual meat due to larger amount of oxygen in blood as result of heavier breathing of animal before it dies, so on and so on . . . animals stunned before they're bled naturally breathe in less oxygen and although more blood drains from their bodies the flesh is darkened by the retained blood. . . .*

'It figures,' he said aloud, and was startled by the noise.

. . . Davidson and Rossman anticipate that when this point is appreciated by Muslim leaders, who are renowned for their sagacity and understanding ['Suck up to them,' advised Z.M. 'My God, they'll never change otherwise.'] *and whose sacred texts bullshit bullshit enjoin them to spare animals unnecessary pain, 'halal' will be performed henceforth only on animals which have previously been rendered insensitive. . . .*

A longer dream, still only the briefest snippet of time, featured his mother. He walked in the front door at

Casuarina Bay and saw blood all up the walls and over the carpets and ran through the house expecting mass murder but discovered Dottie calmly haemorrhaging from the nose, fountains gushing from her while she deftly rolled socks into neat balls.

On the nightclub step he sat upright in his congealing blood and gingerly touched his side.

. . . Normal procedure for slaughter is for the legs to be tied together, and for the animal to be pushed to the ground. Head is pointed towards the east, line of incision is indicated by position of the tip of the ear, and the throat is deeply cut. . . . With a large buffalo slaughtered in this manner five minutes may elapse before the optical reflex ceases to be present. . . .

The pain was bad now, even worse than the pain in his arm, but the flow of blood seemed to have lessened. There was no fresh blood on the step as far as he could see. It was getting light and roosters crowed.

Two Phantoms were flying high overhead. Fighter-bombers. It was silent when they disappeared; the land was still and almost cold. Cullen guessed it was about 5 a.m. A light dewy haze hung over the trees in the mid-distance. Above, the nightclub light burned dimly but the insects had gone. Maybe the tout had intended to return; maybe someone had forgotten to turn the light off.

Against a sharp precise pain, he pushed himself up from the step and tried to stand erect. This stretching of his side and abdomen almost made him black out. Hunched over, breathing hard, he stood for a moment focusing wildly on the ground. It was drying out already, cracking and curling up in chocolate patches. Its crust broke as he took a couple of tentative steps. Around him the mud had set in the night's scars, congealed around bottles, cigarette packets, a torn shirt, other debris. Red betel sputum, which he took at first for more blood, smeared the surface. The tracks of the jeep were sharp.

Roosters crowed urgently but there was still no human movement around the nearest huts and fields. He was anxious to leave before anyone appeared. For the second time in five hours he trudged down the hill, this time his knees buckling against the slope, taking short draughts of air, his body twisted, favouring his wound. New spiders' webs hung between the bushes. Among the vines birds began their noise. About three miles to the macadam, he estimated, and half that again back to town. Difficult, but not impossible. And a taxi or tricycle could happen along when he reached the highway. He patted his pocket. After all that he still had his wallet. Even his little plastic envelope of travellers' cheques was intact. Moving haltingly, apprehensively, down the track, he was aware of an earthy leguminous smell. It was himself: the blood and mud; he smelled like the country.

At the bottom of the hill the path forked. He followed the tracks of the jeep, but it was the route he would have taken anyway; the other turn-off was the one he and the prostitute had taken the night before. The thought of retracing his steps was horrifying. He shuffled away from the turn-off, holding his wound, as quickly as he could manage. In his mind was the image of the tout encased in coagulated clay, face uppermost, the grimace awry and rigid. He anticipated his rapid discovery by farmers, even by the girl herself. With the ding-dong name, whatever it was. He was in great pain but hurried on. The fingers clamped to his side were damp; he could feel the wound seeping again but didn't want to examine it, couldn't dare to or afford the time.

Already he must have struggled along for well over a mile. The sun was now up and he was getting hot. His throat ached with dehydration: his caked skin, moistened, was attracting insects. Around him hung abundant inaccessible sources of food and liquid: coconuts, *buri* palms, *lanzones* with their juicy oblong fruit. Over the track birds fed noisily in a *datiles* tree, dropping small red berries which popped and squashed under his shambling feet.

He had fallen eventually into some sort of rhythm: regular contorted movements like a parody of a jogger. Another aircraft flew over, from its thick roar a troop transport. He didn't look up, but continued on spastically, every limb numb, urging his consciousness away from his body and the zone of pain into the next threshold.

He shuffled on into the insect-hum. Desperately he considered a definite destination, orientated himself with difficulty. He kept his eyes on the tyre marks leading him back to town. They vanished occasionally into stony terrain, reappeared skewing off into the soft shoulders of the track and then centred themselves once more. The track could be the track to the beach. He ran ahead of his parents through the eucalypts. A strip of blue sea was over the hill and Lindy whined behind for him to wait; would follow him anywhere, into deep water, breaking surf. Love and competition could carry her over her depth; her fine hair wound around her eyes and mouth.

His intakes of breath registered on him, fearful asthmatic soughs. *'The Everest of a Himalayan career'*! Ha! A pederast's praise. He slowed almost to a walk and, concentrating intensely, thought suddenly: You could always leave this place. At Casuarina Bay things would be different. This decisive leap astonished him with its simplicity but he found it greatly encouraging. Finish. Out. He thought of Margaret and his optimism increased. Tinged with the usual forced sentimentality of crisis, certainly, but uplifting nevertheless. He saw an idealized younger version of her face, caressed it, dandled his children, years younger, on his knee. No longer would she be sealed off from him. The kids would be at home. She would relax, drop those unfamiliar brittle habits. Nothing is irreversible, my sweetheart. . . .

The sun in his eyes, he had a vision of the beach again, a light nor'-westerly blowing, the currawongs raucous in the bush backdrop, pleasant outdoor parties, drinks, tanned women in bikinis. One of them, olive-skinned, with a face of many faces, touched an amazingly light hand on his arm.

Around the curve of the track, two or three hundred yards ahead, was the jeep. It was stationary by a ditch at the side of the track, but as its presence struck him, as he began to shuffle faster, it started to move slowly off.

His dry shout hardly travelled. He yelled again and jogged

243

after the jeep. Between his shouts his desperate breaths eroded his throat. He swung and waved his aching arms and called again.

He was heard—or seen in the rear-vision mirror—because the jeep braked in the gravel, turned slowly around and headed jerkily towards him. It came to within thirty or forty yards of him, then stopped. He barely remained standing. Three Moro soldiers got out carefully. Another stayed behind the wheel. They were no wild-eyed Muslims swinging knives. Not *bolo*-waving *Juramentados*, naked savages. These men were very young and dressed in MNLF commando uniforms; their long hair fell from under berets and headbands decorated with nationalistic and religious insignia. They pointed new automatic weapons.

'More American,' said one of the Muslims. His cool soft face had a faint frown of curiosity at Cullen's size and condition, a downy adolescent moustache.

Their other sounds, if not their actions, were foreign to him.

Swaying, he began to explain.